Track

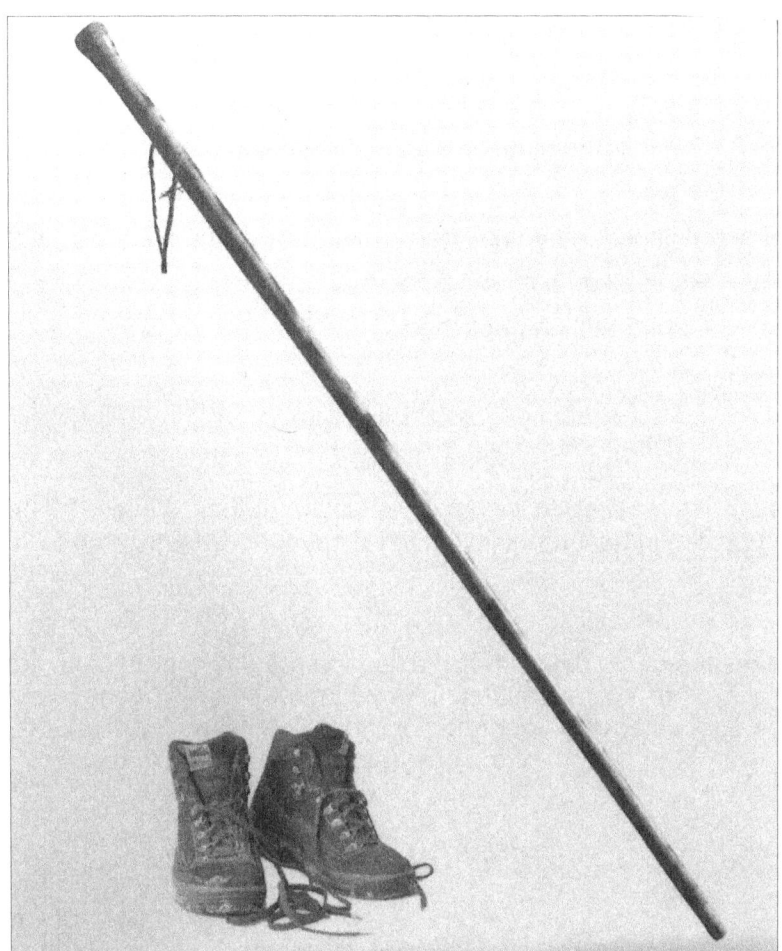

Incorporating the
'The Writer's Diary'

Trevor Cree

Published by Trevor Cree
Steyning, Sussex, United Kingdom

First published in Great Britain in 2005 by agmachine.com Ltd.
Revised edition published in 2017 by Trevor Cree.
Third edition published in 2025 by Trevor Cree.

Copyright © Trevor Cree 2025

The right of Trevor Cree to be identified as the author of this work has been asserted by him in accordance with the Copyright, Designs and Patents Act 1988.

All rights reserved. No part of this publication may be reproduced, stored in a retrieval system, or transmitted, in any form or by any means, electronic, mechanical, photocopying, recording or otherwise, without the prior permission of the copyright owner.

ISBN 978-1-0682103-2-7

Contents

1	Spring Follows Winter	1
2	A Land of Uncertain Climate	17
3	Bare Earth Embracing Sweet Rain	31
4	High Hills and Deep Valleys	52
5	When Rivers Run Dry	57
6	Clear Views to the Near Horizon	65
7	Sun Rising	71
8	A View from Taishan	77
9	Journey to the Mountain Tops	91
10	A Sky Raised on Broad Shoulders	112
11	Far Beyond the Mountain Peaks	122
12	Above the Tree Line	127
13	A Land of Ice and Snow	137
14	Smoke Rising in a Clear Blue Sky	142

Introduction

'Track' - Every year the major walking tracks of New Zealand act as a magnet to thousands of visitors from all corners of the world. A large proportion of those visitors will be backpackers in their early twenties who are testing their adult wings for the very first time. Others may be older and some may be trying to solve the riddle of their lives. And prime among the backpackers are those who travel alone. Sometimes their paths interact with each other in unexpected ways and strangers may become friends, lovers and even victims in an environment that can show its many faces within a single day. Set against the backdrop of the majestic Southern Alps 'Track' follows the story of three such people and the relic of an earlier era, Te Puke. *Te Puke of One Thousand Battles.* And the enemy that they all face is the power of nature itself.

'The Writer's Diary' is a contemporary account of the trials and tribulations, highs and lows, hopes and fears of someone trying to give birth to a piece of writing that others might enjoy, and that might even be successful. The creation of 'Track' was certainly a project born out of necessity. Follow the author on his creative and physical journey throughout New Zealand struggling to create a piece of fiction and see what transpired. Hopefully 'The Writer's Diary' will resonate with aspiring and established writers everywhere.

1. Spring Follows Winter

A shaft of sunlight broke through a leaden sky and played its way along the tree line of the Southern Alps. A solitary Haast eagle soared high in the quiet air until at last it disappeared from view among the mountain tops. And then, far below, a bellbird sang. As clear as a raindrop, as pure as the morning dew.

....

Thursday 25th November 2004

Craig Williams turned over, and as he did so he instinctively placed his forearm over his eyes to protect them from a morning that attempted to force its way into his bedroom through tightly drawn curtains. His mouth felt dry. His headache was, as yet, barely noticeable. But he knew that his relative sense of wellbeing was deceptive. The headache would not go away. It would stay with him, building, taunting him, the whole slow day. Without looking he automatically stretched out an arm and felt that the space beside him was empty. There would be no need for mutual excuses. No embarrassing conversations between strangers of the morning, lovers of the night before. He felt a sense of relief. He could suffer alone. In silence.

It was rather unclear to most how Craig Williams had arrived in Mamoe. Just as it was uncertain how far the bleached driftwood had journeyed before reaching the lakeshore outside of his bedroom window. It seemed as though he had been there for ever but in fact it had been just six short years. Originally trained as a teacher in Wellington he had travelled to London where he had lived and worked, doing anything he could lay his hands on. Bricklaying, bar work, driving vans, anything to make some money to travel around Europe for weeks at a time. Doing the old O.E. After three years he had decided to take time out back in New Zealand to catch up on family and friends. Then it would be back to Europe for good. After all the money was so much better. But he didn't make it. A stopover in Queenstown finished all that. Nine years since he drifted into that town and immediately fell in love with the girls and the vitality of the place. He knew immediately on arrival that he would be travelling no further for quite some time. He had found paradise. Well, paradise from the perspective of a twenty five year old single male. Beer, thrills, women, and yet more beer. For him this was home.

Teaching unruly adolescents was no longer an option for Craig. Queenstown was a place that overdosed on action. Any way you could legally kill yourself was allowed. Even actively encouraged. Sky diving, bungy jumping, whitewater rafting, body boarding, canyoning, off piste snowboarding, you name it and you could do it. But you needed money. You needed time. And teaching kids didn't offer enough of either. So Craig initially did what the other guys of his age did. He became an action bum. Living six to a room, stale socks and all. Working for the various adventure companies for next to nothing, sometimes nothing at all. Just to be a part of the action. Drive the shuttle bus? Sure can. Teach abseiling, no problem. Drive the jet boat, you bet. Along the way most of his younger colleagues burned out, some after just a few months. Too much beer, too many women, too much hash, too little sleep. They just became vacant wrecks. One by one they drifted away, back to the cities where they had come from, to be replaced by fresh new blood. But not Craig. Craig was born for this. He drank, he womanised, he partied. But never beyond the limits that he had set himself. He worked out daily, was always punctual, and his naturally friendly personality made him popular with both his clients and his employers. Before the year was up he had become a full time employee, covering both the winter and summer seasons.

But it was something more than the high voltage lifestyle that held him there. It was the natural surroundings that steadily grew on him and left him in awe. Wherever his work took him he never ceased to be amazed at the beauty, the power, and the mystery of nature. Mountains, rivers, lakes and forests. All had their special qualities. When he arrived in Queenstown he didn't know one tree, one bird, one four legged 'whatsit' from another. They were of no consequence. Having fun was the game. But the longer he worked there the more he wanted to know. Why did the tree types differ in the different valleys? Why did the birdsong change the higher he climbed? Why did he always get wet when guiding in one area and not another? And so he learnt. And the more he learnt the more he came to love his new environment. His workplace.

And then after three years he tired of living in Queenstown. Mentally he had moved on and physically he did the same. One hundred and thirty kilometres as the crow flies, to be precise.

Mamoe. Not as brash or commercial as Queenstown. Not as quiet as Wanaka or Te Anau. Just like Queenstown was said to have been all those years ago. Rough and unrefined. Frontier country. After two short years in Mamoe he had been invited to join the local mountain rescue service and he rightfully considered that to be a great honour. Most of his colleagues were Mamoe born and bred and so he felt gratified to have been asked to join them. The full time job at the local adventure company had to go. He had to be available for any emergency at the drop of a hat. And so he returned to bricklaying and carpentry. Being self-employed gave him all the freedom that he required. He was content.

Apart that was from the occasional hangover. He looked at his alarm clock. It was now three o'clock in the afternoon. Right on schedule the liverish feeling had left his body, the headache had subsided into a distant memory, and he was ready to face the day. Well what was left of it. It was not as if he now drank a lot. Not like the old days. Three pints of Kilkenny was usually his limit. Perhaps that was the problem. It was just that about once a month he seemed to get carried away by the moment, sometimes in Billy Burke's, sometimes in the Gold Diggers. But only when he wasn't on call. The music, his friends, the chat, the girls, and before the night had ended he had drunk far more than he should. Unsteadily he would make his way back to his small house by the lake, usually alone, sometimes with company.

....

Alexander sat on the elevated wooden decking of the Lake Caroline hut and quietly embraced the spectacular view laid out before him. Snow capped mountain peaks, stretching from north to south, were crisply reflected in the stillness of the lake nearby. It had been a particularly hard day on the Ailsa Track for a man of somewhat mature years who had not had time to prepare himself properly for such an arduous exercise. In a few days, the 9th December to be exact, he would be 50 years of age. Fifty not out. A pretty average knock by todays standards, but Alexander was content. He had already had a very eventful life and there was absolutely no reason to complain.

Apart from bloody Osama that was. Or was it his Taliban friends? Or even the Afghan warlords themselves? He couldn't be sure. But a rare opportunity for him to replenish his empty coffers had unexpectedly and rapidly disappeared down the proverbial drainpipe. As he sat there reflecting on the situation he could not decide whether to be angry or elated. The adrenaline rush of Afghanistan versus the unparalleled vista before him. In such circumstances there was only one obvious solution.

He started to rise from the decking but was immediately and painfully reminded of the lower back injury that he had picked up in the Sudan all those years ago. Was it the jarring corrugations on that dirt road between Jebel Hasim and Jebel Himal that caused it? Or was it the couple of times on that same eventful journey that his trail bike had bucked him like a rodeo rider across the rock hard clay soil? That certainly taught him to take more notice of the deep ruts made by overladen trucks in the preceding wet season. Straightening his posture immediately eased the pain and without any further delay he made his way through sweet scented manuka to the mountain stream that bucked and frothed on its melodic passage to the lake below. And there they lay. The two little beauties. Two dark brown bottles of Wanaka's finest pilsner beer glistening beneath the surface of the water. Chilled to perfection. The New Zealand option was a clear winner this time Alexander concluded as he made his way back to the hut. Fate had clearly brought him here. Afghanistan would just have to wait.

Alexander was by no means a walker by nature or inclination. He had, it was true, worn his ancient leather boots at every opportunity in the few days prior to his unexpected departure to New Zealand. But it had been a belated and largely failed attempt to toughen up the soles of his feet for the anticipated trails ahead. His only previous experience of serious hiking, or 'tramping' as they called it here, could be could be counted on just two fingers.

The first occasion had been some 20 years before when he had similarly travelled to New Zealand on an extended vacation. It had been an opportunity to catch up with his younger sister and family who lived in Auckland. Tramping had certainly not been on his original agenda but somehow, like so many others, the literature on the tracks had completely seduced him. The Abel Tasman had been a delight to walk in the 1980s, meandering as it did in dappled shade close to the seashore. Oversized freshly harvested green lipped mussels boiling and opening in his undersized billycan. The camaraderie of fellow walkers from many nations experiencing the track in their own individual way. The peaceful azure sea, undisturbed apart from the occasional waft of wind on sail. The overloaded rucksack, and obligatory blistered toes and heels, which made the final kilometres such a torture for him. And then down south to the glory of the lakes, mountains and forests of Fiordland. And the Mamoe Track. Mamoe. The pinnacle of his limited tramping achievements. A relaxed jaunt for most trampers but an Everest for a novice like Alexander. Memories that had stayed with him for years. Fond memories. Poorly translated by fading photographs which never fully captured the majesty of it all. But for some reason he had never returned to the 'land of shadows' that he had immediately come to love. Until this very moment. Twenty long years later.

The only other tramping experience in his life had occurred just five years before. He had tried to erase it from his memory. A fiasco. An abject failure. For some reason he had had this eccentric urge to trace the route of his own Stewart ancestors all the way back to their origins. He had also wanted to trace his late mother's Montgomery line but a Great Aunt had politely asked him not to do so. He did not know why but he was more than happy to respect her wishes. After all, his Stewart line was more than he could handle. The route of his journey was carefully outlined on a detailed map, starting from his home in the south of England, back to Pembroke in Wales, from there to Cork in Ireland, then to Bangor in Northern Ireland, and finally on to Perth in Scotland. That was where the first recorded history of his particular Stewart family line had been traced some four hundred years before. His mother had always said that he was a strange one. He could not deny it. But he was an experienced hiker, wasn't he, even if his New Zealand experience was by then but a distant memory?

He estimated that the walk would take about three months, allowing for further research into his family history at various points along the way. There might even be a book in it since people liked that sort of thing nowadays. But his willpower, or more to the point, his body was not up to the task. By the end of five days of walking along country roads his blistered heels and toes had once again let him down. Or was that just a convenient excuse for a lack of personal resolve? A lack of inner strength? He couldn't be sure. Others battled on through pain to achieve their desired goals. But the explorer of the Stewart Clan he most certainly was not. Never ever again he vowed to himself. This long distance hiking business is certainly not for me. And so as Alexander sat there on the shores of Lake Caroline he felt very content with the outcome of his very first days walk. It was true that the last hour had been particularly hard, but then that always seemed to be the case. But he was back.

Just at that moment an Asian looking hiker, who Alexander guessed was probably Japanese because he was fully kitted out in the very latest range of Descente clothing, arrived at the hut. Now he really looks the part thought Alexander, who immediately felt very ashamed of his own outdated and rather threadbare kit. But as quickly as he had arrived the newcomer had disappeared, possibly carrying on directly to the next hut on the track. All was again peace and quiet, apart from the occasional piping tunes of a solitary tui in the near distance, eagerly searching for nectar.

Alexander had arrived at his destination so early in the afternoon that he had already inspected the two available bunk rooms. The first under the arched roof of the main building and the other of a more traditional shallow roof design close by. The traditional building was clearly much cooler and so he had laid out his sleeping bag on one of the communal bunks in order to stake his claim for the night. He had vaguely remembered that this was the accepted procedure.

He was just savouring the thought of fetching his sole remaining ice cold beer from the stream when to his left a rotund figure came bouncing through a gap in the bush dressed exactly like a pantomime bumble bee. As this vision rapidly drew closer Alexander observed that it was in fact a young woman in her late twenties, dressed almost entirely in black, tight fitting short sleeved top and shorts. Beneath her black shorts she wore what appeared to be leggings coloured with broad horizontal bands of yellow and black. More like a somewhat obese wasp he now unkindly thought. If Alexander's tramping kit was rather ancient and frayed then this young woman's clothing was verging on the ridiculous. All she lacked was the spring mounted fluffy ball antennae on her head to finish the job off to absolute perfection.

'G'day,' she said jovially as she relieved herself of the weight of her rucksack onto the wooden decking. 'My name's Kathy. Kathy Thomas. Originally from Auckland.'

'Alexander. Alexander Stewart. From Scotland. Well England actually. Very nice to meet you,' he replied rather stiffly. He was about to continue the conversation in a somewhat lighter tone when through the same opening in the trees lightly skipped someone who Alexander could only imagine had recently been cast adrift by the touring New York City Ballet. Lean in stature, jaundiced in complexion, the young man was similarly dressed in black leotards and what seemed from a distance to be black ballet shoes. A cross between Mr Bean and Blackadder, with physical features to match. Alexander was rapidly beginning to feel like a professional tramper compared to these two new arrivals. All he needed was a couple of more days of stubble on his chin.

'Hi,' the young man said in a similarly familiar manner. 'My name's Hoop. Well Hubermann actually, and that's only my middle name. Just call me Hoop.'

'Nice to meet you Hoop. Alexander, from England.'

It appeared that Kathy had already met Hoop since she made no move to greet him. And so the three new acquaintances were soon enjoying mugs of Alexander's freshly prepared tea, mutually reassured in the new companionship that they had found in such a remote location. They talked about the subjects newly introduced trampers usually discuss, the weather, the track, where they had been, where they were going, and so on.

'My husband and I have recently moved down from Auckland to Mamoe,' said Kathy. 'We just needed to get away from the sprawling city life and find some space where we could bring up our daughter in some kind of sanity. We looked at many places in the area, Cromwell, Te Anau, Queenstown and Wanaka, but finally plumped for Mamoe. We just knew from the first moment that we saw it that it was the right place for us.'

'Don't you miss all the excitement of city life?' said Hoop incredulously. 'I'd go crazy without the noise, abuse and congestion. Give me the Bronx any day.'

Hole in one, Alexander thought to himself. Hoop's going to tell us he's the principal dancer next.

'Not a bit of it,' said Kathy.' I feel healthier and fitter already. Can't wait to set up my own backpacker hostel. I really want to make the most of the outback lifestyle.'

If this is the fitter leaner Kathy, I wonder what she looked like before, Alexander pondered before he immediately scolded himself. Why am I being so ungenerous to such warm hearted and friendly people? And then he realised that his unkind thoughts said more about his own character shortcomings than those of his newly found companions.

'Have you walked many of these tracks Kathy?' Alexander inquired.

'Nope. Very first one. My husband, Peter, dropped me off at the start of the Ailsa this morning. I had hoped that he would have joined me but I couldn't change his mind. He's a builder by trade and not really into the outdoor life. The furthest he walks is down to the local bar after work. And anyway, there's our daughter to be cared for if we were both away at the same time. You know I've always wanted to do a real track but somehow the weeks and months have just flown by since the time we first arrived in Mamoe. It was either do it now or not at all, simple as that. I just said to Pete, see you in three days, and he was gone. It was a bit daunting at first.'

'It's also my first, what do you call it, tramp?' said Hoop. 'Shouldn't be here at all really. I took sixteen days vacation from the consultancy company I work for in New York and headed to New Zealand for some trout fishing.'

'You don't look like the fishing sort,' said Alexander, who had already placed Hoop in the stereotypical urban box.

'Just love it. I guess it's due to my early upbringing in Maine. Give me a long weekend and I just pack up my rod and jet off to wherever the fish are reported to be biting. But live in the outback permanently. Not for me. No Sir.'

'So have you been fishing outside of the States before?' asked Kathy.

'I went to Scotland once. About three years ago, Inverloch House in Aberdeenshire. Beautiful river. Lovely people. Lousy fishing. They included a personal fishing guide in the package. I think they called him a *gillie*, but that could have been his name. For three days the old buffer kept repeating, *'Best fishing in Europe, Sar. Best fishing in Europe. Now that's a fine specimen. One of the best this year. Oh thank you very much Sar. A five pound note for a wee dram will help keep out the cold. You're very generous Sar.'* Cost me a fortune. Didn't catch a fish of any mention during the whole expensive trip.'

'So how did you end up on the Ailsa Track?' enquired a still mystified Alexander.

'I haven't got a clue,' continued Hoop. 'I was due to be fishing the Mataura where I had been told that great fish could be had. Flew across the States, changed planes in LA, then down to Auckland. Changed planes again and then I'm in Christchurch. Business class travel is a breeze but by the time I arrived at the Mataura Lodge I didn't know what planet I was on! The owner was a great guy, Rob something or other. Anyway, I was asking Rob where the best fishing places in the area were and he said,

'Why don't you go and take a look for yourself before dinner.'

'But dinner is in twenty minutes, isn't it?' I responded.

'No problem there,' said Rob. *'Just go out of the front door, turn left, and walk about two hundred meters up the track leading off the main road. That's the original coaching bridge over the Mataura. See what you can find.'*

'Sounds a good idea Rob. Anyway I could do with stretching my legs a bit after all that travelling.'

'Without delay I set off for the bridge. It was a beautiful evening and the crimson sun was slowly setting in the west. Great scene, just like the movies. When I arrived I nonchalantly lent over the granite parapet and looked down into the clear water below. It took a while for my eyes to become accustomed to the subdued lighting within the water but what I saw took my breath away. First one, then two and then it must have been five gently waving shapes. I saw them maintaining their station against the steady flow of the crystal clear water. I could not believe my eyes.'

Alexander and Kathy could see that Hoop was in raptures recounting his story.

'They were absolute monsters. Great big beautiful specimens, just lazily holding their position and right below my feet. Brown trout. Unbelievable. A true fisherman's Shangri-La. I wanted to laugh. It was just so ridiculous. I had spent so many largely fruitless and expensive trips just trying to get a single bite from the dammed fish. But they had all been minnows compared to these brutes. I just stood on the bridge and laughed out loud. If anybody had seen me they would have thought I was mad.'

'But that still doesn't explain why you are here?' said a puzzled Alexander.

Hoop's radiant expression took on a sallow hue.

'The next morning it started. The rain that is. You would think that fish and water go together but they most certainly do not. I had been woken up just before dawn by the constant sound of drumming on the Lodge's tin roof and it just didn't stop. It rained through breakfast. It rained through lunch. I was so fed up that I put on my wet gear and strolled down to the bridge to see how things fared. It was difficult to believe that where once there had been a shallow gently flowing river there was now a raging torrent. I leant over the parapet, just as I had the previous evening, but there was nothing to be seen. I even started to think that the fish of the previous day had just been an illusion. Or more worryingly a prank by the owner of the Lodge who simply tethered imitation fish below the bridge in order to have some fun at the expense of his guests. After all Rob had told me that his ancestors had originated from Scotland and as far as I knew he could have been directly related to that crafty Scottish *gillie* who had recommended this place to me. *'Best trout fishing in the world, Sar. Best fishing in the world. Oh thank you Sar. Five pounds will help keep the flu out with a wee dram down at the Fox.'*

Alexander and Kathy could not help laughing at Hoop's sad story. It seemed as if, at least as far as fishing went, that Hoop was simply jinxed. Just born to fail. Hoop could not help but join in the fun because even he could now see the humorous aspect to it all.

'I tried very hard to be philosophical about the whole thing,' he continued. 'But basically I'm a born worrier. Not at ease with myself at all. If only I could have put my feet up by the fire with a good book and a mug of hot chocolate that would have been fine. But I could not. I fretted. Magazines were cast aside half read. After the second day I realised that I was fated. I had come from the other side of the world to escape the northern winter and what had I found. Winter! On the third day the rain abated. However, Rob informed me that it was still raining heavily in the mountains to the west and that the river was unlikely to settle down for at least three days, even if it stopped.

'Why don't you go up to Queenstown for a few days,' Rob had suggested. *'There are plenty of things to keep you occupied there and I'll give you a call as soon as things improve. Or you could try the Ailsa Track. It's a beautiful walk and you can easily hire any gear that you need.'* And so here I am folks, Edward Hubermann Schultz. Intrepid explorer.'

And they all laughed.

'But what about yourself Alexander. How did you come to be here?' inquired Kathy.

'Well, just like Hoop really, I shouldn't really be here at all. I'm an engineer by training, but I've never worked in my home country, only in the developing world. I guess I always found it more fulfilling. Village water supplies, small-scale irrigation, field drainage, dirt roads, that sort of thing. Countries in Africa, Asia and the Middle East, you name them and I've been there. Twenty six in all at the last count over a period of twenty five years. Short-term contracts of one to three months mainly, but never long term. Love my home comforts too much. At this very moment I should be sitting drinking coffee in downtown Kabul.'

'Wow, you wouldn't get me going there in a thousand years,' said Hoop.

'It looked alright at the time,' Alexander continued. 'Certainly not as bad as Iraq. I just kept a very close eye on the daily Afghan news via the internet. Apart from the occasional bomb the country seemed to be making steady progress. The presidential elections had been held in October without any major incidents and so I thought, well, why not. I'd never been there before and I'd heard that it was a beautiful country full of fascinating and diverse people. Exactly four weeks ago today my rucksack was packed, the Afghan visa was in place, medical passed, will updated, and I was ready to go. And then it happened. Just four days before my planned departure three United Nations workers were kidnapped in broad daylight in Kabul and threatened with execution.'

'I read about that,' said Kathy. 'Dreadful.'

'I must admit that I really needed the money,' continued Alexander, 'but it looked as if Afghanistan was rapidly turning into another Iraq with kidnappings and executions to order. I realised that it would inconvenience my potential employers at the United Nations if I pulled out, but not as much as it would inconvenience me if my head was separated from my body by the matter of a few feet!'

Kathy and Hoop laughed as they imagined the gruesome scene.

'I had already told some friends that if they saw me on television dressed in an orange boiler suit then they would know that things were not going as well as I had hoped. But that was a joke. What was happening was reality. And so I pulled out. Well postponed actually since I told the UN that I was still prepared to go once things settled down.'

'You really are crazy!' Hoop exclaimed. 'No way.'

'Not really,' continued Alexander. 'From past experience the news from these countries is often exaggerated and ninety nine percent of the people in the world are just great. It's just the one percent who foul it all up.'

'So how come you came to New Zealand?' asked Kathy.

'Well why not. The UN seemed upset that I had withdrawn at such short notice. My clothes were all washed and ironed. My rucksack was packed. I just thought that fate must have had a hand in it. Twenty years ago I came to New Zealand and walked the Mamoe Track. I'd always wanted to walk it again and it just seemed as good a time as any to revisit the past. Springtime in New Zealand. What could be better. And so within two days of pulling out of the Afghan job I had booked my flight, and within a week I was landing in Auckland. The Ailsa seemed an ideal way to get my body accustomed to tramping again before tackling the more difficult Mamoe.'

'Have you done much tramping?' asked Hoop.

Alexander thought for a moment and his initial impulse was to give the impression, helped by some careful embellishment, that he was a weather worn backwoodsman who thought nothing of ten day tramps with water up to his chest.

'No, not at all. The only real tramping experience that I have is the Abel Tasman and Mamoe tracks. And that was over twenty years ago.'

'Well that's far more than us,' said Kathy. 'Will you walk the track with us? I know that I would feel safer.'

'Me too,' said Hoop with apparent relief.

'Sure, I'd be only too pleased,' Alexander replied somewhat gratified. 'It will be great to have the company.

'Where can we buy some food?' said Hoop. 'I'm starting to get hungry.'

Alexander and Kathy looked at each other, and once again burst out laughing. They looked again at Hoop and they could see by his expression that he was deadly serious.

'Well, I would guess that if you follow that track over there for about thirty kilometres, that should just about do it,' said Kathy mischievously.

'You cannot be serious!' exclaimed Hoop, in what easily passed as a perfect McEnroe impression. 'Well how does anyone eat?'

'Well, we carry it all in with us,' said Alexander feeling once again like a seasoned campaigner. 'There's bottled gas in the huts, flushing toilets and bunks. But that's about all.'

'Why didn't anybody tell me?' Hoop continued looking rather agitated.

'Did you ask?' said Kathy knowing full well that he had not. But before he could respond Kathy said, 'I've got more than enough tucker, you're welcome to share mine, if you like.'

'And mine,' Alexander quickly added.

'This tramping business is pretty complicated,' continued Hoop shaking his head, 'I really had no idea. Well thanks for your help. That would be great. Jeez, I feel like a real Homer Simpson.'

'No worries,' said Kathy.

Hoop had no idea what Kathy meant but it sounded reassuring. 'I think that I'll just go to the rest room. That's what they call it here don't they?' said Hoop, and as he made his way towards the toilets he turned and said, 'They do have toilet paper here, don't they?' looking at them with more hope than conviction.

'No problem there,' said Kathy.

'Well thank goodness for that, these fern leaves look awfully rough,' Hoop chuckled as he made his way along the path.

'How about another brew, coffee this time?' said Alexander to Kathy, and without further ado they again made their way back to the kitchen area of the main hut. They sat down at one of the bare wooden tables as they waited for the water to boil.

'I met Hoop at the start of the track,' Kathy explained 'and after passing and re-passing each other a few times we decided to walk together. In fact I was rather scared about losing my way.'

By this time Hoop had rejoined them and continued Kathy's story.

'I travelled on the Mercury Express bus from Te Anau to the start of the track in the company of a number of other backpackers. I had a great time during the hour long journey to the drop off point. However, it came as a huge shock to me when it turned out that I was the only one getting out at the start of the track. The rest were all carrying on to stay at Gunn's Camp. I just didn't know what to do. I just stood there looking at the track disappearing into all that dark forest. Alone. I just had no idea what sort of dangers lurked within that gloom. I'd read about poisonous snakes, crocodiles and spiders. But maybe that was Australia? For sure we have them all in the States. Well alligators, not crocs. Anyway I just didn't know. I just stood and stared at the entrance for what must have been fifteen whole minutes. And then I made a decision. I'd just catch the next bus back to Te Anau. Easy. I'd be back in the comfort of the motel within a couple of hours. But when I looked at the timetable the next bus was tomorrow morning! God, it was rapidly becoming a nightmare. Hitchhike, or wave down a tourist bus? Now that's the answer, I thought. If anyone asked I could pretend that I'd just finished the track from the other direction. I tried to wave down a number of tourist buses but they all just waved back. I must have waved at virtually every nationality on the planet, Korean, Dutch, you name it!'

Alexander and Kathy laughed at Hoop's vivid description.

'And as for cars, they were virtually non-existent at this time of year. And camper vans won't pick you up. I was stuck. And then I saw Kathy's car draw up and noticed that her husband was unloading her rucksack. I quickly walked about fifty metres into the forest until I made sure that Kathy was actually going to start the track and not disappear again. As soon as I confirmed that she was I continued further up the path making sure that my pace was slow enough not to lose contact with Kathy. However, the slower I went the slower it seemed that Kathy went.'

'I saw the tramper up ahead,' said Kathy to Alexander. 'I thought great, I'll just follow close behind and I'll be alright. But he just seemed to go slower and slower until we were walking along at a snail's pace, still fifty metres apart. And then he stopped. I had no choice but to say a cheery 'Hi' and then continue on my way. After a short while I looked behind and there he was, fifty metres behind me. Whenever I sat down for a rest he would pass me and whenever he sat down I would pass him. It seemed that neither of us wanted to lead the way. And so the next time he was passing I just said, 'Hi, my name's Kathy. Do you mind if we walk together.' I could see the relief on Hoop's face, as no doubt he could see the same on mine.'

'You bet,' said Hoop.

'I know that feeling exactly,' said Alexander. 'When I did the Abel Tasman all those years ago it was just the same. A journey into the unknown. Would I be able to finish the walk? What would happen if I twisted my ankle or worse? I didn't want to make a fool of myself with all those experienced trampers around, but everything came right after a day or two. I'm sure it's the same experience for everyone new to walking the tracks.'

'Well I tell you I'm reassured meeting up with you two guys,' said Hoop. 'I'm really looking forward to this adventure. I had to buy my sleeping bag and so that would have been a waste of money if I hadn't carried on. The rucksack I hired. It's not bad but they only had a ladies model. I don't know if there is any difference?'

Neither Alexander nor Kathy could shed any light on that particular question. By now the sun had fallen even lower in the early evening sky and the shadows had begun to lengthen. Together they explored the combined kitchen and dining room area and tentatively tested their limited outback cooking skills before the more experienced trampers arrived to commandeer the facilities. Alexander managed to expertly demonstrate to the others how to burn his fingers in a failed attempt to light one of the complicated gas burners, whilst Hoop, not to be outdone, subsequently demonstrated how it was best not to hold onto a boiling pan of water for more than an instant. All in all these mini disasters, or 'meaningful learning experiences' as Hoop later described them, helped to strengthen the fledgling bond between them. They were no longer alone. They were part of a team. A rather inexperienced team.

After their early dinner Alexander was once more sitting on his own on the wooden decking enjoying the last warmth of the setting sun and his sole remaining beer. Then unexpectedly from his right, the opposite direction from which he and his new companions had come, a young woman came striding purposefully along carrying what seemed to be an exceptionally heavily loaded rucksack. She had beautiful golden hair tied in a long pigtail and was wearing a bright yellow T-shirt, blue shorts and sturdy walking boots. He could not help but notice that she had a shapely body, so fully developed and so very feminine. 'And God created woman,' he thought to himself. She was indeed quite stunning. She also looked every part the professional tramper, fully at home in this environment, totally in control.

Alexander did not see her again until about thirty minutes later when this time she emerged from the direction of the lake. Her long blonde hair, wetted from what must have been a swim in the icy water beyond, now hung loosely over her shoulders and cascaded like a tumbling golden waterfall down her back. Even the thought of swimming in the lake made Alexander shiver. But he was immediately smitten. It was a sensation that he had rarely experienced before and then only every decade or so. As in the past, there was absolutely nothing he could do about it. It just happens that way.

Throughout the late afternoon and early evening further walkers of every nationality continued to arrive until the hut buzzed with noise and excitement. Most were clearly experienced backpackers who gave the outward impression that they had been travelling for many months, if not years. Their skill at preparing appetising meals made of recently purchased fresh vegetables and more exotic ingredients made Alexander, Kathy and Hoop's boiled rice, tinned chilli con carne, and plain biscuits look pretty dismal efforts. Still they did not mind. They were pleased to be part of this newly formed community within the outback.

....

Te Puke leant against the bunk room wall of the Lake Caroline hut. He was not amused. In fact he was downright angry. That Rita Ata Whenua had a lot to answer for. For over one hundred years Te Puke had had pride of place on the wall of Rita's small ancestral home in the Parnell district of Auckland. And now she had given him to a complete stranger, who was not even one of their people. *Te Puke of One Thousand Battles*. Given to a complete stranger. *Te Puke of One Thousand Battles*. What would her ancestors say if they could only speak? Given away as a simple walking stick. Pa! He vowed then and there not to accept this indignity without a fight. And with that he slowly slid down the wall and rolled under the lower bunk into the farthest recesses of that space.

2. A Land of Uncertain Climate

Friday 26th November 2004

The night turned out to be far colder than expected and even Alexander's down sleeping bag had not quite managed to keep out the chill. There and then he resolved to wear more clothes the following night, particularly his socks and thermals. Waking at first light, as he usually did, he looked across the bunk room and saw the unmistakable figure of Hoop, fully dressed, wearing a snug woollen hat, busily packing his ladies rucksack. My goodness Hoop is keen thought Alexander, as he rubbed the night out of his eyes. Getting ready for the track at first light. Impressive. Alexander turned over to get a little more rest and Hoop disappeared in the direction of the kitchen. The next thing Alexander knew was when he heard the sound of Kathy whispering from her bunk on the opposite side of the room. It was strange how her whispers resonated so loudly.

'You can't go back now Hoop. It would be such a pity having got this far. If you were so cold you should have cuddled up to me,' she added mischievously, guessing that the female form was not Hoop's first preference.

'No, I've made my decision,' Hoop replied rather loudly, 'and I'm going back. I nearly froze to death last night and it was certainly no fun. No fun at all. I'll just get back to the fishing or the nightclubs in Queenstown. That's what I know best.'

'You can borrow some of my spare clothes tonight if you wish,' Alexander intervened, sorry to lose a recently made companion.

'Thanks Alexander, but no. I've made a firm decision and that is that. I have to get a move on to catch that bus back to Te Anau, and then on to Queenstown. Nice to have met you folks. Bye now.'

And with that the illustrious Hoop disappeared through the bunk room door and was gone. As quickly as he had entered their lives he had left. Later Alexander and Kathy would both agree that he had made the right decision in the circumstances. No point in going on if you didn't enjoy it they both said. No point at all. But privately they both felt that Hoop's hasty retreat had increased their own achievement, however limited that had been. They had lasted the first night. It certainly increased their mutual determination to finish the track.

In the meantime the weather had taken a turn for the worse. Alexander could see the path that would ultimately lead them to the next hut rising steeply up the far side of the valley until it disappeared into lowering clouds. Knowing that todays walk would be high above the tree line Alexander proposed to Kathy that they should start as soon as possible, to which suggestion Kathy readily agreed. A quick breakfast of instant porridge, washed down with black coffee, soon made them feel ready for the task ahead. It was then that Alexander realised that he had mislaid the hiking stick that had been given to him by Rita in Auckland. She was a long time friend of his sister and her husband.

'Where is that damn stick?' said Alexander out loud as he tried to remember where he had put it the night before. For an instant he thought that someone might have taken it.

'Have you seen my stick Kathy? I'm sure that I leant it in the corner last night.'

'You mean that beautiful pole? I said to Hoop last night that it was really special. All those shades of brown, gold and black. No, I'm afraid not. How did you come to own it?'

'It was given to me by an elderly Maori friend of my sister who I first met some twenty years ago. When I previously left the country she had said to me,

'Welcome you back again.'

'Just those exact words.'

'Welcome you back again.'

'It was quite moving since I could tell that she really meant it. A Maori, with generations of history in this land, sincerely wishing for me to return. I never forgot it. When I met her this time she said to me, *'Where have you been Alexander?'* as though I had just been out to buy a bottle of milk and had been longer than expected. I said,

'Rita I've been away twenty years and yet you greet me as if I have been away for twenty minutes.'

'I knew that you would come back,' Rita replied. *'It was your destiny.'*

'She then exchanged with me the traditional Maori greeting and we sat down in the warmth of her little home for a long talk. Rita hasn't been in the best of health these past few years but she battles on. Must be in her late eighties now. We talked about many things until I mentioned to her that I was planning to walk the Mamoe Track again. She looked at me knowingly. Unsteadily she had then risen to her feet and walking over to the huge open fireplace she gently lifted an old wooden stick from where it hung in pride of place on the wall.'

'I want you to have this Alexander. It has been in our family for over three hundred years. His name is Te Puke. Te Puke is just not any old piece of wood Alexander. Te Puke is a weapon of war, a Taiaha, which has been used by our leaders for generations. Please accept Te Puke as a gift from my people.'

'I couldn't possibly do that Rita. I'm really moved that you have offered this beautiful stick to me but I couldn't possibly take it. It belongs to your people and no one else. What would happen if I lost it? I would feel dreadful.'

Rita laughed. *'You cannot lose Te Puke. And even if you did he would find his way home. By stream, river, lake or sea.'*

'But what if I broke it?'

'You cannot break Te Puke. He is made of kauri. He has outlasted generations of my family and he will outlast both you and I. No, take Te Puke Alexander. It is my firm wish.'

'Well I don't quite know what to say Rita. It's a wonderful gift. And I know that it will come in really useful in the mountains and for crossing any fast flowing streams.'

Alexander had been full of admiration for his gift. It was beautiful to behold with colours that ranged from walnut brown to cream along its length. The bottom five centimetres were encased in copper whilst a silver coloured coin of ancient heritage had been let into the head. The flowers engraved on the coin seemed to Alexander's eye just like the snowdrops that he knew from home, but he could not be certain. Rita told him it was in fact a native plant, a Kowhai. The Maori Pukawa, that Rita told him was engraved on the other side of the coin, had no way of protruding its fearful tongue out at him.

'I know Te Puke will be a good companion for you Alexander. After all he is going home to the land of our fathers. That is where our tribe lived for generations. Close to the shores of Lake Mamoe. Our people made their way there shortly after the first canoes arrived from Hawaiki. We lived off the land, the sky, and the waters of the lake and its rivers. And then our peace was disturbed. For sixty years our people, the Ngati Mamoe, fought the tribes from the north who wished to steal our birthright. Our pounamu. Our greenstone. We

fought many great battles. Te Puke was there. Te Puke of One Thousand Battles. Until we could fight no more. Those who were not killed or enslaved went into exile. My family arrived here in Auckland many generations ago but we have never forgotten our origins. We have never forgotten our land. And now I am the last of our pure line. The last of the true Ngati Mamoe.'

'Wow,' said Kathy. 'That's really a special story.'

'It certainly is,' agreed Alexander. 'I feel very honoured to have been entrusted with such an heirloom. But I've only had the damn thing for two weeks and already I've lost it! I knew that I should never have accepted it as a gift. All it does is get in the way. Doesn't easily fit into taxis or buses. It's just a damn nuisance. Now where are you Te Puke?'

And with that Alexander got down on his hands and knees and peered into the darkness beneath the bunks. At first he couldn't see what he was looking for but then, in the far corner, he just made out the shape of the object of his search. Alexander reached under to capture his quarry.

'Got you, you good for nothing piece of wood. Now behave yourself in future.' He then proceeded to strap Te Puke tightly to his pack. 'Now get out of that Te Puke of One Thousand Battles.'

They set off on schedule at eight o'clock in the morning taking good account of the six hour journey time which they had read that it would take them if all went well. It was going to be a hard day. The other trampers remained oblivious to their departure and still lay like dormant polar bears on their icy communal bunks. Alexander suggested that Kathy lead the way to ensure that she set a pace with which she was most comfortable. Almost immediately their path took them through thick native bush where they had to scramble over moss covered tree roots, twisted and distorted, as if transplanted from a scene of some frightening witches tale. But soon the path settled into a regular incline and this allowed the pair to adopt a more relaxed rhythm.

Looking up from the hut the previous evening the climb had not appeared to be as severe or as long as it was now proving to be and both were soon breathing and perspiring heavily. Occasionally the clouds would part and they could see the snow capped peaks rising far above them whilst the hut below was by now just a small dot dwarfed by the mountainside above. It seemed so vulnerable. Up and up they climbed closely hugging the narrow path as it made its way along the top of ragged bluffs which dropped precipitously to the valley floor below. After an hour or more of continuous effort they finally reached their immediate goal, a flat area of tussock grass above the tree line which marked the beginning of the long traverse, and which would continue along the Ailsa valley for at least another three hours. Kathy seemed intent on plowing on and so Alexander called out,

'Hey Kathy! Time for a short break,' to which she readily agreed.

Alexander undid the straps of his rucksack and lent Te Puke against a nearby rock. He then delved inside to locate his gas bottle, matches, saucepan, water, coffee and sugar. At just that moment it seemed as if sudden gust of wind blew up out of nowhere and rolled Te Puke along the rock face. In one bound Alexander's trusty hiking stick had slipped over the edge of the path, cartwheeled once and seem destined to end up in a fast flowing stream which ran far below the point where they stood. Whether it was pure luck or not they didn't know but just when it seemed that all was lost the hand cord at the head of the stick snagged on a single gorse bush that grew in splendid isolation on an outcrop some fifteen meters below them. And there Te Puke hung.

'Well that was lucky,' said Kathy. 'I thought that you had lost your stick for good this time.'

Alexander was not amused. 'It's becoming more trouble than it's worth Kathy that damn stick. Perhaps it would have been better if I had lost the darn thing.'

And with that he carefully climbed down and retrieved Te Puke from the gorse bush.

....

Te Puke was distraught. Where on earth had that ugly yellow bush which had foiled his escape come from? He had never seen anything like it before and they certainly weren't around when he last passed this way over two hundred years before. All those horrible yellow flowers and prickly growth. The opportunity had been so good. Below lay the stream which would have taken him safely away from the stranger, and it had taken little effort to conjure up that wind. It was just bad luck, that's what it was. Bad luck.

....

'Blimey, that climb was hard,' Kathy said as she gratefully slipped her rucksack onto the coarse grass. 'I'm absolutely knackered.'

'You've done very well,' Alexander continued. 'You've now basically completed the hardest climb of today's walk.'

'You're kidding? You're not kidding. Wow! '

Alexander could see by her expression that she was absolutely delighted. She literally beamed with pleasure. As he tended the gas burner he continued,

'You've actually reached the highest point on the whole Ailsa Track. From now on it's fairly level, apart from one or two minor inclines. And then it's a steep downhill drop to the next hut at Ailsa Falls where we will stay tonight. Tomorrow it continues downhill until it levels out and follows a fast flowing river to the very end of the track. Simple as that.'

Kathy rested her sizeable backside on her rucksack, stretched out her dumpy legs, and let the intermittent rays of the sun warm her body. For what seemed a long twenty minutes they sat there engrossed in their own thoughts. The rest and mugs of hot coffee revived any aching limbs and soon both were eager to continue the journey along their appointed path.

Alexander had previously sensed that there might be a deeper reason behind Kathy's solo adventure. So in order to give her as much time and space as she required he made an excuse and suggested that she should walk on ahead for a while. He said that he would follow as soon as possible. He reassured her that he would be close at hand if anything untoward happened. In any case Alexander's stout walking partner was proving to be far faster than himself and her strength belied her physical form. He was therefore more than happy to pursue his own path at a pace more appropriate to a man rapidly approaching fifty. *'Cannonball Run Kathy'*, he thought. Now that's an appropriate nickname in more ways than one.

On occasion Alexander would catch a glimpse of the *'Cannonball'* in the far distance passing around some rock outcrop or stopping to chat with the trampers travelling their path in the opposite direction. After failing to see her at all for some considerable time Alexander began to worry that his charge had suffered some kind of dreadful mishap. But there she was once again buzzing busily around some distant bend on the route, even further ahead. There was really no stopping her now.

Alexander had always considered himself to be a particularly relaxed sort of person. Friends often described him as being so laid back he was almost horizontal. But it was only now that he realised what tension he had been carrying with him in recent weeks. The clear mountain air that he breathed, the sweat that he exuded, the effort that he expended all seemed to have contributed to a new level of peace within himself. A very large weight had been gradually lifted from his shoulders and for the very first time he felt totally relaxed. It was indeed so good to be alive he thought. It was so good to be free of his recent Afghan concerns, which had been far deeper and more profound than he had realised. But suddenly his reverie was abruptly broken by a shout.

'Where have you been slowcoach?' Kathy bellowed good-naturedly from a small rise in the near distance. She had reached the key point in the day's walk where all that remained was a stiff two hour descent to the Ailsa Falls hut. Alexander could clearly see the exhilaration on Kathy's face. She was going to make it. Big Kathy Thomas, the butt of so many unkind jokes since childhood, was going to bloody well do it. She was going to knock the bastard off.

They both sat on a large rock outcrop for a while, looking far down into the valley from where they had so recently come, and behind them into the valley where their path would soon take them. Spirits rising they got to their feet and commenced their steady descent to the unseen hut below. Descending proved far harder than Kathy had imagined and on more than one occasion she had slipped abruptly onto her substantial rear. The laughter that inevitably followed reassured Alexander that no lasting harm had been done. And then at long last they could both see the dark green tin roof of the hut below them and when they finally achieved their goal and entered the bunk room it was clear that none had preceded them. Alexander assumed that earlier starters, if any, had taken one of the optional side paths to particular vantage points along the route. But Alexander and Kathy were more than satisfied with their six hours of sustained effort. It was time for them both to have a short and well deserved siesta before the others arrived.

....

Te Puke reluctantly had to admit that he had actually enjoyed the day. After all he was getting closer to his homeland and many of the features that he now saw were very familiar. Above all, he hadn't had to do a single thing. The stranger, Alexander, had slipped a few times and occasionally knocked his knee against the odd rock or two, followed by a few expletives, but what was that to do with him? If he chose not to make use of my skills then that's his business. Yes, it had been quite a satisfactory day.

....

The most popular way to walk the Ailsa Track was in the opposite direction to their own path. Therefore, of the occupants he had seen at the Lake Caroline hut the previous evening Alexander noticed that there were only five other familiar faces at the Ailsa Falls hut that night. This clearly constituted an informal group with a common history and therefore the six of them, an English couple named Pete and Jan, an Australian called Andy, the beautiful young woman who Alexander had previously seen at the Lake Caroline hut, Kathy and himself, all sat at the same table during their evening meal.

As he slowly appraised all of the occupants of the hut Alexander became aware that he had eyes for only one person, the young woman sitting close by. From her accent he had guessed that she was either German or Austrian but she remained somewhat aloof and self-absorbed during the early part of the evening. Later on Alexander had the opportunity to talk to her, as he did with all the others, in order to be friendly but without being too forward. Her name, it transpired, was Sonja, and she was indeed German, from a small town in Bavaria. She had been in New Zealand for just over four weeks and was planning to stay a further three months, mainly walking the appropriately titled 'Great Walks' of the country. She told him that she had just finished the McKenzie Track that led directly to the Lake Caroline hut where Alexander had first observed her striding past the day before. After briefly explaining his own plans Alexander did not press her further since he sensed that at this particular moment in time she did not wish to volunteer any further information about herself.

In the meantime the Australian member of their group, Andy, was unintentionally impressing their small gathering by opening up a number of small plastic containers each full of a separate delicacy, olives, artichokes, macadamia nuts and the piece de la resistance, Baileys Irish Cream liqueur. Now here was a real professional at work Alexander thought to himself as he tried to forget his own meal of curry flavoured noodles which he had enthusiastically prepared and consumed together with Kathy. The next time he vowed that he would do better. Much better. Andy turned out to be a very interesting and informative source of knowledge on the art of tramping, particularly concerning his recent experiences in Tasmania, but in a commendably modest sort of way.

Later in the evening, whilst the babble of conversation milled around him, Alexander suddenly found that he was at a complete loss for something to do. He had failed to bring a good book to read during the long hours that would be spent at each hut after every day's tramping. It remained light until past nine o'clock in the evening and so there were many vacant hours to fill. It was a pretty basic omission, but just one of many that he had made. He had by now read his backpacker hostel guide, bus timetable, and track information leaflets from back to front. At just that moment Sonja lent across the table to him and asked if he would like to go outside for a short walk since she said she was becoming bored. They left the others and walked back up the track a little way until finally they sat down by a small waterfall. At first they talked about nothing in particular. It was then that Alexander unexpectedly turned and could not help but notice that there was a certain moistness in her eyes, not tears as such, but that moment when tears are in the very balance. She turned partly away but in a show of confidence in him that Alexander had not expected she said,

'I'm so homesick. I don't know why but I feel so unhappy.'

In an instant Alexander's perception of this young woman changed from one of aloof Germanic strength to one of vulnerability.

'I think that it is only to be expected Sonja,' responded Alexander uncertainly. 'After all, this is the first time that you have travelled so far away from your home country. We have all felt the same at one time or another.'

Sonja stood up and began throwing pebbles into the tumbling stream below.

'I don't think that it's normal,' she continued.

Alexander so wanted to give Sonja the support that she so clearly needed but he felt completely inadequate to be able to do so. The only thing that came to mind was to recount his own personal experience of homesickness. He had rarely mentioned this to anyone before.

'When I was eleven years old,' he began 'my parents sat me down and asked me if I wished to join my elder cousin at a boarding school many miles from where we lived. In fact it was in another part of the country. Our family were not well off and so the cost of paying school fees was extremely difficult for them both. A sacrifice no less. But, of course, I was unaware of that fact at the time. My cousin seemed to be very happy at boarding school and so there was no doubt in my mind that I definitely wanted to join him. And so it was settled. The first one or two days of school were fine since the novelty of it all was so exciting. We new boys arrived a few days before the rest of the school so all was relatively peaceful and homely. And then suddenly all was chaos. Hundreds of rowdy boys arrived all rushing around, shouting loudly, completely at home with their surroundings. It was only then that reality hit and I realised that I would not be returning to the comfort of my home and the loving care of my mother for a very long time. Someone who had been with me all of my life until that moment.'

Sonja looked at Alexander inquisitively. It was strange to hear this grown man, who must have been about the same age as her own father, being so open and frank. Freely exposing his weakness to her.

'And then it started.' Alexander continued. 'The misery and the tears. I was just so unhappy. I think I shed enough tears to overflow the river which ran below the playing fields at the bottom of the school.' Alexander laughed at the memory. 'I think I must have cried virtually every day for two years.'

'But why were your parents so cruel?' asked Sonja.

'I certainly don't think they meant to be cruel Sonja. After all they had left the final decision to me. They just knew that I would never receive such a good education at my local school. They put my future before their own.'

'But didn't you ask to leave?'

Alexander laughed again. 'I must have written at least ten letters in the first term alone saying what a good boy I would be and how hard I would work if they would only let me leave. I'm surprised that it didn't break my mother's heart. I'm sure that it must have hurt her deeply. My father as well, perhaps. But they were right not to let me leave you know Sonja.'

'How could they be right to cause you such pain?'

'I would never have achieved what I later did without that education. I'm sure that I would have just become one of the gang if I had gone back to my local secondary school. Afraid of being called the school swot, of being left out, unwittingly derailed into a dead end career. I would never have made university and the opportunities that were later presented to me.'

'It seems like a high price to have paid,' said Sonja. 'We don't have such outdated schools in Germany.'

'It certainly left a few scars. But no, it was a price worth paying. My parents were right not to give in.'

Somehow Sonja's own unhappiness seemed to subside as she realised that she was not alone in feeling how she did. If this old man could be homesick then clearly it was only natural that so should she from time to time. She felt reassured by this. She felt reassured that this complete stranger had opened up his weakness to her. She felt stronger. Twilight was now upon them but still they sat and talked.

'I had a nightmare of a journey to New Zealand,' recalled Sonja. 'Sheer hell!' she said quite forcefully to emphasise the point. 'It was madness really. I bought the cheapest ticket available and that was on Korean Airlines, via Seoul. No stopover, just straight through. I cannot complain about the airline. I guess each one is much the same as any other. I don't know. But I was sick you see. I have no idea what it was but from the moment I passed through immigration in Frankfurt I began to feel ill. Some sort of fever, but worst of all diarrhoea.'

Sonja looked at Alexander and for a moment she thought that she should refrain from such intimate detail. But then again he had been so open with her.

'I have tried to work out what caused it. Perhaps it was the emotion of leaving my boyfriend and family. I can't remember anything that I ate could have caused it. But whatever it was, I certainly had it. But what could I do? My ticket was non-refundable and so I just had to get on with it. Twenty six hours of absolute hell. The stewardesses did what they could to help but I was a complete wreck. I spent half of the time in the toilet. Everybody must have thought that I was quite mad. How I survived the journey I just don't know. When I finally arrived in Christchurch they could have just tipped me out onto the tarmac, I wouldn't have cared. I just wanted to die there and then. Or just return home as soon as possible.'

'It certainly sounds like a dreadful experience,' said Alexander. 'What on earth did you do then?'

'The people at the airport were very helpful. I went to the medical centre and they did some tests. It seems that I had caught some sort of undefined bug that they felt would clear up after a day or two. Nothing too serious. They gave me some antibiotics that they hoped would solve the problem. And the silly thing is I'm a trained nurse and I had no idea what it was.'

'I hate air travel at the best of times,' continued Alexander 'but as you say your flight was a complete nightmare.'

'The tourist office at the airport were very helpful and they arranged a taxi to take me to a nearby bed and breakfast. After the best hot shower that I have ever had I just slipped between the clean cotton sheets and slept and slept. I must have slept for two whole days. Molly, the owner of the house, was very kind. She basically cared for me like her own daughter. After three days I had started to regain my energy and the thought of catching the first plane back to Germany seemed to recede into the background. It would have been such a failure. After all I had been planning this trip for over twelve months and so to give up immediately was not an option for me. I don't think I could have faced my boyfriend telling me, *'I told you so.'* And with that Sonja laughed out loud. A long booming laugh which echoed across the valley. It was good to hear her laugh.

'My first trip after my recovery was to Kaikoura where I swam with the dolphins and watched the whales rise and fall to the depths of the ocean. Have you ever swum with the dolphins Alexander? No. Oh it's just amazing. It's one of the best experiences I have ever had. The dolphins did more for my spirits than any human being could have done and they banished all negative thoughts from my mind. That is until this evening when my sadness returned.'

'I think that homesickness is just a natural part of a traveller's life,' said Alexander. 'I would be more worried if you didn't miss your friends and family.'

They did not talk for much longer since it was by now quite dark but before they left Alexander suggested to Sonja that she join himself and Kathy for the final part of the track. He said that they were both novices and they would really welcome the company of someone as experienced as herself. Sonja readily agreed to this proposal and with that they both returned to the hut to join the general throng. Sonja felt reassured that she was no longer alone in a strange land.

They had hardly sat down in the dining room area again when a commotion broke out outside of the window. A small group of well dressed people of varying age and sex seemed intent on peering in through the windows like so many visitors at the zoo. They were all dressed in the very latest *'adventure wear'* procured no doubt from leading stores in New York, London and Paris. It was immediately obvious to all of the aptly named 'freedom walkers' inside of the hut that this gaggle were from the official guided walks group whose private lodge was located only a short distance away. The group had no doubt just finished their prepared evening meal with accompanying choice of cheese, wines and liqueurs. Bolstered by their alcoholic intake they had clearly decided to go and have a look at how the poorer half of humanity lived. Not for them the indignity of carrying their own overloaded rucksack over such difficult and annoying paths like a common labourer. No, that night they would be sleeping in their own individual rooms under warm duvets prepared for them in advance by the lodge staff. All they had to carry was a very small day pack to hold their freshly prepared pre-packed lunches.

Lowered tones were not the overriding characteristic of this particular section of society and those inside could hear them squawking,

'Its really awful you know. They all sleep in the same bunk rooms on communal beds. Men and women!'

and

'Do you see they are actually cooking for themselves!'

None of this greatly perturbed the trampers inside who just returned to their individual conversations, cooking, reading quietly or playing games of cards. They knew very well that the people outside were paying over one thousand dollars for their luxury whilst the 'freedom walkers' were only paying a fraction of that to experience the very same magical sights. Those peering in from outside were the real losers but the majority of them wouldn't have been able to recognise the fact if they tried. Not in a thousand years. Perhaps privately, in a quieter time, one or two might come to appreciate what they had missed. Gradually, one by one, the strange assortment of unwanted guests trailed away back up the path to their cocktails and their material lives. It had been good entertainment for all concerned. On both sides.

3. Bare Earth Embracing Sweet Rain

Saturday 27th November 2004

The next morning Alexander awoke early to the howling of the wind and the hammering of the rain on the metal roof of the bunk room. A real old storm was in progress and he considered it fortunate that he, Kathy and Sonja were heading directly down the valley and not up onto the exposed ridge lines where they had walked the day before. How suddenly the weather can change in the mountains, he thought, and he promised that he would pay closer attention to the weather forecasts in the future. As they were preparing their breakfast the hut warden came in and advised the walkers going in the opposite direction to delay their start until at least midday since conditions on the tops were potentially dangerous. After that time it was expected that the situation would improve.

Following a hearty breakfast taken in the warmth of the dining room area, Alexander, Kathy and Sonja put on their full wet weather gear, double checked their rucksacks, and commenced their steep descent through a forest of mountain beech. The trees gave considerable shelter from the wind but the rain was torrential. Kathy *'Cannonball Run'* Thomas was soon far ahead of the other two winging her way back home to her husband and daughter with a newly discovered confidence in herself, her marriage and her life. Alexander meanwhile fell in behind Sonja and soon found that her pace was virtually identical to his own.

At one point they passed a major landslip, which in years past had crossed the track without a moments warning taking with it any animate or inanimate object in its path. Unwary trampers would not have been excluded. This again reminded Alexander that the mountains should never be taken lightly and this train of thought was soon reinforced by a huge silver beech tree that had been blown across their path within the last few hours. Shortly after negotiating this obstacle Alexander and Sonja could hear the distant sound of a mountain stream in full flood. As they rounded a corner in the track they came upon Kathy who was standing quietly bemused before a raging torrent. Everywhere they looked the stream, of about fifteen metres in width, bucked and foamed with no obvious safe place to cross. For about ten minutes they searched for easy crossing points above and below the track line but none could be found. It was clear to them all that one slip in the fast flowing stream with a fully loaded pack could prove disastrous, possibly fatal.

Kathy's experience of stream crossing technique was clearly non-existent. Alexander's only previous experience was limited to hopping from rock to rock in a usually vain attempt to keep his feet dry some twenty years before. Even so that past experience had stimulated him to try and imagine what he would do if he had to cross a fast flowing stream whilst tramping on his own in the future. Whilst in Wanaka on that previous visit he had therefore looked at various expanding walking poles that he had seen the more experienced trampers carrying. They were, however, all too expensive and he did not want to spend so much money on such an infrequently used item. It was then that Alexander remembered Te Puke.

....

Te Puke was having a great time. At that very moment he was dreaming about fighting past battles and about the beauty of the Maori maidens that his many owners had once known. His new master had ignored his presence and he had never had it so easy. It was just at that moment that his dream was rudely interrupted when the stranger began unfastening the straps that held him tightly to the rucksack. Things had decidedly taken a turn for the worse.

....

'We can use Te Puke to help us across,' Alexander exclaimed with a certain pride.

'What on earth is *'Tey Puukee'?'* responded Sonja whose knowledge of the English language had apparently failed her.

'My hiking stick,' said Alexander who was by now holding Te Puke firmly between both hands.

'You mean that you have given your hiking stick a name?' said Sonja wondering if Alexander was perhaps not quite as sane as she had first thought.

'Well no, not exactly. I didn't actually give him a name myself Sonja. He already had it. But it is a long story and I'll explain everything later. I don't think that we will find any better place to cross this torrent than where the track approaches the stream,' Alexander continued rather unconvincingly. 'I'll walk across testing the depth with Te Puke just to make sure it's safe. What do you think Sonja? You have far more experience than I in these situations.'

'I think that what you propose is correct,' said Sonja in her stiff Germanic tone and without any further delay Alexander warily entered the ice cold water supporting himself against the torrent with his stout pole Te Puke. As his boots filled up with ice cold water he suddenly thought that perhaps experienced trampers removed their boots and put on their walking sandals for such crossings. He really would have to learn much more about this bushcraft business before he really landed himself in deep trouble, or more pertinently, in deep water. Alexander was particularly surprised at the force of the stream and step by slippery step he waded deeper and deeper until the water passed his thighs and approached his midriff. He knew that if he went any deeper the fast flowing stream would strike hard against his rucksack with potentially devastating force. Just at that moment his left foot slipped and it appeared that all was lost. Te Puke immediately sprang into action and dug himself deeply into the gravel at the base of the stream. He was a pillar of strength, immovable, a veritable Thracian column. *'You're a damn fool Stewart,'* Alexander thought to himself silently. Fortunately, with Te Puke providing solid support, the crossing continued. He descended no deeper and step by careful step he slowly emerged from the water on the other side of the stream. Absolutely soaked through but safe and sound. He felt exultant.

'Well done Te Puke. Well done,' said Alexander out loud. Sonja looked at him despairingly. He was now talking to his stick. The English. Eccentric or just mad, she did not know. Perhaps both.

'Whoopee,' shouted Kathy.

'Well done Alexander. I think Kathy and I should also use your stick to cross,' Sonja shouted above the roar of the torrent. So Alexander threw Te Puke like a novice javelin thrower to the other side of the stream quietly praying that his new found friend would not fall short and flow out of his life forever, so soon after he had entered it. But he had no need to fear for his arm was true. Kathy, being somewhat stouter and much shorter than the other two, was not so sure about this unscripted adventure. Everything had been going so well until this point. Nevertheless, she did as Sonja instructed and holding each other firmly they entered the water with Te Puke once more acting as their guide and support. Fortunately their crossing was uneventful except for a loud expletive from Kathy as the water reached her sizeable bosom to the effect of *'Jesus, this water's bloody cold.'*

When safely on the other bank they all laughed at the thrill of it and stood there for a few moments in the torrential rain taking in what they had just achieved. Totally soaked through. Basking in the moment. Another unforeseen test had been successfully passed and with that they resumed their former path with the *'Cannonball'* speeding off once again until the sound of her squelching boots could be heard no more. It was not long before they finally reached the end of the track and the pick-up point that was conveniently located next to a rudimentary shelter.

....

Te Puke felt more like his old self. After so long hanging on the wall even the great Te Puke had some fears that he might have lost some of his powers. But not a bit of it. The moment the stranger had slipped, there he was as quick as an arrow from a bow, into the gravel to grip the earth tight. As much as the water demons fought him he had held his own until his master was safely to the other side. And this stranger, Alexander, or whatever he called himself. Green as a new sapling. But strong and wiry as a sapling. And not afraid to lead. Perhaps he had potential after all?

....

'Sonja, I really did enjoy walking the Ailsa,' said Alexander, as they sat down inside the shelter. 'It was great to discover a new track, see such beautiful sights and to make such good friends. I enjoyed it so much that I am really determined to do the Mamoe next.'

Sonja had earlier told Alexander that she planned to walk the Mamoe Track within the next few days. What Alexander was clearly trying to convey to her was, *'I know that I was always going to walk the Mamoe anyway Sonja, but I would really love to walk it with you. People like us meet up all the time for just a few days but then go their own separate ways. It's just the way backpacking friendships are. Short lived and short-term. But I really don't want to say goodbye.'*

'Why don't you join me?' Sonja replied without hesitation. The very words that Alexander had been hoping to hear but had feared would never be said. It was truly pathetic. After all he was a grown man and she was just a girl. But he couldn't help himself. He was enchanted by her company and he just could not bear for her to walk out of his life so soon after she had so randomly walked into it. After all, such encounters were rarer than the nuggets of gold lying hidden in the river beneath them.

'Oh, that would be great,' he said, trying hard not to sound too ecstatic. 'It would certainly be much better for me to have someone with alpine experience to walk with.'

In order not to omit their newly found companion from the proceedings Sonja asked Kathy if she too wanted to walk the Mamoe with them.

'I'd really love to,' she replied, 'but I think that I should get back to my family just now. Next year for certain.'

They had all made good time on the descent and so they took off their supposedly *'waterproof'* outer clothing in the small shelter and after drying themselves they delved into their sacks to retrieve dry socks, cotton shirts and trousers. With a due degree of modesty, stranger changed in front of stranger, as if they always did that sort of thing, so familiar had they become with each other over the past few hours. The bus was not due for another hour and so Alexander unrolled his sleeping bag and instead of dressing immediately he dozed in the warm down cocoon comforted by the thought that he could look forward to at least another four days in the company of the young women for whom he had developed such tender feelings. It was ridiculous for a man of his age but there was nothing he could do about it. It had just happened.

Just as Alexander was finally dozing off he was rudely disturbed by a loud shout,

'Wake up lazy bones,' Kathy called out. 'The bus is leaving!'

With a large degree of panic Alexander emerged from his sleeping bag in his underwear to find to his horror that he was surrounded by a large group of trampers who had just arrived on the shuttle bus and were in the process of getting ready to commence their own walk in the opposite direction. They found it hugely amusing as he rapidly half pulled on his trousers, stuffed his rucksack in great haste, and left the shelter with his trousers hanging around his ankles shouting, 'Wait for me. Wait for me!' The Santa Claus boxer shorts, that a Dutch girlfriend had given him years before, were the only thing that protected his modesty. He felt such a fool with Sonja, Pete, Jan, Andy and Kathy just sitting there laughing at his antics. It was not an impressive performance and so he just sat at the back of the bus the whole seventy kilometres to Mamoe, staring out of the window, cringing with embarrassment. Choruses of *'Jingle Bells, Jingle Bells,'* and other seasonal Christmas tunes boomed out from the front led by the main villain, Kathy *'The Traitor'* Thomas. Bastards, he thought and laughed.

....

Te Puke had to laugh. It was just like that time Rangi got blind drunk on all that fermented honey. Ah, those were the days. How many years ago was it now? He couldn't remember. But this Alexander bloke, he's not such a bad type after all. He may have dragged his trousers through the dirt but he didn't drag me. He's even started talking to me at last. *'Come on Te Puke. Let's sit at the back away from this ungrateful rabble,'* he said. No more slumming it with all those rucksacks and parcels in the luggage compartment. No. He sort of respects me now. We're a team.

....

When the shuttle bus finally arrived in Mamoe, at about three in the afternoon, each of them went their separate ways. Kathy was met by her husband and daughter, both of whom gave her huge hugs. Alexander and Sonja had already arranged to meet Kathy and her family that evening for a celebration dinner and so final goodbyes were unnecessary. Andy, Pete and Jan were dropped off at the YHA and shortly after that the bus arrived at Alexander's backpacker hostel which was appropriately named, Screaming Ned's. As he left the bus he said a quick 'I'll meet you as arranged at about seven Sonja,' and before she could reply the bus had departed taking her the small distance to Scooby Doo's backpacker in Ship Street.

Alexander's experience of backpacker hostels was fairly limited but they were certainly great value for money. Mostly he would take a bunk bed in one of the dorms but when he really needed a bit of peace and quiet he would take a single room. After two nights sharing communal bunk beds with twenty other people on the track Alexander felt that he really needed that space just now but unfortunately Screaming Ned's had no single rooms available. The best they could offer was a four bed bunk room which he was to share with two Israelis and a girl from Latvia.

Alexander wearily lugged his rucksack up the stairs and on entering the room he said a cheery 'Hi' to the two young men inside. One was lying on the top bunk reading a book and the other was texting someone on his mobile. Silence. Absolute silence. He felt as welcome as an Englishman at an Al Qaeda safe house. Well this looks as if it's going to be a bundle of fun thought Alexander to himself. At least it's only one night. He spread his sleeping bag out on the vacant lower bunk and trying once more he said,

'So where have you both come from?' to which question there was again absolutely no response. Well there you go he thought to himself, it takes all types. A long hot shower soon took away his disappointment and most of his aches and pains. Surprisingly his feet were in good shape and this augured well for the much tougher Mamoe Track which Sonja and he were due to start in just over two days time. Overall Alexander concluded that he had found his tramping legs and starting with the Ailsa had been a really good decision. He was pleased to discover that the passage of twenty years had not dulled his physical abilities as much as he had feared. Somehow everything seemed to be slipping into place and Afghanistan now seemed but a distant memory. He decided to go downstairs, make some coffee and send a few emails.

The backpacker was clearly filling up as people returned from their daily outings or arrived by bus or car from other locations throughout the south. The various individual paths that they had previously trod in their lives momentarily crossed at that one geographical location on the planet. The backpacking community was indeed very special. It was as if they were pieces of flotsam and jetsam washed up on the seashore. Some stayed a day, some a week and some for months. But most stayed for one or two days after which the receding tide would take them out to sea once more to be deposited further along the coast at some later date. It was a microcosm of humanity, mixing and mingling freely. The *lingua franca* was English and throughout the room different accents coped in different ways with that most frustrating of languages, with its many mysteries of spelling and pronunciation. But lines of communication were established, acquaintances made, and friendships forged. The kitchen and the lounge were conduits for reliable information, just like the underground news sheets of the Honecker days. The backpackers relied on this daily feedback more than they did on the official guidebooks to determine their plans for the days ahead. Alexander sat down at a solid wooden table and slowly stirred the sugar into his cup of coffee. He was preoccupied with his thoughts.

'Hi,' said a young women sitting opposite. 'How's your day been?'

Alexander looked up to be greeted by the smiling face of yet another beauty. He could not quite understand it but all the girls in backpackers seemed to have tanned healthy complexions, beaming faces and long blond hair.

'Oh good, thanks,' Alexander replied. 'I've just finished the Ailsa. Stunning scenery. And yourself?'

'Oh, I'm just resting up here for a week or two. I've taken on a bit of housekeeping work at the backpacker in exchange for free lodging. Helps save a bit of money.'

'How long have you been travelling?' Alexander asked.

'Must be about ten months now. I started in Asia and have just arrived in New Zealand for the summer. Then on to Aussie.'

The long-term traveller had always impressed Alexander, especially those who travelled on their own, girls in particular. They were so different from the majority of backpackers who travelled for four to six weeks in a single country, before they returned home to their secure jobs and structured futures. These were in it for the long haul, leaving family and friends for months, even years. He knew that he could never do it himself. Alexander had previously reached the conclusion that those who travelled to far away lands for extended periods changed for ever in some way or another, even if they did not fully admit it to themselves. The person who left home would never be the same as the person who returned. Somehow friends and family would be viewed in a different light. Sometimes ties became stronger, sometimes weaker. But above all the traveller would become a different person due to their own individual experiences, both the good and the bad. Many would find it difficult to settle back into their former lives again and would remain forever restless. As indeed he was himself.

People in backpackers often talked for hours without exchanging names. It often seemed superfluous information. But Alexander felt that it was as important as Captain Cook exchanging tools and beads with the native pacific islanders. The attainment of a new level of trust.

'I'm Alexander, from England.'

'Hi, Melissa, from Canada.'

And with that the gifts had been exchanged, anonymity dispatched to the waste bin standing in the corner.

'So, Melissa from Canada. How was travelling in Asia?'

Alexander had previously worked in a number of the countries in the area and so his interest was genuine. South-East Asia in particular he loved, Malaysia, Indonesia, Laos, Thailand and Vietnam. The diverse peoples, the food, the humid warmth, the lush tropical vegetation, the different faiths. All had left a lasting imprint on his mind and on his soul.

'Oh, they were just huge,' Melissa replied. 'Loved every minute of it. Somehow New Zealand seems too much like home for me. Provincial. Nevertheless, I guess that I love it in a different way.'

It turned out that Melissa had studied anthropology and commerce at university and so was well prepared for her travels. Alexander admired her ability to observe. It was something that he had failed miserably to achieve during a lifetime of travel. Travelling with eyes wide shut. It was as disappointing as his failure to keep a diary. What a story his experiences, accumulated over a lifetime, would have had to tell. An opportunity missed. Never to be regained.

'So what do you think that you have learnt from your travels?' Alexander asked with interest.

'Well I had hoped to resolve a few major issues regarding my life and career. But somehow I'm just as confused as I was when I left Vancouver,' she laughed. 'It's a strange thing really but I'm sure that it will all work itself out before long.'

Alexander could not really be of any help with Melissa's particular dilemma. He had spent a lifetime trying to understand what it was all about and totally failed. Some found their relief in drugs, some in the environment, others seemed to take refuge in some religion or another. It was so much easier to believe in one guiding light. Jesus, Mohammed, Mao, Karl Marx. But Alexander was too stubborn to let go of his freedom of thought, his freedom of movement, his freedom of expression. There was no doubt about it, he was a lost cause. And so they talked for a good hour, exploring each others strengths and weaknesses, doubts and fears, hopes and illusions. And then, as easily as they had met they went their separate ways. It was just the way it was.

....

Just before seven o'clock that evening Alexander arrived at the reception area of Scooby Doo's where he had agreed to meet both Sonja and Kathy.

'Would you be Alexander by any chance?' the girl at reception asked when he arrived.

'Yes, that's right,' he replied.

'Oh good. I've got a message for you from Kathy. She says she's sorry but she cannot make it tonight.'

'Did she say why?' Alexander asked.

'No, she didn't say.'

'Oh. Well thanks for taking the call.'

That's a pity Alexander thought. After all it was Kathy who was the one who suggested that we all got together with her husband to celebrate her very first tramping achievement. I guess she was just happy to get home to the comfort of her family or perhaps she was just too tired. But above all Alexander knew that something very special had occurred in Kathy's life. Someone who had carried the taunts about her size and lack of sporting prowess all her life was now an achiever. And no one knew that more than Kathy herself. Nothing more needed to be proved to herself or to anyone else.

Alexander sat down to wait for Sonja. The minutes ticked by one by one until the clock on the opposite wall indicated seven thirty five. Alexander had been inwardly fretting for some time. It was just his nature. When he arranged a time to meet someone it was from his perspective an unwritten obligation to keep his word. A matter of honour. And after all he liked to keep things simple since life was too complicated as it was. For the women in his life it appeared exactly the opposite. Timing was just a vague point of reference, an indicative mark of no particular significance. Alexander knew this very well but, however hard he tried, he could never stop himself becoming at first fretful, and then annoyed, even angry.

A further ten minutes passed before Sonja arrived downstairs completely oblivious to the fact that she was over forty five minutes late. She smiled at Alexander, who as hard as he tried could not conceal a frown of disapproval.

'What's wrong Alexander?'

'Oh, nothing really. Kathy can't make it I'm afraid. She didn't say why.' He wanted to say, 'Why are you so late Sonja. It's nearly eight o'clock,' but as usual he didn't want to make a fuss.

'Oh that's a pity. She was good fun and I would have liked to have said goodbye to her properly.'

'What type of food do you fancy tonight Sonja. There's plenty of choice according to the local guidebook. Thai, Indian, Italian, Japanese?'

'Anything. Absolutely anything. I'm *famined*. Correct expression. Yes?'

Alexander smiled. 'Correct expression. Yes, I couldn't have described it better myself.'

And with that they set off on the short walk into town. They looked at the menu boards of a few restaurants before they finally agreed on a small trattoria that had a picturesque balcony overlooking the street. As they sat down to watch the passers-by Alexander said in a fatherly way, 'It's my treat.'

At first Sonja looked blankly at Alexander because she hadn't got a clue what he meant. At last she worked out the meaning and quickly responded in a firm manner, 'No Alexander. I cannot accept that. We must share the bill.'

Alexander could see from the determined look on her face that there was no point trying to force the issue. She had clearly spoken her final word on the subject. After that the dinner went really well and it was clear that they had made a very good choice of restaurant. A bottle of imported Bardalino helped and they sat and enjoyed a balmy evening until the sun had finally set in the western sky. Conversation was relaxed and they both felt at ease in each others company. It was by now nearly nine thirty and Alexander was reluctant to end such a special evening so early.

'Why don't we go for a drink somewhere? I believe that there's an Irish pub down by the lakeshore.'

'That's a great idea Alexander. But first I must telephone my parents and my boyfriend. I always do that after completing a track. Just to let them know that I am fine. They worry about me otherwise.'

And with that they paid the bill and made their way down towards the lake to a point where Sonja had previously noticed a payphone kiosk.

'You go ahead to the bar.' Sonja said. 'I think that I know where it is.'

'No, that's OK,' responded Alexander. 'I'll just go and sit over there. I'm in no hurry.'

Alexander watched as Sonja entered the kiosk and although he could not hear her words he could tell that the first and shorter call was to her parents. The second call was much more animated and even the enclosed kiosk could not contain the sound of her characteristic booming laughter. Clearly she was excited to be calling her distant lover. The light illuminated her blushing features that appeared full of contentment. At one with the man she loved. But if she loved this man so much then why had she left him to travel alone to the other side of the world? Perhaps she was not yet ready to commit herself totally to one person? Perhaps there were a number of important issues for her to resolve in her life before she was prepared to settle down? Perhaps she had doubts? Who could say.

After she had finished her call she seemed somewhat surprised that Alexander was still there. She had anticipated that he would wait a few minutes before heading to the bar. Most of her friends would not have waited. In fact she was disappointed that he had not done so since she was beginning to feel a little crowded by his presence, however congenial. She had always jealously guarded her space and this new companionship was beginning to invade it, however kind he had been. As they arrived at the bar they could see that it was very crowded. Every night at Billy Burke's was busy but Saturday it just pulsated.

'What would you like to drink Sonja?' Alexander asked after he had squeezed his way into a rapidly closing space at the bar.

'A Guinness please,' she replied.

Alexander hated the hurly burly at the bar since more often than not he felt that the invisible man had more success attracting the attention of the staff than he did. Perhaps he was just too polite. Perhaps others were simply more forceful. However, on this occasion the dark haired girl with the broad Irish accent noticed him immediately and asked, 'What would you like my darling?' Alexander did not think that she could be talking to him but to a broad shouldered hulk of a man who stood towering over him from behind. He nearly lost his chance but managed to blurt out, 'Two pints of Guinness please.' The girl with the romany features glided away to the other end of the counter and he watched as she expertly pulled two pints of the black velvet liquid, finishing the head off with a perfect shamrock.

'That'll be fourteen dollars thanks.'

Alexander then squeezed back through the throng to where he had left Sonja. But she was nowhere to be seen. It was not easy to make his way through the mass of bodies with two hands full of the creamy black liquid but Alexander went off in search of her. It was very dark in the room and the throbbing multi-decibel music meant that it was virtually impossible to hear what people were saying to each other. But above the hue and cry Alexander at last heard her distinctive laugh and by heading in that general direction he found Sonja animatedly talking to a small group of people who were sitting in a concealed alcove. Through the gloom Alexander soon made out that it was the English couple that they had so recently met on the Ailsa Track.

'Alexander, it's Peter and Jan,' shouted Sonja from the place where she was now sitting. 'And this is? Sorry I didn't get your name?' said Sonja leaning across to a man sitting next to Jan.

'The name's Craig. Craig Williams. I ran into Pete and Jan about ten days ago, just before they did the Ailsa. And you are?'

'Sonja. Sonja Schneider. And this is Alexander. We met on the track.'

'G'day Sonja, Alexander. How do you like Mamoe?' Craig continued.

'I just love it,' said Sonja. 'There's just so much to do and see. And the atmosphere here is crazy.'

Alexander found a space next to Pete and they started to reminisce about their shared experience over the last few days. Pete was a keen ornithologist and so whilst Sonja, Kathy and Alexander had hurried along the track, he and his partner Jan had ambled along, stopping as and when they felt like it. They usually arrived at the huts just before dusk and this meant that they were left with the worst bunks, often far apart but they never seemed to mind. Somehow Alexander felt that Pete and Jan had both gained more from the tramping experience than he had.

Occasionally Alexander looked across the table to where Sonja was sitting and it was clear that she was having an animated conversation with Craig. Alexander could not see him clearly in the gloom but it appeared that Craig must have been in his early thirties. A dark complexion on a rugged and muscular frame. He had the handsome features so characteristic of part Maori part European descent. Every so often people would come up to Craig for a brief chat and it was clear that he was well known in Mamoe and that he had many friends. A large proportion of those who spoke to him were attractive young girls of varying nationality. Alexander assumed that they were doing temporary work during the season or that they were backpackers, like himself. From their body language it was clear that a number were clearly attracted to Craig. By now the dance floor was a mass of heaving bodies gyrating in concert to songs that Alexander had only vaguely heard before.

'Want to dance Alexander?' Sonja shouted across to him.

'No, you go ahead Sonja. I'll sit this one out.'

Without hesitation Sonja turned and said, 'Dance Craig?' and they were on their feet and making their way to the dance floor at the far end of the room. Even from a distance Alexander could see that Sonja was a very good dancer and what was even more obvious was that she absolutely loved to dance. In sad contrast dancing was not one of Alexander's favourite pastimes. In fact he loathed it. And that was loath with a big L. He would have given anything to be able to get up there now and do the John Travolta bit but he knew from years of painful experience that he just didn't have what it takes. He just felt so self-conscious and lacked any natural rhythm. Girls had often said to him in the past, 'Come on Alexander. Of course you can dance. It's easy.' And so encouraged he would get up and try his best. But to no avail. Like Steve Martin in the film *The Jerk*, he just had to accept that he had absolutely no rhythm. There was nothing he could do about it. It must have been in his genes. Soon it became apparent to the girl that what he had been telling her all along was true. And when he gave his apologies and sat down again they did not object. Within a short while they had completely forgotten him as they lost themselves in the music with another partner.

Alexander was convinced that if he had been able to dance his past relationships with women would have been much more successful. With few exceptions girls just loved to dance. With men, with each other, even with the wall. It just didn't matter. It was as if music tapped into some primeval vein in the female psyche. Dance to the music. Dance to the music. At least Alexander was not alone in his aversion to dancing. The clubs of the world were littered with sad men like himself, leaning against the bar, warm beer in hand, watching from afar with barely concealed envy. But there were certain men who had that natural rhythm and they knew how to use it. Like sharks in the sea they cruised the dance floors looking for that night's catch. Bastards thought Alexander. Lucky bastards.

And Craig was clearly one of them. Alexander could see by his movements that he was a natural. And Sonja was clearly responding to his lead. From slow dance to fast, from country to rock, they were both into the music and into one another. They did not return to the table. Occasionally Craig would go to the bar to buy them both a drink and then off they would go again. It was like a single ritual mating dance performed amongst a multitude of ritual mating dances. And at that moment Alexander realised that he had absolutely no chance.

It was now close to one in the morning, and making his apologies to Pete and Jan, Alexander left by the back entrance and broke out into the cool clear air. The throbbing music slowly receded into the background as he made his way back to Screaming Ned's. His emotional roller coaster had hit rock bottom once again. 'Pathetic. Alexander Stewart you're just a pathetic wimp.' And with that he entered the dormitory and crashed out in the company of his two other roommates, both snoring profusely. He never did see the Latvian girl.

Sonja hadn't had such a great time for years. Time lost its significance. Just the incessant beat of the music had meaning. And this Craig, great dancer, she thought. Good looking too with an easy smile. And when she occasionally looked into his eyes they just held her. It was like a game of dare, which she always lost as she looked away. Sonja had never been one for drinking. She used to tell her girlfriends jokingly that a couple of glasses of wine and she was easy. But she had never been easy. She had never slept around even though she knew that she had a high level of sexual desire that needed to be satisfied. It was just something that she wanted to save for serious relationships, and not for casual encounters. She was as aware as anybody that she was physically attractive to men. But she never flaunted her sexuality. Never teased men with it. She was just, well, herself.

As the evening progressed Craig had observed every detail, every contour of his new companion's body. He had been immediately attracted to her at first sight but no more than the steady stream of beauties who passed through Mamoe on a regular basis. They rarely tried to speak to each other above the clamour but when they did Craig felt an affinity with this girl which he hadn't felt in a long long while. Sonja was not just the typical budget bus type travelling from place to place, sinking the bevies with the men, hopping from bed to bed, thrill seeking all the way. It was clear that Sonja, well, she was in many ways similar to himself. Very much the outback type whether it was tramping, skiing or whatever. On each fragmentary point of discussion her interests seemed to match his own like pieces in a jigsaw puzzle. But Craig was not the relationship sort of guy. It just wasn't worth the grief. Fun times. That's what he was after. Fun times. Love them and leave them. After all, they all moved on from Mamoe in the end. Back to the family, the trusting boyfriend, or possibly just the cat.

So engrossed was Sonja in Craig and the music that it was past one thirty before she glanced across to where they had been sitting earlier in the evening. She could see that Alexander, Pete and Jan had long left and that their seats had been occupied by a set of unfamiliar faces. No matter. She was sure that they had had a great time too. At about two o'clock people seemed to drift away and the atmosphere took on a relative air of calm. Even the music changed to a slow romantic pace and the remaining couples held each other close as they moved around the dance floor.

'Do you fancy a cup of coffee at my place,' Craig said as they both made a move to leave.

'No thanks Craig. I'm fine. I should be getting back now because I've an early start to Queenstown in the morning and I haven't even packed yet.'

'Well I'll see you back to where you are staying. Scooby Doo's backpacker isn't it?'

Normally Sonja would have insisted on returning on her own but she wasn't exactly sure where her backpacker was located.

'OK Craig. That's very kind of you.'

The two of them left the bar just as the staff had started to pile up the wooden chairs onto the tables and commence sweeping the floor. A solitary couple on the dance floor continued to hold each other close, more for mutual support than anything else.

'We're closing now,' shouted the girl with the only authentic Irish voice in the place. Can you drink up now please!'

By this time Sonja and Craig were far away and they walked along holding each other close. When they finally reached the main door of the backpackers it was clear that, apart from the security light, all was darkness inside.

'Well thanks Craig. I had a great time,' said Sonja. She felt unusually reluctant to say goodbye.

'So did I,' said Craig. 'Perhaps we can meet up again when you come back from Queenstown?'

'Yes. Why not. I'll look forward to that. Billy Burke's. Right.'

'Right,' said Craig. And then he abruptly drew her towards him and holding her tightly to his body he gave her a long lingering kiss. Sonja did not resist. She just willingly gave herself up to it. When he finally drew away she was confused. It might have been the excess of Guinness that she had had that night. She was not sure.

'Well, good night Craig, and thanks again.'

And with that she felt inside her pocket and withdrew the key. Placing it in the lock she attempted to turn it, without success. She tried again without any better result.

'Craig, I can't seem to unlock the door. Will you have a try?'

Craig took the key and likewise had no better luck. It was then that he noticed a rather insignificant notice pasted to the inside of the glass window. *'For the security of our guests this door will be locked and bolted after one o'clock. Please do not attempt to force the door and do not, under any circumstances, ring the bell. Remember, be back before one!'*

Craig was familiar with all the backpacker hostels in town and he was aware that the owner of this particular one had a reputation for being a right misery. He knew that Sonja could ring the doorbell until dawn broke without getting any response.

'I'm afraid you'll have no luck here Sonja. She's a right pain this owner. I guess you'll just have to take me up on that coffee. I have a comfortable sofa that you can use.'

She looked at him and knew that it would be alright. And anyway if it wasn't she knew how to look after herself. 'Well, coffee at your place then. Is it far?'

'No, not far at all. Just about a kilometre along the lake. Nice little place. I've lived there for about five years now.'

And so they walked through the night to the gentle sound of waves lapping on the rocky shore.

Craig's place, when they arrived, was as cozy as he had described. In fact Sonja was rather surprised at how tastefully it had been decorated and furnished. It was not what she had imagined at all. She had expected a real bachelor pad. She looked into the kitchen, a real giveaway with most of the men that she knew, expecting to see the obligatory pile of dirty dishes. But here were a row of neatly stocked shelves with an extensive selection of herbs and spices, extra virgin olive oil, balsamic vinegar, a full rack of fine New Zealand and Australian wines and so forth. All was clean, neat and tidy.

'This is a beautiful little house Craig. I'm really surprised. It's quite feminine.'

'Well thanks *daaarling*. One tries to do one's *besst*,' he said in the most camp voice his vocal chords could manage. 'I think that I'd better just make the coffee.'

And with that he opened one of the cupboards, studied the numerous glass jars carefully, before withdrawing one with *'Colombian dark roast'* hand written on the label. The aroma suffused the air as the little electric coffee grinder did its work.

'Do you mind if I look around?' Sonja said.

'No, feel free. The coffee will be a few minutes. I'll put some music on.'

Craig walked across to his extensive CD collection to look for something mellow and appropriate. Very soon the sound of Enya was quietly washing over the room in harmony with the hour and the evening that had preceded it. Images of times past entered the room, of Celtic tribes, of ancient lore, of mist covered mountains and of wet lowland pasture.

Sonja had by now taken in every detail of the lounge, so restful and relaxing. The extensive quantity of books on the neatly stacked shelves were equaled only by their quality. Craig, she thought, you are indeed a man of surprises. She drifted into the only bedroom and turning the corner her eyes were immediately drawn to a large original oil painting of a reclining nude hanging directly over the bed. Two dimly lit spotlights highlighted the female form that was expertly rendered. In the bottom right hand corner she could just make out the signature of the painter. C. Williams. 1998. Oh my, she thought. How wonderful it must be to be painted with such skill. I wonder who she was. Someone very special I think. The only other light in the room stood on the bedside table and directed its beam downwards in an irregular fashion across the bed cover and onto the floor, highlighting warm tints and gradations of colour. It all looked so very welcoming.

Sonja was quite startled when Craig appeared quietly behind her and said in a gentle voice, 'Coffee Miss?' Saying her thanks Sonja slipped back into the lounge and sat down on the cream damask sofa. Craig did not sit next to her but in a deep leather armchair opposite. Sonja was somewhat disappointed as she had grown used to his closeness.

'If you have a spare sleeping bag I'll be quite comfortable here,' Sonja said after a short while.

'I won't hear of it,' said Craig, 'you can sleep in my bed and I'll kip here. I'm used to roughing it in the mountains and my sofa is pure luxury in comparison.'

For a short while the sparring continued with each not wanting to inconvenience the other. 'Look, as long as you behave yourself we can both share your bed. I don't know how many men I've slept with in the mountain huts back home,' she laughed, 'and all at the same time! It's just like the tracks here. You all just bunk down together. Stranger with stranger. Male with female. It's just not an issue.' She could hardly believe what she was saying.

'That sounds fine with me Sonja. As long as you don't try to take advantage of me,' said Craig. Sonja laughed and simultaneously threw a cushion in the general direction of the armchair.

'So who was that old guy you came to Billy Burke's with tonight?' Craig inquired.

Sonja was unsure who Craig was talking about until she said, 'You mean Alexander? Alexander's not that old.'

And it was true what she said because before that moment she had never given much thought to his age. He was just a fellow tramper who she had met by chance. A person she now considered as a friend, even as a confidante.

'We met on the track two days ago and he helped me with one or two things. He's a really nice man, you know.'

Craig sensed that he had hit on a sensitive subject and so he changed the direction of their conversation to what type of music she liked and so on. Before long Sonja glanced at her watch and was surprised to see that it was already close to three.

'Well, I'm going to call it night Craig. As I said I've got to be off at seven thirty in the morning. Sorry, I mean this morning. And I haven't packed anything yet. Can you set your alarm for six?'

And with that she discreetly wandered into the bedroom, took off her jeans and bra, kept on her long tee shirt, slid under the cotton duvet, and turned out the bedside light. A short while later she heard the sound of Craig undressing and soon he was lying close beside her. Close but not touching. She could sense his warmth. She lay there willing him to touch her. But at the same time she was willing him not to touch her. She was so confused. And as she thought about this she felt him move closer and then she felt his body touching hers along the length of her back. She did not object. It felt warm and good. They lay there for some minutes until Craig gently placed his arm around her waist. It seemed so natural. It seemed so innocent. But she would go no further. She determined it to be so.

As Craig drew close to her he knew that he wanted her. He wanted this woman more than he had wanted anyone in a long time. He wanted to take her slowly. But above all he wanted to give her pleasure. His own needs were not important. He had moved from the me to the you. It was a place that he had not been for such a long time. He felt the slow rise and fall of her breathing. He felt protective and enveloping. He moved his hand from her waist until he was gently caressing Sonja's firm well formed breasts with the lightest of touch. Slowly back and forth. Her nipples erect and taut through the cotton T-shirt. He felt her take a sharp intake of breath and although it seemed as if Sonja wanted to say something no words broke the silence. It seemed as if they had been caught somewhere, suspended in transit. At last, with the last remnant of willpower, she managed to speak.

'No Craig. I care for you. I think that I care for you deeply. And that is why I would rather not.'

There was no sudden movement. No sudden outburst of surprise. No turning to confront the man with whom she shared her bed. She just lay there calmly and at ease. Craig also lay for a while feeling the warmth of her body. Slowly he withdrew his hand, then his arm, then his body. Finally, he tenderly kissed the nape of her neck saying, 'Sleep well Sonja,' before he turned over onto his back. Eyes wide open. He would stay that way until dawn. Something had happened to him. Something that he did not quite understand.

4. High Hills and Deep Valleys

<u>Sunday 28th November 2004</u>

When Sonja awoke with a start to the shrill alarm she found Craig standing over her with a steaming mug of coffee. Craig knew from years of encounters that most girls were not at their best in the mornings, at least not the ones that he knew. Conversations had to be short and brief.

'Coffee Sonja? Be careful it's very hot.'

And with that he returned to the kitchen to prepare a quick breakfast for them both. Freshly squeezed orange juice, local cheese, ham off the bone, and toast and marmalade. Natural yoghurt if she wished. That should be plenty.

Sonja soon came out of the bedroom as she had slept, her long T-shirt acting as a perfect nightdress, her lean brown legs leading the eye down to her bare feet. She disappeared into the bathroom for a few minutes and emerged fresh and radiant. Only her eyes betrayed her tiredness. They ate in silence but Craig would occasionally look across at her with pleasure. He knew that in a few minutes she would be gone. And he knew that he wanted her to stay. If he were quick he would catch her smiling to herself as if she was remembering a private joke. But as she caught his gaze she became embarrassed and after that he tried not to make her feel uncomfortable. The minutes quickly passed and before long Sonja had dressed and without further delay she had left his house. There was barely time enough for her to say, 'Thanks again Craig. You're very special. Tomorrow at Billy Burkes. Seven thirty, right?' And then she was gone.

As she approached Scooby Doo's Sonja was still trying to work out the wonderful and mysterious events of the night before. It was just like a dream. Her emotions were strung taught like the strings of a mandolin. But of more immediate concern was how she would be able to get to her room since the main backpacker doors were not officially opened until seven thirty, exactly the time her coach was due to leave for Queenstown. Just at that moment of indecision the front door burst open and a painfully thin Korean jogger emerged with next to nothing on, except his shorts, skimpy top and fluorescent headband.

'Wait, wait,' shouted Sonja, 'I forgot my key.' The young man, who she had briefly spoken to the night before, held open the door for her.

'I tink you hav gud tim last right,' he said without a trace of malice, more like appreciation.

'Thanks,' she said as she rushed up the stairs two at a time.

She made her way to the bunk room that she had been due to share with three other girls. Thankfully the door had not been double locked from the inside and the security chain was off. But when she entered it was completely dark. The three sleeping forms were totally oblivious to her presence. Rather than disturb them by turning on the light she felt for her things and as swiftly as possible she made a pile of the various items on the hallway floor outside. It appeared that she had everything and so as quickly as possible she packed her rucksack. It was not the usual precise pack that Sonja invariably undertook but she could sort everything out when she finally arrived at her next destination. She then remembered that she should have confirmed the planned rendezvous in Te Anau with Alexander. Well it was too late for that now. And without further delay she heaved her rucksack onto her back, dropped the room key into the box located in the empty reception area, and headed off to the bus stop on Emerald Street.

Sonja's three hour journey on the antique Bedford bus from Mamoe to Queenstown was quite special. Soon after it left the town the bus had to climb hairpin bend after hairpin bend up what seemed to be a sheer cliff face. The driver shifted the ancient gears easily, double de-clutching as and when necessary, a single missed shift threatening to plunge them all back towards the point where they had started their journey. Even though it was relatively early in the morning the elderly driver seemed as bright as a button and he gaily entertained his six passengers by recounting a series of stories about cars, RVs, and indeed buses, which had taken various shortcuts down the mountainside. Budget travel in New Zealand was such a different experience for Sonja since she had only been used to the luxury coaches that effortlessly cruised the autobahns between Munich and Berlin, Dusseldorf and Hamburg. At last they reached the summit of the climb where the driver pulled over into a lay-by so that they could all take some photographs. The view was quite just amazing. Mamoe seemed but a small dot sitting quietly by the dark waters of the lake. All around the mountains seemed to rise sheer out of the water, apart from a few points where fantail estuaries led off into steep sided valleys full of mystery. Sonja looked down on the place where at that very moment Craig would be preparing for his day. It already felt like home.

What had seemed so simple on her departure from Germany, an extended exploration of a new country and walking a selection of its major tracks, had suddenly become so complicated so very fast. Perhaps her distance from home had made her particularly vulnerable. Perhaps her recent sense of loneliness had made her susceptible to the warm embrace of a sympathetic man. Whatever it was thoughts of Craig would not leave her mind. Within one short night, Herman, her boyfriend since childhood seemed just that. A boy. The beckoning of the driver broke the train of her thoughts as he called out, *'All aboard folks.'* Onward they travelled for a further two hours through classic sheep and deer farming country. Occasionally herds of alpaca would greet them with some surprise. It was certainly a bountiful and beautiful land.

When she finally arrived in Queenstown Sonja was very pleased to be met by a distant cousin of her mother, her cousin's husband and their small family. It was such a relief to speak German again. No longer did Sonja have to strain to listen to the various English accents of so many different nationalities, process the words into German, and then back again into English. A dam of pent up language flowed and she felt that she could not stop talking. So much had happened to her in such a short time. The afternoon and evening went quickly as the family busily interrogated her for news from home. The meal that the mother prepared was true Bavarian cuisine from Sonja's home area and at the end of the feast she felt that she had eaten and drunk far too much. Nevertheless it was a wonderful interlude. But for all their generosity she could barely wait for the morning to arrive and her return to Mamoe.

....

By the time that Alexander had stumbled out of his bunk at Screaming Ned's Sonja was already well on her way to Queenstown. He had spent a number of days in Queenstown on his previous visit to New Zealand and although he would have very much liked to have seen the town again he felt that he had to give Sonja the space that he felt she so clearly needed. And anyway she would be fully occupied with her relatives.

They had already agreed to meet in the small lakeside town of Te Anau some one hundred and sixty kilometres distant, which also marked the starting point for the Mamoe Track. Geographically Te Anau was much closer to Mamoe but such was the effect of the intervening Munro and Fraser mountains that it could only be reached by the circuitous route. Sonja had informed Alexander the night before that she had already made a booking at Grumpy's backpacker in Te Anau but when they had looked in Alexander's guide book they could see no reference to the place. They therefore agreed that it must be the Lakefront backpacker since he knew from his previous visit that it was certainly located on the lakeside, and perhaps it had changed it's name. Backpackers did that all the time, whether it be through a change of ownership or a change of fashion. Sonja's departure from his life did not worry him unduly since he knew that in two days time they would be together again.

On finishing the Ailsa Alexander had felt like a genuine tramper with a three day growth of stubble on his weathered features. It felt good to have made the transition from the tourist mode to the veteran tramper mode. Someone who had sweated over mountain tracks and struggled through forests just like an early pioneer. He had previously wondered whether the passage of twenty years since his last tramp in New Zealand would have taken its toll but he was thrilled to discover that he felt exactly the same as he had all those years before, totally and utterly shattered. Running on empty at the end of every single day.

Alexander's bus to Te Anau was not due to leave until two in the afternoon and so he took time to relax in the air of Mamoe. The warm morning sunshine made it pleasant to walk around the town dressed only in his T-shirt, shorts and newly acquired leather sandals. However, after a while he started to feel much more like a tramp than a tramper. One sight of his frightening reflection in a shop window confirmed his worst fears and he resolved there and then to return to the backpacker to have a shave and get his haircut at the nearest barbers, without further delay. Much refreshed by these activities Alexander finally boarded the Mercury Express bus for Te Anau with the primary objective of arranging the necessary hut passes and transport to and from the track for both himself and Sonja. He also intended to find a place for himself to stay at Grumpy's backpacker so that they could be together just prior to the walk in order to finalise arrangements.

However, upon his arrival in Te Anau Alexander was shocked to discover that Grumpy's backpacker was not actually in Te Anau at all, but some thirty kilometres out of town at a remote location called Te Anau Downs. It was the main staging point for the Milford Track, but certainly not the Mamoe Track. It also happened to be on the road to Milford Sound. What was he to do? He had already arranged to meet Sonja at the main Te Anau bus stop off Miro Street at ten minutes past five the day after tomorrow. According to their carefully conceived plan she would be returning from her round trip from Mamoe to Milford Sound. And if they missed each other at the bus stop they had agreed that they would certainly meet at the tourist information office at five thirty. It had all seemed so failsafe. But now all their carefully arranged plans were in jeopardy. What if Sonja were to be helpfully informed by the bus driver at some point in her return journey that Grumpy's backpacker was not actually in Te Anau at all, but at Te Anau Downs? She would then leave the bus at that place and they would have no easy way of contacting each other. This had the potential of rapidly turning into a disaster. However, on reflection, Alexander decided that there was little more he could do that day but book places for them both in the Lakefront backpacker and hope for the best.

5. When Rivers Run Dry

Monday 29th November 2004

Alexander sat alone on the edge of Lake Te Anau looking out across the still water towards the distant mountains. For the first time in many days he thought of his only child. In early February she would be twenty two. He guessed that Sonja must be about the same age but in recent years he had found it far more difficult to guess the ages of people, both young and old. Men and women in their early twenties could just as easily have been young adolescent teenagers as far as he could tell. Minnie. What an unfortunate name to land a girl with for the duration of her life. Minnie. He had never liked it. His American wife had been quite insistent though. Beautiful little Minnie, with her natural tanned complexion that always made her look so healthy. Where that complexion came from neither Alexander nor Linda his wife knew. Genes were a mysterious thing.

'Why do we have to have such old fashioned names Alexander? Just because your ancestors followed tradition for hundreds of years that is no reason we should.' And so they compromised. Well he gave in really. Minnie Elizabeth Mary Stewart. His ancestors had always taken particular care not to upset any one faction of the Scottish crown. If you wanted to keep your head it was always best that way. But Minnie!

Alexander's marriage to Linda did not last long. Four years and she wanted out. She was tired of dreary old England, and as for that backwater of Scotland, well that was even worse. She wanted to return to Boston where her parents and many of her friends still lived. University in Oxford had been a stimulating experience, as had the chance to explore Europe. But now that they had a child she wanted her to be brought up in a civilised country and with a proper American education. Transatlantic marriages. He should have known better. They should have known better. But they were young. Alexander dutifully tried the 'home of the free' for two years but he disliked it intensely. The wealth hierarchy seemed so alien to his own more familiar, but no more equable, class hierarchy. Material wealth on its own all seemed so shallow and pointless. Who cared if your Cadillac was slightly longer than your neighbours? Who cared if you had a limited edition of an Andy Warhol on your wall? It really didn't matter one microscopic bit to him. It didn't make the world a better place. But unfortunately it mattered very much to Linda.

The fact that his only way of earning a living was overseas didn't help matters. He made sure that he kept his assignments to no more than two months but rapidly they drifted apart. And when Linda met him at the airport, something she never did, he should have known something was up. But he was too simple for that. He just thought that it was a wonderful surprise and that perhaps they could make it together after all, if they both tried harder. But no. They had hardly got into their car when she came right out with it.

'I think that it is best that we separate Alexander. There's nobody else. It's just that we don't seem to have fun any more.'

He had wanted to argue. He had wanted to propose that they give it another try for Minnie's sake but he knew that what she said was true. Their marriage was dead. It was without feeling. It was without emotion. Whether or not it was shock he could not tell but there and then he agreed.

'You know that I would never try to keep you in a relationship that you were unhappy with Linda,' was the best that he could manage.

Two months later he left the States and went back to live in England. Regular access to Minnie had been guaranteed. But of course there was another man. Perhaps there always had been. Before he left Alexander had had an unrealistic vision of Linda bringing up Minnie in dutiful isolation and chastity. A divorced woman living quietly alone with her child. It was nonsense of course. But when Brad, or whatever his name was, moved in barely three weeks after Alexander had left the country, that hurt. It hurt him deeply. To have another man bringing up his own daughter. It drove him quite mad for a time.

Access was never easy at the space of a few thousand kilometres. But whenever his overseas work allowed he would travel economy class to Boston just to savour a few precious hours with his daughter. At first he used to go to Linda's apartment to collect Minnie. But after a while he just got so angry after being greeted at the door by yet another new boyfriend. It was then agreed that Linda would bring Minnie to his hotel. He didn't blame Linda. She was desperately searching for happiness, just like everyone else. But it was clearly taking its toll on little Minnie. She always seemed so thin and drawn when he met her. Frightened even, as if he was just another of Linda's boyfriends.

Finally he felt that he could certainly do no worse than Linda and applied for custody. Over the next two years his legal expenses rose in direct correlation to how his fragile relationship with Linda fell. She fought him bitterly every step of the way. The American legal system fought him every step of the way. And then it was all over. The funny thing was that he had never smoked dope, not even cigarettes. At least not since a few boyish experiments with cigarettes during his schooldays. It was 1990. He was just enjoying a quiet evening at the home of some friends after a visit to the pub. His companions were smoking hash, as they usually did to mellow out after a hard week, and they asked if he wanted to try. Why not, he thought. Life's been pretty miserable lately with absolutely no progress in the custody battle. What's the harm?

The harm was the door suddenly caving in and four heavyweight policemen in body armour standing over them and threatening them with an uncertain future if they moved one inch. The subsequent search found small but, in legal terms, significant amounts of hash. And two sachets of cocaine. His two friends looked at him apologetically. But Alexander just wanted to laugh out loud. It was just so typical of the direction his life had been heading lately. He couldn't help but see the black humour in it all. And he hadn't even had a chance to inhale. The correspondence from Linda was abusive and exultant. If she had known he was a junkie she would never have married him. And as for seeing eight year old Minnie again, he could forget it. Her lawyers would see to that. And the American immigration service also saw to that. His one month suspended jail sentence for being an accessory to the fact saw to that. Banned from entry to the United States. Indefinitely.

Alexander soon pulled his life around. It was the sort of shock therapy that he needed. There was nothing that he could do but get on with it. Work was plentiful and travel to remote corners of the world took his mind off his more personal problems for a while. But he never forgot Minnie. Wherever he was. Every two weeks he would write her a long letter telling her where he had been, what he had been doing, and why he was doing it. It was as if he was trying to justify his reason for existence to himself. And of course he told her how much he loved her and that one day they would be together. On her birthday and at Christmas he would send her a collection of little gifts that he had collected on his most recent travels. Simple gifts. Special gifts. Made by special people. A hand carved hardwood dish from a villager in the Mekong delta, bone jewellery from the cattle nomads of the Sudan, baked earth figurines from the caves of Ningxia Hui, dried rose petals from the hills of Lebanon. Only once a year did he receive a reply. At least Linda had the good grace for that. Short, simple, hand written letters whose words he treasured. Whose contents he kept safely like sacred texts. And photographs. Each year a single photograph taken on her birthday. Professionally taken. Formally posed. His little girl. Daddy's little girl. Daddy's sad looking little girl.

But for over six years, since her sixteenth birthday, he received not one letter. Not one photograph. Just a curt message from Linda stating that Minnie had ungratefully left home directly after finishing grade school and was having some 'behavioural problems'. Just like her father. Substance related. Serious substances. And then last August, out of the blue, a simple crumpled note arrived by post.

'Dear Dad, I'm going to make it. Just for you. All my love, Minnie.'

Nothing more. No address. Nothing. But those few words gave him the first real hope in years. And he knew in his heart that she would do it. She would get well again. She would make it. And life for them both would be better at last.

And as he sat there his thoughts turned to Sonja. He wondered for the first time if the love that he had felt so strongly for her over the past few days may have been a misdirected love. There was no doubting that it was real love. But was it the substitute love for his long lost daughter? The same age, the same looks, the same vulnerability. Had Sonja unknowingly filled a yawning void in his life, the daughter that he had never really known?

....

Te Puke was very disappointed with Alexander. All this self-analysis was a complete waste of time. It was clear that he was in love with Sonja so why didn't he just get on with it. Rangi wouldn't have stood for such nonsense. He would have just used Te Puke to give any rivals in love a few sharp blows on their heads to help them on their way to join their ancestors. And then he would have thrown Sonja over his shoulder like a sack of kumara and taken her away and ravished her. Nobody could have resisted Rangi and within a short time she would have come to love and respect him. Women liked that. Could man have changed so much during the hundred years or so that he had have been hanging on that wall, Te Puke pondered. No. It just wasn't possible. Women needed someone strong and decisive. A born leader and protector. A worthy father of their children. That's what they needed.

....

Sonja arrived back in Mamoe late in the afternoon. The short break in Queeenstown had been very welcome but somehow the town was rather too commercial for her tastes. Making money as quickly as possible seemed to be the overriding mantra, whether from visiting tourists, housing or from various other developments. The prices in the shops reflected that particular obsession. She had been told that the super rich often jetted into Queenstown from far off countries and if the weather was less than perfect they jetted straight out again the very next day. It all seemed such a waste, such a vacuous existence where boredom was only a hairs breadth away. She instinctively felt that she had little in common with most of the people that she passed in the street but then she realised that it took all sorts to make the world go around. Perhaps it was wrong for her to be so judgmental?

But Mamoe was clearly very different. For a start it did not have an airport and could only be reached by rather badly maintained gravel roads. The government had talked loudly about upgrading the infrastructure for many years but various feasibility studies had clearly demonstrated that it was uneconomic. Why bother when Queenstown, Te Anau and Wanaka still had another twenty years potential left in them. The property developers were disappointed but the locals certainly were not. They loved it just the way it was. And Sonja could fully understand why since it was populated by real people leading real lives. People of the land, working people. And the backpackers that appreciated it were of exactly the same breed.

On the journey back to Mamoe Sonja began to think about Craig. The painting on his bedroom wall, the attractive girls who had approached him in the Irish pub, the many friends that he had in the town. Perhaps she had been foolish to believe that he might have similar genuine feelings towards her that she had rapidly developed towards him? Perhaps she was just another potential conquest that might take a little longer to catch? To be thrown back in the pool with all the others? She did not want to be hurt. She did not want to be made a fool of. She had too much respect for herself for that. It had just been a very pleasant interlude. A little too much Guinness perhaps but no harm had been done. In any case tomorrow she would be moving on and in a few months she would be leaving the country for good. By the time that the bus had reached the outskirts of Mamoe she had resolved not to meet Craig at Billy Burke's that evening. She would have a quiet night in at Scooby Doo's and make her final preparations for her trip to Milford Sound and the Mamoe Track. That would be best for everyone. She was convinced of it.

....

Craig arrived at Billy Burkes well in advance of seven thirty, the time that he had arranged to meet Sonja. He bought an ice cold Pepsi and sat down at his favourite place on the bench directly opposite the fireplace. He was preoccupied with his thoughts. Sonja had only left his house just over twenty fours hours before but it seemed like a lifetime to him. He just couldn't get her out of his mind. It was quite something. He looked at his watch and by now it was seven forty five. That's a surprise, he thought, I had assumed that Sonja would be the punctual sort of girl. Various local characters that he knew came up for a chat as they had a quiet drink before proceeding onwards to their own homes and families. Monday was always a slow night in Mamoe. Eight thirty and another Pepsi and still no sign of Sonja. Craig was not used to being stood up. In normal circumstances he would not have cared since there were always pretty girls eager for his company. But these were not normal circumstances. I'll give her until nine and then I'll go home and listen to some music or read a book, he thought to himself. Who cares.

But he did care. On the stroke of nine he left Billy Burke's and rapidly walked the short distance to Scooby Doo's backpacker. The owner was a bit of an eccentric and normally she wouldn't allow outsiders into the backpacker premises. However, she knew Craig very well and after a bit of banter she allowed him to see if Sonja was in the lounge area. Craig walked through the door and could see Sonja sitting there quietly reading a book. Numerous other backpackers of varying nationalities talked together in small groups, surfed the internet or just generally milled around.

'Sonja, can I talk to you please?' Craig said as he stood a few feet from her.

Sonja seemed to ignore him.

'Sonja, can I bloody talk to you please?' Craig said rather too loudly.

'OK,' responded Sonja curtly, rather annoyed and surprised by his bad language, 'Go ahead.'

'In private, if that's alright with you?' Craig continued rather more civilly.

They walked out of the backpacker entrance and stopped a few metres away under the street light.

'I thought that we had a date Sonja? Did what happened between us the other night mean nothing to you?'

'I had many things to sort out for the next few days. I didn't think that you would mind,' she responded coolly.

'Mind, Sonja! Mind! I think that I bloody love you, you silly girl. I haven't been able to think of anything but you since the moment you left. I don't care if I'm making a fool of myself. I don't care if the ground opens up and swallows me right now. The only thing I care for is you. Nothing else matters.'

Sonja looked at him. So it wasn't a dream. It wasn't an illusion. He truly did care for her. Even love her. The way she loved him. She stepped forward a pace and placing her hands gently into his she whispered,

'I'm so sorry. I'm so sorry. I just couldn't believe that you could feel the way that I feel for you. I just don't understand what is happening.'

Craig looked into her clear blue eyes and knew in that instant that what she said was true. He drew her closer to him and they held each other tightly. Some Japanese girls walked passed giggling at such a romantic scene but Sonja and Craig were oblivious to anything but each other.

'Move along now,' called out Irene the backpacker owner, 'you'll be giving my place a bad name Craig Williams.'

Sonja and Craig laughed. It was indeed time to move on.

'Have you eaten?' Craig asked.

'No, nothing. I seemed to have lost my appetite. Until now that is.'

'Great. Neither have I. This calls for a celebration. How does the best sirloin steak that you have ever tasted sound?'

'Sounds just perfect. I guess that you'll be the cook?'

'No way. The French restaurant around the corner just can't be beat. Absolutely superb with a bottle of the finest Martinborough pinot noir.'

And with that he ran off with Sonja chasing him just like two young children on their way home from school. They were the only ones in Nina's restaurant that night but they didn't mind one bit. The owner tended the log fire while the chef, who Craig knew very well, came out and sat at their table. All three sat talking for a while whilst drinking the best wine out of the finest fluted glasses. After they had ordered, the chef returned to his kitchen whilst Sonja and Craig just looked at each other. It couldn't be true. It just didn't happen in real life.

As Craig had promised the food was superb. Unbelievable. They said their goodbyes to their host and without the need for any words they made their way to Craig's house. There was no need for coffee. There was no need for soft music. There was no need for conversation. They made their way to the bedroom where they slowly undressed each other. They would not make love that night. They just held each other in a sleep filled embrace until the dawn. They had a lifetime together for such things.

6. Clear Views to the Near Horizon

Tuesday 30th November 2004

Craig stood at the open doorway of his house and watched as Sonja walked down the street to catch the bus to Milford Sound. As she reached the corner she turned and waved, smiling at him in her own beguiling way. And then she was gone. He had not asked her to stay. She had not offered to remain. It was just an unspoken understanding between them that she had things that she must do. After Milford Sound it was the Mamoe Track, then on to Stewart Island, followed by a leisurely passage up the Catlins so that she had time to fully take in the beauty of that remote landscape and the varied sea life. In three weeks she would be back. Then they would have time to sit down and discuss their future together. There were no fears in separation. They knew they were one.

Alchemists had tried to make gold out of base materials for centuries and failed. It was the same with love. You could marry gold with silver in the most exquisite jewels but they would never be one. To the external observer the combination would look perfect but both gold and silver knew in their hearts that there would always be an insurmountable barrier between them that could never be overcome. An enduring incompatibility of spirit. But take copper and tin. Not as glamorous perhaps but bring them together in the right circumstances and they become one. Each giving to the other until an unbreakable bond is formed. You see them sometimes. The elderly couple quietly walking down the street hand in hand.

Craig closed the door and walked over to his CD player. He was taking the morning off to reflect on events. It was a Mahler mood. Some might think it melancholy. Others might think it romantic. Craig just thought it appropriate for that particular moment. He sat down in the expansive leather armchair and let the music envelop the place. The events of the last few days had been so unexpected. It was as if he had been struck between the eyes by an unforeseen blow that had shocked him to his senses. He was in love. It was such a unique and ridiculous sensation, one that he had never experienced, and had therefore never missed.

After all, until that moment, no one could have been happier than Craig. He had everything that he needed. He enjoyed his work that brought him into direct contact with a wide range of people who respected his professional skills. His commitment to the mountain rescue team had allowed him to put something back into the very community that had welcomed him with open arms. His small house by the lake was more than a construction of wood, brick and glass. It was home. And as for his social life he had everything that any man in his early thirties could ever want or need. Single life was so enjoyable and so uncomplicated that he never envisaged that he would ever wish to enter into a permanent lifetime relationship.

He had loved many women. But he had never been in love. He remembered every girl that he had ever slept with and genuinely respected every single one. After all they had given themselves willingly to him, and he to them. A number of girls had fallen in love with him and his friends could only admire, even envy, the particular type of women that he attracted. Intelligent, independent and invariably beautiful. He had never misled the women in his life, always explaining at an early stage that he was not the marrying kind. Nevertheless, rather than discourage them, this fact made them more determined. Those who went out with him for more than a few weeks felt that they could, given time, make him love them. Persuade him to marry them. They could picture the future clearly. But the longer the relationship continued the more Craig needed to have his freedom back. His three elder sisters had virtually given up on him ever finding a suitable partner, even though they still schemed to introduce him to eligible girls on the rare occasions that he visited them in their disparate towns throughout New Zealand.

Love? Perhaps his own parents broken marriage had had a more profound effect on his life then he had fully comprehended. After all he was the youngest child and was only five years old when the arguments started and only seven when the final split came. His sisters had tried to protect him from the emotional turmoil but he had just watched all the unhappiness from a distance. The two people that he loved most in the world arguing so intensely. He had wanted to shout Stop! Please Stop! But he had just stood there silently in the corner with his hands in the pockets of his baggy short trousers. Bewildered and lost. Perhaps, deep down, it had marked him. Scarred him. Created an unbridgeable Berlin wall that could never be breached. And then suddenly that wall had come tumbling down. And he was free. Free to love.

Later that morning Jenny would be coming over. Her portrait hung in the bedroom. Once a lover, now a true friend. It was a routine arrangement. Sometimes Craig would take Jenny's deeply glazed pottery over to Wanaka, each piece accurately reflecting the earthy colours of the surrounding land. On other occasions she would take his art. It was strange how so many people could only see the superficial limitations in others, Craig reflected, whereas his school teaching years had taught him only to see their potential. He admired the craftsmanship of the true line of the bricks in a well built garden wall, the close fitting joints at the end of the massive wooden beams of one hundred year old barns, the precision engineering of the thrusting pistons of the Wakitipu steamer. Everyone had potential. Everyone had skills. People looked at his tradesman's hands and saw only that. A tradesman. Those who saw the magnificent paintings in Wanaka signed by C. Williams did not relate them to him. It just didn't fit their perception. It couldn't be Craig? Not our Craig?

He never exhibited in Queenstown. Only in the arts and crafts co-operative in Wanaka. It suited his philosophy. He exhibited among friends. Even so he still loved Queenstown, notwithstanding all the bad press that it had received in recent years. It was just the random development that he disliked. And especially some of the architecture. The hillside behind the town seemed more like a Sao Paulo shanty town. It was as if a Damien Hirst clone had been let loose in an architect's office. Rather than *'The Colonial'* or *'The Canterbury'* it seemed as if clients had been offered *'The Favella'* or *'The Shanty'*. In many ways it was amusing. And in others it was simply the New Zealand way.

Perhaps, Craig thought to himself, perhaps it is nearly time to return to teaching. He had always loved it. It was just that life had got in the way. He could still do weekend relief on the mountain rescue and provide cover during the holiday periods. He would discuss it with Sonja on her return.

....

The morning had arrived bright and clear. Alexander had thought long and hard but there was very little that he could do but wait. If Sonja didn't arrive on the Milford Sound bus, and did not turn up later at the tourist office, then he would just have to telephone Grumpy's to try to make contact. But he knew that they would only take his message and place it on a notice board. What if she did not see it? Alternatively he could travel to Grumpy's some way or another but what if she had gone out for a walk, or realising her mistake had herself travelled on to Te Anau? She had no way of knowing where Alexander was staying since he hadn't booked anywhere and so their well laid plans were inexorably taking on the appearance of a complete and utter mess. There was nothing he could do but wait for the bus.

He sat on the bench on the opposite side of the road to the bus stand on Miro Street and started to apply much needed waterproofing to his ancient boots. This was the direct result of a good humoured telling off that he had received in Mamoe from a lady in an outdoor activity shop. She had informed him that his boots were an absolute disgrace, so dry and cracked had they become. When he recovered from his initial surprise he had reflected that the life of a professional tramper was certainly not an easy one. He had so much to learn.

And so he sat there doing his penance. Normally he absolutely loathed cleaning his shoes at home and he thought that this said something quite significant about his undisciplined character. But very quickly he began to feel a sense of pleasure at the sight of his boots turning into something presentable, from scuffed dry white into shiny brown. As he sat there busily polishing away, a number of coaches stopped at the roadside opposite and a regular procession of tourists, mainly Japanese, trailed dutifully into and out the opaque closed doors of the exclusive gift shop opposite. It seemed to Alexander that wherever he had travelled, Rome, Paris and beyond, the same buses full of the same Japanese tourists had spent all their time doing exactly the same thing. Arrive, travel, photograph, exclusive shop, travel, photograph, exclusive shop, leave. It wasn't necessarily wrong. It was just, well, different.

He looked at his watch for what must have been the twentieth nervous time and at last, from around the corner, came the bus making its daily return journey from Milford Sound to Mamoe. Right on schedule. Alexander scanned each window as it pulled to a halt but he could not see the familiar face that he longed to see. He walked across the road full of suppressed foreboding but through the open door of the bus he could at last see Sonja's smiling face as she gave him a shy wave. His heart beat a little faster and he was overcome with an enormous sense of relief that their planned rendezvous had occurred without a hitch, when, for the last few hours, it had seemed to him that so much could go wrong.

Sonja skipped down the steps of the bus and strode quickly towards him. Alexander was not sure how best to react to his recently departed friend since he did not want to cause her offence by being too forward. However, Sonja soon dismissed these thoughts from his mind by embracing him warmly in her arms so that he could feel her soft body pressing against his chest. She really did have some genuine affection for him, Alexander thought with pleasure. His reverie was, however, rapidly shattered when Sonja turned and said,

'This is Jurgen.'

Alexander tried not to show his disappointment but he had no doubt that his expression gave away his true feelings, as it always did. He had already lectured himself that he had no right to be close to this young woman.

'Nice to meet you,' Alexander quickly responded. 'Will you be joining us on the Mamoe Track?'

'No,' Sonja said before Jurgen could respond, 'I have arranged to meet Jurgen in Invercargill for the Stewart Island Track in five days time. We met on the boat trip at Milford Sound but Jurgen has to return to Christchurch for a few days.'

'Oh that's a pity,' Alexander said with as much conviction as he could muster but deep within himself he could feel his heart leap. How much longer he could endure these wild swings in emotion he was not quite sure. Affairs of the heart certainly took their toll.

'Sonja's a very strong walker,' Alexander said jovially at a loss for something better to say.

'Not as strong as myself,' Jurgen replied stiffly.

A few minutes later it was time for the bus to leave on its way back to Mamoe and soon it was disappearing into the distance and away, taking Jurgen with it. Alexander's wave was perhaps rather too enthusiastic. She looked at him and said,

'Do you always wave goodbye to complete strangers?'

His hand was suspended in mid-air, caught in the act.

'Of course. It's the custom in my country. It's only polite.'

She looked at him sideways with a questioning look. Without any further delay Alexander picked up Sonja's walking boots and her day pack and said to her,

'Do you want the good news first or the bad news.'

Sonja looked somewhat bewildered but said, 'The bad news', possibly expecting that the Mamoe Track huts were fully booked and that they would have to rearrange or even cancel their plans.

'Grumpy's backpacker is located at Te Anau Downs which you must have passed some twenty minutes ago. It's thirty kilometres from here.'

Her look of surprise was just as Alexander had hoped but straight away he continued,

'But the good news is that I have booked you into the same backpacker as myself, in one of the four bed female bunk rooms. The transport and huts are also all arranged and so we can start the track the first thing tomorrow morning, as planned.'

Sonja laughed at her mistake. It was that deep laugh which Alexander had come to know and love. Sonja did not say so but it was clear that she appreciated all of the arrangements that her newly found companion had undertaken on her behalf. And with that they made their way the short distance to the backpackers in order to prepare for the following day.

When they had completed their preparations, and Sonja had had a chance for a refreshing shower after her very long day, they walked back into the centre of town to find somewhere to have a good hearty meal before their next tramping adventure. This was not a great problem since Te Anau basically consisted of only one street that contained two or three good restaurants. 'Italian again?' queried Alexander feeling happy with whatever Sonja wished. 'They say pasta is good for building up your energy.' 'Wonderful,' she replied and with that they entered the Firenze Trattoria. Various Italian scenes on the wall, red and white chequered table cloths, a well stocked antipasto counter, the rotund Italian mother taking orders, and the subdued background music all went together to give the place a truly authentic atmosphere.

7. Sun Rising

<u>Wednesday 1st December 2004</u>

The dawn again greeted them with cloudless skies and the gods were looking down kindly on Alexander and Sonja. The usually unpredictable springtime weather was as good as they could ever have hoped for. The air was still and the lake provided a mirror image of the mountains and forests rising opposite, just as it had the day before. A leisurely breakfast was soon to be followed by the short walk back into town to the tourist information office, weighed down by their fully provisioned rucksacks. This was the location where Alexander had previously arranged for them to be met at eight thirty by the local track shuttle bus that would take them some twenty kilometres north to the wharf at Pleasant Bay. A launch would then take them to the start of the track on the distant banks of the South West Arm of the lake, directly beneath the slopes of Mount Pisgah.

A solitary Swiss girl was also patiently waiting for the same bus but soon the three of them were on their way. Alexander's sensitivity to the feelings of others had always been particularly acute and he was concerned that the Swiss girl looked quite apprehensive about what lay ahead. And so he broke the ice by initiating a conversation with her, about nothing in particular. Indirectly he was trying to let her know that she was not alone and that they would be close at hand should she need support. Sonja appeared oblivious to such sensitivities.

The boat journey passed enjoyably but uneventfully and soon they were all assembling their few possessions on a pebble beach. The first six kilometres of the track passed through verdant rain forest never straying more than a few metres from the lakeshore. It was without doubt a peaceful and leisurely introduction to their re-formed walking partnership. Since Sonja was the most experienced walker Alexander once more asked her to take the lead since he still lacked confidence in his own natural pace and abilities, whether or not his pace would be too slow for Sonja, or far less likely, too quick. Within a short space of time he was again reassured that indeed their natural rhythms were as one.

As they made their way through giant ferns, their fronds dappled with filtered shafts of sunlight, Alexander had time to observe the young woman pacing along just a few metres in front of him. He reminded himself there and then to savour these precious moments since in another three days it was almost certain that polite goodbyes would be said and that he would never see or hear from her again. He admired the graceful way in which she seemed to glide over the path before him, assured and confident. Her movement might best be described as athletic, physically strong, yet not overly muscular, her long limbs moved in an easy relaxed manner. She was, Alexander thought, exactly the type of woman that he had been searching for in vain for a lifetime. Her natural habitat was, like his own, the open air, far from the hustle and bustle of city life.

They had been walking for over an hour now and so they decided to take a short rest beside the lake at Campbell Bay. The Swiss girl seemed to be taking it at a steady pace since they had not seen her since the start of the track. Far across the water they could still clearly make out Miller Peak. But soon it was time to resume their trek and shortly thereafter the track took an abrupt turn to the left and they both knew that the long climb up to the tree line had begun. The growing sense of confidence which Alexander had quickly gained along the flat part of the track suffered its first test as his pack suddenly felt like a lead weight, his leg muscles became tighter, and his breathing more laboured. However, by focusing solely on Sonja's rhythmical steps directly in front of him Alexander soon found some relief. He immediately became aware of the benefits of following a path rather than leading one. Sonja's walking boots were having a trance like effect on him so much so that he failed to notice how the sweat was by now freely running down his forehead and neck.

Up and up they climbed until after a further thirty minutes Sonja stopped and reached for the water bottle that was conveniently slung from her slim waist. Alexander, not being as organised in these matters, had to drop his rucksack onto the ground and struggle to retrieve his bottle from inside the top of his pack. Although they were still in the beech forest they could occasionally catch a glimpse of the deep blue lake below and it was clear to them both that they had already climbed a considerable height.

'Would you like me to take the lead for the next part?' asked Alexander somewhat hesitantly, unsure whether or not Sonja preferred to take the lead at all times.

'That would be good,' she replied.

And so with renewed energy and confidence Alexander led off trying to mentally remember what pace Sonja had previously set. In the end he just settled into his own rhythm and since he heard no sound of complaint from behind he assumed that his pace had been declared acceptable by his more experienced partner. Higher and higher they climbed, alternating the lead like a pair of alpine mountaineers, until at last and with little warning they suddenly broke through the tree line. Alexander marvelled at how one moment they were completely immersed in thick beech forest and then the next there was not a shrub or bush to be seen. They both quietly acknowledged that a milestone had been reached. They had spoken but few words on the climb but it was clear to them both that their new partnership had started well.

They sat down on the tussock grass for a short break and Sonja withdrew a crisp red apple from her pack. Alexander again realised that yet another important item was missing from his food supply, fresh wholesome fruit. Somehow Sonja seemed to sense this fact for without hesitation she removed her knife and sliced the apple cleanly in two, passing one half to Alexander as its clear juices dripped onto the soil below.

'Thank you Sonja,' he said but Sonja showed no sign of acknowledgement. It was by now about midday and the sun shone fiercely in the clear blue sky above. After savouring their short rest they continued on their journey. Further and further they rose until the lake below and mountains above revealed themselves in their full splendour. High jagged peaks of black rock contrasted sharply with pristine white snowfields on their more sheltered southern slopes. Fantails sang their shrill warnings high above the alpine meadow whilst exotic flowers paraded themselves to the spring sunshine.

Alexander estimated that they had now been walking steadily for about five hours and all being well they would reach their goal, the Anson hut, within the next hour. He felt well pleased that their individual paces were in harmony and that augured well for the days ahead. And then at last, around yet another bend in the track, the hut finally revealed itself to them. The objective that they had been aiming to reach for over six long hours was now within their grasp. They always say that it is better to travel hopefully than to arrive but Alexander could not agree. It was with the greatest relief that he unfastened his rucksack and heard a dull thud as he lowered the heavy pack onto the wooden decking. It had been a hard climb and for the last hour his leg muscles had continuously screamed at him to stop.

A short while later, whilst he sat recovering from his exertions, Alexander could not help but notice a disjointed stream of trampers making their laboured way up the same steep path. 'They look like Korean tourists,' Alexander remarked to no one in particular but someone to his right said, 'Americans.' Alexander could immediately see that the latter opinion was indeed correct. They came around the corner of the track in an intermittent file, in ones and twos, like the survivors of the Battle of the Little Big Horn. Alexander immediately recalled that there were no survivors of that historical event but the image stayed with him. As they approached closer he could see that they were a disparate group of people, ranging in age from pubescent to geriatric. Well from about sixteen years of age up to seventy to be more precise. From pencil thin to pudding plump, from foghorn loud to reflective quiet, accents ranging from New England to Latino Californian. Within this small group it appeared that every stereotype of the American nation was fully and fairly represented.

Early evening in the huts is often a period when new friends are made over boiling water, burnt rice and curried noodles. It soon became apparent that the Nevada Club, for that was what the American group were named, had a definite team leader. She was a matronly woman of about sixty years of age who took control of her charges as if they were a group of young offenders.

'Now I want Conrad and Mary to do the cooking tonight and don't forget it's your turn to do the washing up Morton. You flunked it last night, remember!'

Communal cooking was clearly the order of the day for the group. Individualism was out. Definitely out. To emphasise the point the team leader, whose name was Nancy, commandeered three gas burners on one side of the kitchen area and clucked backwards and forwards like a mother hen warning off other trampers who strayed too close. She did not have to say anything since her stern look and piercing eyes made words unnecessary. The remainder of the Nevada group sat at their tables obediently waiting for their meals to be served, like children at a second rate English public school.

Alexander and Sonja found a place for themselves at a table occupied by two members of this group. One was a handsome fair haired young man, late twenties, by the name of Ted. The other was a sad looking figure, with bulging eyes, obese, late forties, and for all the world one of life's unfortunate losers. This indeed was the very same Morton who Nancy had previously scolded.

'How y'all, my name's Morton Prebble, from Charleston, South Carolina,' said Morton as he proffered his podgy damp hand to Alexander and Sonja in turn. 'Where're you folks all from?' Alexander and Sonja duly responded and the conversation developed. It appeared that the group came from all over the US and had not met one another until their separate arrivals in New Zealand. It transpired that the Nevada Club arranged various tramping expeditions to all corners of the world, but this particular selection of individuals did not seem to be your typical tramper types, thought Alexander to himself. Perhaps this was the singles tramping package but Alexander did not pursue that line of enquiry. He was just thankful that he had not joined an organised party and there and then he promised himself that he never would. Ted informed them that the group had already completed an obscure walk in the North Island and just a few days before they had finished the renowned Milford Track. The Mamoe was to be their final track before they returned their separate ways to wherever they came from in the States.

Alexander and Sonja watched with barely concealed astonishment as the Nevada Club dinners, or more accurately rations, were distributed to each in turn. Not a murmur of dissent, just thankful to have received their fair and just portion. Alexander then decided he had been quite wrong to make comparisons with an English boarding school. The food was more like that described in the gulag in *'One Day in the Life of Ivan Denisovich.'* The final flourish came when Nancy walked around to each in turn and handed them a single piece of a milk chocolate that they duly accepted without comment. There was not a single, 'C'mon now Nance, we've busted our guts walking up this damn mountainside and this is all we get to eat! Get real.' Complete and obedient silence. Why some of them had not already decided to prepare their own food when and where they liked Alexander could not explain. The world was indeed a strange and varied place.

As they continued chatting Alexander and Sonja were proudly informed by Morton that he was a terrible snorer and that the others in his group had long ago banished him to a different bunk room from themselves. It was with some relief that Alexander and Sonja were able to confirm that Morton would not be in their own bunk room that night. Snorers were the bane of many a backpacker hostel and tramping hut. Alexander had already been astonished at how many snorers there were in the world since the opportunities to discover such facts in normal life were clearly very limited. Mostly men it was true, but he could not forget the low volcanic rumble of the Icelandic girl in the Nelson backpacker.

It took his mind back to a friend's fortieth birthday party in England when a large number of the guests, including himself, had crashed out on the dining room floor in their sleeping bags in order to avoid driving home in an alcoholic haze. At about two o clock in the morning they were all awoken by the loudest snorer one could ever imagine, Rodney Parks. Alexander had the name etched in his memory for ever. Quietly everyone present at the party had carried their sleeping bags into the adjoining room from where they could still hear Rodney snoring away throughout the remainder of the long night. Rod had only recently separated from his wife. The following morning all those present could only express their greatest admiration for her resolve in having endured such inhumane treatment for so many years. People had appeared in front of the war crimes tribunal in The Hague for less.

A pleasant evenings socialising in the Anson hut finally drew to a natural close as the dusk fell and darkness descended upon the place. A few stalwarts stayed and talked quietly by candlelight but most were relieved to make their way to their respective bunk rooms for a well deserved rest.

8. A View from Taishan

Thursday 2nd December 2004

As usual Alexander awoke early. His night had been characteristically fitful with prolonged periods of wakefulness. It seemed that he was simply incapable of making himself comfortable for more than a few minutes, wrapped as he was in the constraining cocoon of his sleeping bag. When tiredness finally carried him into sleep it was usually for no longer than two or three hours. And then he would lie awake and look across at the indistinct form of the young woman who lay on the communal bunk sleeping so soundly beside him. So peaceful, so at home in this environment. Some time later he too would drift off to sleep again until the hazy light of dawn finally woke him for good. Yet still the others slept. Alexander marvelled at how his companions of the night could sleep for so long.

He rose as quietly as he could and made his way to the nearby toilets. To flush or not to flush, for that was always the question. For to flush was to risk awakening the sleeping masses. Not to flush would be in extremely bad taste. It's a half flush he decided and with that Alexander went outside to take the early morning air. The surrounding landscape was completely shrouded in a white mist and although he could not yet see the sky he could tell that it would be another fine day.

When Alexander finally entered the dining room area he was shocked to discover a scene of carnage. Bodies lay everywhere. Well four bodies actually, fast asleep in their sleeping bags on the hard wooden floor. Morton had clearly wrought havoc in the night, forcing these poor souls to seek refuge at the furthest point from him. Alexander dare not look into the other bunk room fearful of what he might find. People driven to madness or suicide, or who had simply expired from the shock. Morton *'the Terrible'*. Alexander made a mental note to add earplugs to his survival kit should he ever tramp again in the future. It was rapidly becoming a very long list.

Apart from the sleeping refugees the dining area was empty when he entered it but as he prepared a saucepan of boiling water for a cup of tea one or two other early risers soon joined him. Brief pleasantries were exchanged but it was far too early in the day for anyone to engage in extended conversation since the waking process had to take its natural course in very individual ways. Much fortified by the tea Alexander returned to the bunk room to quietly delve into his rucksack for something edible for breakfast. As he did so Sonja turned over sleepily and said in a long drawn out singular word, 'Alex-an-der'. She said it with such easy intimacy. It had no meaning to the others in the room but for Alexander it was as if she had read him a love poem. This girl who kept her emotions so hidden had captivated him entirely. 'Did you sleep well?' he responded quietly, completely at a loss for a more appropriate reply. She did not reply but just turned over and seemed to drift once more back to the beautiful place from where she had just come. Two more days Alexander thought. Two more days and this delightful girl will be gone from my life forever. And there is absolutely nothing I can do about it.

Approximately forty minutes later Sonja entered the kitchen area but Alexander made no move to speak to her. He was instinctively aware that she also needed time and space during this period of the day and so he went outside onto the balcony. Sonja was always so reserved and distant whilst he just wanted to converse with her about anything that came to mind. The early morning passed and in ones and twos the individual trampers lifted their heavy rucksacks onto their backs and headed up the track and away into the still enveloping mist. Alexander knew that there would be a significant amount of hard climbing again that day before they would finally reach the point where the final steep descent to the Isolation Pool hut began. The brief guide to the track indicated a journey time of five to seven hours, not counting the optional side diversion to scale the extra two hundred metres to the top of Mount Anson.

At last both Alexander and Sonja were ready to leave. It felt good to be on the move again and soon they regained their steady rhythm as Sonja led the way. Up and up they climbed until they finally broke through the blanket of cloud and distant snow capped peaks dramatically revealed themselves to them for the first time, sitting majestically above a sea of white mist. It was as if they had been transported from the earth world to the sky world. They both stopped, made speechless by the beauty of it all. How fortunate they both were to be walking the track in such fine weather when fate could just as easily dealt them torrential rain and a raging gale. Alexander took a photograph of Sonja that caught her unawares and she said,

'Don't do that Alexander. You know that I don't like it.'

Alexander said nothing but as she continued to lead up the track he continued to take the occasional photograph of her out of earshot, as the view and the moment dictated. He felt sure that she would appreciate such a record of their little adventure at some time in the future, whilst he himself, well, memories and photographs were all he was likely to have.

The harder the climb became the more Alexander's thoughts turned inwards. It had been over twelve years since he had last fallen in love and he had not expected to be touched by that bitter sweet feeling again during the remainder of his days. It seemed too much to ask, for he had already been far more fortunate than most. It had been his experience that real love only came every decade or so, but he knew that for many it just never came at all. To have never experienced love, that was more than sad, it was tragic. Even now he continued to search for that elusive match but he knew that time was against him.

Was it really so wrong for him to be attracted to the beauty of a young woman, so fresh, unspoiled, and unwearied by the years? No more, he thought, than the desires of an older woman for a young man with the body of the statue of David. It was only natural and right. But for a young woman to love a much older man, or for a young man to truly love a much older woman? Now that was just improbable. Not inconceivable, not impossible, just plain improbable. Alexander knew that he was no gnarled film director or global mega-publisher. The matter of a few million dollars saw to that.

But then again there was James. James from Alexander's group of friends in England. Battered and bruised by a vindictive wife for a lifetime he had kept to his vows. But when retirement came at sixty, and the children had all completed university, he just walked out and left. To the astonishment of all concerned, most notably his wife. It was no easy exit. He still had his financial obligations to his partner of so many years. And so it was a damp and cold caravan for James among a multitude of similar faceless caravan dwellers. When the gas canister froze up that winter all his friends thought that it was just a matter of time before he returned home to the warmth of the central heating and the chill of his relationship. But he didn't. And then fate took a hand. Driving along a local by-pass he was hit head on by a lady distracted by her baby's wailing in the back seat of her car. Intensive care for a while, then on to the main ward to start his recovery. How much bleaker could his future be?

And then by chance he was visited by a friend of his who ran the nearby English language school. Why on earth his friend took along one of his students to visit James no one knows. It seemed too improbable to believe. But he did. Frieda. That was her name. Frieda. A German repertory actress of no great fame. Late twenties. Attractive. Sensitive. And there it began. A love affair. She with her painting. He with his pipe and garden. The last Alexander heard they were still living down in Cornwall. Happy as doves. Eight years later.

And so to experience feelings of love for Sonja was not so unnatural for a man of his age, was it? It just happened. One could not dictate when and where love might strike. It just happens. Or could it simply be that what he felt was the love that a father felt for his daughter? Paternalistic love? No more, no less. Only one person could provide the answer to that question, and that was Sonja herself. He could not and would not press the matter. He would leave it for the fates to decide.

Since it was still early in the day Sonja and Alexander decided to make the short diversion to climb Mount Anson. A large number of rucksacks already lay on the ground at the foot of the climb where the early starters had left them, and Alexander and Sonja followed suit. The view when they finally reached the summit was stunning and in the far distance they could just see their original point of departure, Te Anau, revealing itself through the rapidly clearing mist. Mount Anson was to be the highest point for the whole day and from here on in Alexander thought that it would be relatively easy going. Returning to their rucksacks his optimism was not however rewarded, for after regaining the track and descending for some considerable distance they passed around yet another bend where to his dismay he could clearly see the track rising and rising yet again until it disappeared from view.

He was leading by now and made no comment to Sonja. There was nothing for it he thought. One step at a time, one foot in front of the other. The sun was by now rising higher in the sky and he stopped to remove his fleece that he had needed to combat the early morning chill. The back of his shirt was now damp with his own sweat but he felt good. He looked at Sonja and smiled. She returned his smile and said, 'It's just so beautiful, isn't it?' Alexander just nodded his head and said, 'Indeed it is. Incredible' and then without further ado he lifted his rucksack once more onto his back and they were on their way. As the walk progressed Alexander was gratified to see that they were gradually passing the early starters who seemed to stop to rest more often than they. Te Puke seemed to give him so much support. Perhaps there's still life in the old dog yet, he thought.

After a further two hours it was time for a short lunch break and so making another short diversion in search of seclusion they climbed up to a small rock outcrop. There they lay back and watched minuscule black specks in the far distance making their weary way along the path which Alexander and Sonja had so recently trod. It was not a race by any means but somehow Alexander derived a great deal of satisfaction from the fact that they had led the way up the not inconsiderable final climb. Perhaps being nearly fifty years of age was not so bad after all.

'Apple?' Sonja asked as she once again offered him a half of her own. 'Thank you. Chocolate?' Alexander responded but she declined saying that as much as she loved chocolate she had to resist the temptation this time. After finishing his lunch Alexander was feeling somewhat impatient to carry on but said nothing since Sonja was clearly enjoying her rest and just lay soaking up the afternoon sun. He watched as many people passed them on the path far below until finally Sonja roused herself and it was clear to Alexander that it was time for them to continue. From their vantage point he could clearly determine that down really meant down this time for he could see the valley far below wherein the goal of their days effort lay. Isolation Pool hut.

Within fifteen minutes they came upon the Nevada Group who had rendezvoused at an appointed spot on the track for their allotted rations, the second emergency shelter. They seemed happy enough but such a regimented trek still did not appeal to Alexander. A cheery greeting to one or two familiar faces and down they both descended until the tree line, which they had left the day before, once again enveloped them. The overhanging branches provided much appreciated shade from the now intense sun but as they descended further the temperature rose. Finally, to their mutual relief, they reached the valley floor and after a further hour of relatively easy walking the Isolation Pool hut finally came into view. It was with great satisfaction that Alexander offloaded his rucksack, sat down, and removed his walking boots. They both inspected the two available bunk rooms and Sonja was of the same opinion as Alexander, the downstairs one was far better and with that they once more staked their claim on one of the communal bunks.

Near to the main door of the hut a signpost pointed the way to an isolated swimming hole that the track guide stated was a short twenty minute walk through the surrounding bush. Alexander hoped that Sonja might be ready for a cooling swim after their recent exertions through the late afternoon heat. But when he asked as casually as he could she just said in a rather disinterested way,

' No you go. I'll have a swim later.'

Somehow the swim, which he had eagerly looked forward to during their descent to the hut, didn't seem so inviting but nevertheless he gathered up his towel and set off for the nearby objective.

The narrow well-graded path meandered quietly through the forest and each step of the way was undertaken in the cool shade of giant ferns and towering beech trees. The silence was occasionally broken by the distinctive call of the ubiquitous tui, in addition to grey warblers and tomtits. Alexander soon became aware of the distant sound of cascading water. When he finally arrived at the pool he discovered that not only was there a wonderfully deep swimming hole but that the pool had been clearly formed over the millennia by the power of a waterfall which plunged out of the canopy of trees and bush some ten metres above. Alexander stood for a moment astounded by this site of such natural beauty and isolation. He had not expected it to be so special. It had the feel of a secret grotto hidden in the depths of a fairytale landscape. At the extremity of the pool the calm water changed to a fast flowing stream that dropped steeply, cascading over and between large rocks and boulders until it disappeared from view around a bend on its ultimate course to the distant sea. Alexander approached the waters edge and kneeling down he tested the temperature with his hand. It was excruciatingly cold. It hardly seemed possible that this could be so, such was the air temperature of the sun drenched spot where he sat. But then he recalled the snow clad mountain peaks high above from where the stream would have begun its journey just a matter of hours before.

Alexander had never particularly enjoyed swimming. As a child he had often been taken to the local beach by his mother and her friends. There was usually a small group of children who made the same short railway journey to the coast and they used to take a small picnic lunch of a few sandwiches, biscuits and orange juice. The beach primarily consisted of stones and pebbles but somehow what sand there was invariably seemed to find its way into their sandwiches. The English summer rarely encouraged swimming and the families often had to take shelter from the prevailing westerly wind behind huge wooden breakwaters that partitioned the beaches one from the other. After a great deal of protest his mother and aunt would finally convince Alexander not to be such a baby and he would tentatively enter the water. After the shortest of immersions in the freezing salty sea he would stand on the shore clutching his small wiry body and just shiver. 'You're a softy,' his mother would say. 'Go and get dried.' The other young children seemed oblivious to the cold and just splashed and played until their parents had to virtually force them out of the water.

And so Alexander sat on the side of the deep black pool and firmly decided that he would just take his sandals off and soak his weary feet in the icy water. Even this was more easily said than done such was the numbing effect of the pool. Nevertheless, if anyone asked, he could truthfully say that he did have a short dip, without going into unnecessary detail.

Just at that moment there was a sound directly behind him and he just prayed that it would be Sonja. But it was not. It was the New Zealander who he had spoken to briefly at the hut the night before. To Alexander the man looked quite old but it was in just such situations that Alexander usually found out that he outdated the same person by some years. It was all very discouraging. He had concluded that this was the man who was acting as the local guide for the Nevada group and he certainly did not envy him his role.

'G'day. How's the water?' said the man in the usual friendly Kiwi manner. 'My name's Jack.'

'Alexander. Nice to meet you Jack. The water's fine. I just haven't had a chance to get in yet,' responded Alexander.

At this point Jack bent down and tested the water with his hand. 'Jeez mate, it's bloody freezing. Still never mind I've been looking forward to this for the last couple of hours.' Without further ado he stripped off every piece off clothing he had on and plunged head first into the pool to surface a moment later spluttering, 'Jesus! Jesus! Jesu Bloody Christ!' whilst laughing out loud.

'Come on in Al, it's great.'

There was nothing for it. His planned strategic retreat with the short dip storyline for Sonja had been completely and utterly scuppered. Painful childhood memories rushed in on him again. Slowly stripping to his underpants he contemplated the options. A gradual immersion was out of the question since it would just prolong the agony. The plunge it had to be then. Splash. In he went, down and down. His whole body immediately went into a state of extreme shock. One moment he was sitting on a large rock sunning himself contentedly in the warm rays of the late afternoon sun and the next he was inflicting some kind of sadistic water torture on himself. There was only one thing for it. Scream. 'Aaagh! Aaagh!' and then he too was laughing his head off. His body slowly started to adapt itself to the new situation and for an instant he began to think that perhaps this was not so bad after all. But this was not your typical beach in the temperate climate of England. This was ice cold mountain water which a few hours before had started its journey from the snow line. In order to retain some degree of national pride Alexander made a few quick strokes, this way and that, before climbing unsteadily out of the water and thrusting his shaking hand towards his towel.

'That was great Jack. Really great,' Alexander said lying profusely.

After drying himself as quickly as possible he sat there with an undeserved sense of pride, bordering on smugness. Childish really for a mature man but he didn't care. 'Yes, he had been to the swimming hole. Yes, it was really great. Cold? No, not really,' he imagined himself saying to one and all back at the hut.

For a while Jack swam backwards and forwards in a leisurely and unhurried way. He gave the appearance that he was fully enjoying the experience and he could have been swimming off Bondi beach in the height of summer as far as one could tell. At last he pulled himself partially out of the water and just hung onto a large rock waiting for the sun to dry his back. Jack looked around, and after confirming that nobody was close at hand he said,

'Bloody Nevada Club. They're driving me crazy. It's just like being in charge of a kindergarten. This is the last time that I'm getting involved with that lot.'

'I know what you mean,' responded Alexander. 'Sonja and I found the whole set-up amazing.'

'Are you two together then?' Jack asked.

'Oh no,' replied Alexander. 'We only met the other day. We're just walking the track together.'

'It just seems, well, that you are really close,' continued Jack.

Alexander had not realised that it was so obvious and just replied,

'No, not really. No. I don't think so. I'm old enough to be her father.'

But Alexander liked the idea that someone had concluded that they were a pair. It gave him a warm glow inside. However his brief enjoyment of that thought was immediately broken by a young women's voice but it clearly was not Sonja's. It was a girl that he had barely registered even though they had talked together for some time the night before. His thoughts were always trained in another direction. But even so it was apparent that in some way she, Melanie, was attracted to him. Life's certainly confusing sometimes. He would have guessed that she was in her late twenties, petite, certainly pretty, without being stunning. She had told Alexander that she was involved with some sort of social work in her home town of Wellington, although she had recently returned from four years in England, London to be precise. In different circumstances Alexander could easily have warmed to her but in his present state of mind it was as if she barely existed. Another time. Another place.

'How's the water?' she asked as Jack pulled himself further out of the water as he unsuccessfully looked for his clothes.

'It's great. Really great,' said Alexander. 'Why not take a dip?'

'I don't have a cozzie,' she replied.

'Jump on in in your undies. We did. Well I did,' said Alexander as Jack was busily reaching for his underpants, again without success.

'Pass me my shorts mate,' said Jack with a slight sense of embarrassment.

'Sorry Jack?'

'Pass me my shorts, Al.'

Alexander made as if he still had not heard until Jack shouted, 'Pass me my bloody shorts mate or I'll throw you in.'

Alexander laughed and threw Jack's underpants over to him.

'Nice tattoo on your bum,' said Melanie to which remark Jack responded, 'You're a couple of bastards,' and they all laughed.

'Oh well,' said Melanie, 'if you two jokers can do it, so can I,' and without any hesitation she stripped down to her underwear and entered the water one slow step at a time. Both Alexander and Jack could not help but notice what a trim little figure had been hidden beneath that loose shirt and baggy shorts. Very trim indeed. Melanie swam up and down the pool taking great care not to wet her hair. It was once again very peaceful. Jack and Alexander warming their bodies up again whilst Melanie continued her steady strokes, oblivious to the cold.

After about ten minutes she left the water and borrowing Alexander's towel she dried her naked body in a slow and satisfying manner. They looked away out of politeness but somehow, inadvertently, their gaze returned to this figure drying herself in this Gauguinesque setting. It was a very special moment.

But that moment rapidly passed. Soon all three were on the path making their way back to the hut, much refreshed and enlivened. Within the space of a few minutes they heard the chatter of two people walking in the opposite direction, laughing and joking loudly. Alexander recognised Sonja's laugh immediately and he soon saw that the other person was the young American who they had spoken to at dinner the night before. Ted. He was indeed extremely good looking. Too damn good looking from Alexander's point of view. And of a similar age to Sonja herself.

'Hey, Alexander. How was it?' Sonja asked.

'Really fantastic Sonja. You really shouldn't miss it.' And Alexander could see that indeed she would not pass the opportunity by. She was already wearing a figure hugging blue bathing costume with a towel discreetly wrapped around her waist.

Ted did not appear to be prepared for a swim at all but carried an expensive looking camera with a huge telephoto lens.

'Modelling for Playboy Sonja?' Alexander said as a nervous joke and immediately the words were out of his mouth he wished that he had kept quiet. He also wished that he had not left the pool just a few minutes before. He wished that he could just turn around and go back to where they had recently come from. But he knew that he couldn't. God he wished that he didn't feel the way that he did.

When they arrived back at the hut Alexander sat on the veranda and toyed with an official guide to the flora and fauna of the Mamoe track. Bugger the flora and fauna he ungenerously thought. He immediately reprimanded himself for being so small minded. And with that admonition the flora and fauna were freed to speak to him. So engrossed did he become, so open was he to absorbing this new knowledge, that he failed to notice that Sonja and her new friend had arrived back at the hut. He did not even notice footsteps behind him or the fact that his name had been spoken in those familiar tones.

'Alex-an-der.' It was only when Sonja repeated his name that he was transported back to the present. 'Alexander. Do you wish to eat now? I have too much food for myself. We can share it if you like?' He looked up at her, standing there, her shapely legs bronzed by the sun. Those neat fitting walking shorts, the tight fitting yellow top which she had worn on the very first occasion that he saw her. Her beaming face with its natural friendly smile. And God did indeed make woman, he again concluded.

'Yes, I would love to. Thanks. Just tell me what you want me to do,' he replied.

'Not much really. Just sort out the dried mushrooms and boil up a pan of water. I'll do the rest.'

'OK Sonja. Then I'll do the washing up.'

And so they set about their individual tasks. Standing one beside the other in a homely sort of way. Not speaking. Just concentrating on the job at hand. Once he had finished his small contribution Alexander returned to his book. Soon he was once again fully engrossed in the subject. Sonja sat on a bench close by, occasionally rising to check on the progress of their dinner. By now the kitchen area was quite busy with fellow walkers, politely vying with each other for the available gas rings. But Alexander was oblivious to them all. They did not exist.

When Sonja called him and presented the dinner he was amazed at how such a delightful meal could be prepared using just two small cooking pots. He had often admired how master chefs on television took a few ingredients, a chop here, a slice there, a sprinkle of this and a pinch of that, until *voila*, there before them stood a wonderful dish made from next to nothing. And there placed in front of him, miles from the nearest outpost of civilisation, was the very same. Sonja was completely unaware of the look on Alexander's face. It was one of pure wonderment.

'Fettucini con fungi porcini a la crema,' Sonja announced theatrically, 'con piselli e pane.'

'Bellisimo,' said Alexander, 'multi bene Sonja.'

'It's nothing,' Sonja replied, somewhat self-consciously.

But Alexander had a surprise of his own. For the last hour a bottle of sauvignon blanc had been chilling in the nearby stream. He triumphantly brought it in and with an appropriate flourish he withdrew the cork. And as he did so he winked at Morton who had so generously sold him what was to Morton becoming to feel like a lead weight. The last but one bottle of his smuggled wine supply.

'Wow!' exclaimed Sonja. 'Stupendo!' She gave him a big hug and they held each others gaze and laughed. Everybody enjoyed the entertainment.

Later that evening, as they sat together, Alexander withdrew a frayed sheet of paper from his daypack. They had been discussing the next day's route that would involve a gruelling two hour climb to a nearby ridge followed by a further three hour trek to the Paradise Ridge hut. It was indeed a beautiful route which crossed and re-crossed the Eyre river at various points utilising a number of swaying suspension bridges. Most people stayed the night at the Paradise Ridge hut before tackling the final three hour walk to the track end the following day. But Sonja and Alexander had both agreed to give the Paradise Ridge hut a miss. Instead they planned to continue by following the river down to the pick-up point. After that Sonja intended to make her way directly to Bluff to catch the ferry to Stewart Island the following day whilst Alexander had yet to decide what to do.

Alexander carefully unfolded his crumpled piece of paper until they could both see the heading, *'The Scorpion's Tail Route'*. But what took Sonja's interest most was a simple word written in capital letters. 'WARNING'. She read on, *'The Scorpion's Tail route is an alpine crossing and should not be attempted in adverse weather. Steep snow grass slopes on the Muller river side become treacherous when wet or covered with fresh snow. Sudden cold storms bringing snow can affect this area even during the summer months.'*

'This looks interesting,' Sonja said at last. 'I've never seen this alternative route publicised in the tourist information offices.'

'No, they keep it very quiet and it's not marked on most maps. I found it by accident in a backpackers some twenty years ago,' Alexander continued. 'I found out that the Kiwi tramping clubs like to save some of the best routes for themselves. Understandable really.'

'The track description is wonderful Alexander. It sounds just like some of the routes that I do in the Alps.'

'I actually walked it when I was last here all those years ago. It was a brute and at some points I almost gave up and retraced my steps. And I was twenty years younger then. It was the original Maori greenstone hunters' route and was subsequently used by European settlers looking for gold.'

Alexander then proceeded to show Sonja on the map how the track diverged from their planned route and followed the Mamoe river up to its source at the Mamoe Glacier. The track then veered sharply right and climbed up and up until it reached the Scorpion's Tail Saddle itself. From that point on it continued for a number of kilometres above the tree line until it finally dropped steeply down rejoining their original route at the Paradise Ridge hut.

'How did it get such an unusual name, Alexander?'

'Basically you can see from the map that it starts from here at the Isolation Pool hut, and curves around to join the original route, just like a scorpion's tail which is ready to strike. I think that the warning notice also relates to the dangers of the scorpion's sting. It took me ten hours to the Paradise Ridge hut the last time. I have never been so exhausted in my life. I was literally on my last legs. I just thought that I would show you.'

Alexander felt a sense of satisfaction that he had been able to demonstrate to Sonja that even he, old Alexander, had managed to tackle some serious tracks in the past. He had particularly enjoyed pointing out to her the sentence, *'Strictly for Experienced Trampers Only.'* It was all rather immature, but then doesn't the blackbird fluff its feathers up to impress a potential mate.

'But we must do it Alexander. We cannot waste this wonderful opportunity. After all the weather is so good and such a chance may not come again. Please Alexander?'

Sonja looked at him imploringly. He immediately regretted ever getting the stupid battered piece of paper out of his pack. He only did it because he felt it might impress her in some way or another. That even he had once accomplished something of note. But he had been young and fit then. Alexander thought for a moment and in his mind he worked out a list of ten good reasons why they should not do the Scorpion's Tail route. And then he looked up and saw Sonja's eyes and he could see none.

'We'll have to leave very early,' he said. 'And since there is no warden here we'll have to write our revised intentions in the book. I don't think that they will throw us out of the Paradise Ridge hut even though we haven't booked,' he laughed. 'We will just have to pay the extra fees for not booking ahead.'

'Oh Alexander. That's fantastic. It looks absolutely great. I'm really excited.'

As Alexander lay in his sleeping bag that night excited was not a word that came to mind. Apprehensive seemed more appropriate. He had no doubt that Sonja would find their revised routing relatively easy. But what about himself? He could still remember his bursting lungs and screaming leg muscles as he tackled the moraine slopes at the base of the glacier. At times he had only managed five steps before he had had to stop. Five steps stop. Five steps stop. It had been his own personal north face of the Eiger. He had survived it once. But twice? But there was nothing he could do. Chance had thrown them together and fate had dictated that the Scorpion's Tail route was to be part of their shared future. And with that thought he drifted off to sleep.

....

Beneath the bunk Te Puke lay back and pondered the recent discussion that he had overheard between Alexander and Sonja. The ancient coin in his head glowed a luminescent blue green that lit up the space immediately above him. So they were going to tackle the Scorpion's Tail in springtime? Te Puke had travelled that route hundreds of times, sometimes in battle, sometimes in search of greenstone, sometimes in search of the few remaining mountain moa. He was apprehensive. Yet he was proud. He was apprehensive because no one knew better than him the dangers of that route. Yet he was proud because he was returning to the very heartland of his people, after all these years. He knew that he had to prepare for battle. Slowly, oh so slowly, the coin in his head turned. The gentle flower of the Kowhai that had previously projected itself to the world was replaced by the fearful vision of a tattooed warrior, *Taiaha*. Eyes bulging. Tongue extended. A countenance to make any foe quiver with fear.

9. Journey to the Mountain Tops

Friday 3rd December 2004

The next morning Alexander and Sonja rose just after five and being as quiet as possible they packed their rucksacks on the veranda decking and sat down on the steps to have a quick breakfast. Alexander had estimated that it would take them about ten hard walking hours to reach the Paradise Ridge hut by their new routing and therefore they should arrive in the late afternoon. Plenty of time for any eventuality since dusk would not fall until past nine in the evening. At one point they thought that they heard the distant rumble of thunder but they immediately realised that it was just the sound of Morton snoring in the adjacent bunk room. The sun was rising in the east into a clear ice blue sky. Just perfect for the trek that they were about to commence. At six o'clock precisely they left the hut leaving their sleeping companions to their dreams. It felt great to be on their way long before the others since they would have the wilderness to themselves.

Sonja led them along an easily graded path for the first kilometre until the point where the two alternative routes on Alexander's tattered map diverged. The Department of Conservation signpost on the side of the path simply read Mamoe Track with no reference at all to the existence of the alternative Scorpion's Tail route, and certainly no signpost revealing its existence. Alexander could see their original route meandering backwards and forwards up the slope directly in front of them until it reached the distant ridge line. That was the route that the vast majority, if not all, of their fellow trampers would take that day. Only one or two knowledgeable Kiwis might follow their own path. It would then drop down into the Eyre river valley beyond and straight on to the Paradise Ridge hut. A relatively easy five hour tramp for most. Their own less distinct path led to a steel rope swing bridge that traversed the raging torrent of the Mamoe river. And beyond that Alexander could see the bleak rock strewn valley that gradually rose in height until it disappeared around a bend in the far distance. It immediately brought painful memories of suffering flooding back into his mind. Could it really have been twenty years ago? With a wistful glance at the easier route he struck off towards the bridge with Te Puke measuring his stride. 'Alexander Stewart,' he thought, 'sometimes you just don't know when to keep quiet.'

Alexander knew from his previous experience that they had to keep to the right hand side of the Mamoe river all the way up the valley. Their only guide would be intermittent rock cairns located every few hundred meters which marked the general direction of their route. But rock cairns in a rock landscape are not that easy to see and he had to regularly stop to locate the next one. Sometimes this task proved impossible and so they just kept on heading up the valley travelling more with hope than conviction. Alexander had told Sonja that there would be streams to cross and he worried a lot about these potential barriers to their path. When he had successfully tramped this route so many years before it was midsummer. Even then the crossings were deep and the footing unstable. But this was springtime when the first melt would be in full flood. At least there would be two of them to overcome these obstacles this time. Perhaps he should have brought a climbing rope so that if one of them slipped the other could catch the fall and at least they would not be washed downstream. But of course the thought had not crossed his mind. And since they had not planned to take this route there was no reason why it should have.

After about an hour a distant observer would have only seen two ant like figures dwarfed by a towering landscape. The further they walked the steeper the two sides of the valley became. The opposite side of the river looked far more dangerous since huge snow capped cornices projected from the rock face above and seemed to hang over the river like a canopy. At any moment it seemed that tons of ice would plummet down onto the exposed path below. Nevertheless they were making very good progress and each was enraptured by the experience. It was Sonja who spotted the first of the torrents that threatened to block their path. She stood motionless on the brow of a hill as Alexander struggled up behind her breathing heavily with the exertion.

'This looks to be our first test Alexander,' she said looking at him with excitement. When Alexander saw the raging stream, or more accurately river, his first reaction was one of horror. Compared to his previous experience this was a monster. One slip and it was goodbye Alexander Stewart.

'We'll just have to do a quick recce upstream and downstream again to find the safest place to cross,' Sonja said decisively. 'Maybe we can find a place where we can still scramble from rock to rock and so on. You go up and I'll go down.'

And with that they dumped their packs and proceeded to explore in either direction. As Alexander climbed higher he concluded that it was pretty hopeless. One slip with a heavy pack would be disastrous, almost certainly terminal. And then a warming sense of wellbeing entered his thoughts. Their path was blocked right. They had tried their best but what could they do? They would just have to return by the path they had come and take their original easier route. Alexander could picture himself now sitting in Billy Burke's with a pint of Kilkenny recounting the tale to anyone who wanted to hear.

'Yes, we gave it our best shot. But it was just impossible. In the mountains you have to make decisions all the time and we both decided that retreat was the only option. Yes, we were both bitterly disappointed.'

It was with this reassuring thought that he descended to the point where he had come from just in time to see Sonja moving with graceful ease up the slope. He was about to express his sincerest disappointment about having to abandon their joint adventure when he heard Sonja shout, 'I've found a crossing point Alexander. It's not easy but it's the best that I can find.'

Alexander's heart sank and along with it thoughts of supping beer by a roaring log fire that very night. 'Oh, that's great Sonja,' he responded with as much enthusiasm as he could muster. 'Bloody hell. Bloody, bloody, bloody hell,' he mumbled to himself.

'What's that Alexander?'

'Oh nothing. I was just talking to myself. The first sign of old age you know.'

And without further discussion they heaved their packs onto their shoulders and headed downstream. The place which Sonja had identified as a possible crossing point certainly looked better than any that Alexander had seen. For a start it was wider and somewhat shallower. But shallower was a relative term and Alexander could see that they would have to wade up to their waists in the icy cold water. It immediately made him shiver.

'Sonja, are you sure that there is no other point where we can cross?' said Alexander imploringly.

'Look Alexander. This is clearly the original crossing point since there are still old rock cairns on either side of the stream.'

'Game, set and match,' thought Alexander. 'We can use Te Puke to help us cross,' he continued realising that he had no chance of changing her mind. 'I read somewhere that if we cross shoulder to shoulder and both hold on tightly to the pole held horizontally it will give us a lot more stability.' He meant to say more but his voice petered out as he became aware that what he was saying might be complete nonsense.

'Very good Alexander. Very good. I'm sure that what you say is correct.'

And with that they gingerly entered the water and as it rose numbingly above Alexander's boots he again had the feeling that he should have removed them and walked barefoot or worn his new sandals. It was all very confusing this tramping business. They walked shoulder to shoulder as intended and he could feel the surge trying its very best to up end them both. Deeper and deeper they stepped until Alexander became certain that they had misjudged the depth and that any moment the torrent would reach their packs and sweep them both away. So intent was he on this thought that he did not notice the freezing ice cold water enveloping every part of his lower body. For a brief moment he felt completely at one with Sonja. She depended totally on him and he on her. Their fates were momentarily entwined. And then as quickly as it had started it ended. They were now entering shallower waters and before long they had reached the safety of the other bank.

'That was fun!' exclaimed Sonja. Alexander looked at her questioningly. 'Fun?' he thought. 'Fun? Maybe for a masochist,' but he kept those sentiments to himself. For there was the little matter of his freezing lower half and the chattering of his teeth. 'I'll get a brew going Sonja. It's about time we had a break and we certainly deserve it.' Fortunately the sun was now rising higher in the sky and they could both feel the rays warming their backs. As they sat there waiting for the water to boil they had a chance to take in the stunning vista. The snow clad peaks of the mountains surrounding them glistened in the reflected sunlight. The crystal clear air seemed to give the blue sky a far deeper hue. It was paradise. It was what it was all about.

'I'm so glad that you suggested that we came this route Alexander. Wunderbar!'

'I didn't suggest it Sonja. I was just showing you where I had trekked all those years ago.'

'Oh well, I'm so very glad that you did,' and she looked at him and they both laughed.

The short break was a tonic for them both, even if they had consumed the last of Alexander's gas supplies. They had already walked for two hours and he estimated that it would be at least another three before they made the Scorpion's Tail Saddle. He also knew that they would be the hardest three hours of the day. They did not bother to change their clothing because it was apparent from the map that they would have to cross another two or three streams within the next three kilometres.

And as they finally reached them they took them in their stride. Each was challenging but none was as deep or as dangerous as the first. As they crossed what would prove to be the last Alexander looked up and noticed a single puff of white cloud making its track across the sky. It reminded him of home. It reminded him of lying on his back at the boundary of the cricket field watching that small piece of cotton wool cloud making its passage from west to east. He liked to think of them as scouts in the wild west spying out the land ahead for danger. He also knew that these insignificant wisps of moisture heralded the imminent arrival of a change in the weather as frontal systems made their rapid transit from the distant Atlantic Ocean. But that was England and this was New Zealand.

Making the most of the opportunity they both changed into a new set of dry clothing and soon both were feeling warm and yet at the same time refreshed. By now they had reached the bottom of the glacier moraine and they could observe milky blue water appearing as if by magic from its depths. It was with some relief that Alexander saw the path now turned sharply to the right and directly upwards. He had become more and more concerned about the bluffs that seemed to tower directly above their heads from the other side of the river. One unfortunate rock fall and they would be as they say, history. However, his relief was soon tempered by the fact that up really meant up. Furthermore they had now left solid ground and were climbing up fine pulverised rock that had been ground out of the mountain by years of glacial erosion. It seemed to Alexander that it was again five steps up and two steps back. His pack was beginning to feel as if he was carrying a few of the rocks himself. His legs and lungs screamed at him to stop. Take a rest. Don't be too hard on yourself. He remembered how twenty years before he had nearly turned back at this point. How he had kept going he did not know. After all, then he had been going into the unknown alone. A place that he had read was for experienced trampers only, which he was certainly not.

It was Te Puke who was now his strength. Alexander looked ahead and saw Sonja rising step by deliberate step. If Sonja could do it why not he?

'Come on Te Puke. We can do it. I need your help like I've never needed it before. Come on Te Puke of One Thousand Battles.'

It was indeed a continual battle between the positives and the negatives. Alexander focused on a particular rock some ten metres ahead and made that his target. When he reached that point he had his promised rest for a few seconds. And then he would identify another rock and repeat the process. He barely had time to look around, so focused was he on the ground a few metres ahead, but soon it became clear that they were rising high above the valley floor. The sights were becoming more astonishing since by now the glacier, which had previously towered above them, was now beneath. He was mystified as to how the black rock spoil came to be on the top of the lower part of the glacier but that question would have to wait for another day.

After another hour of torture they at last came to a small rocky plateau area. The severity of the slope finally seemed to be receding and it was clearly time for another break before the final push to the Saddle. For the first time they felt the chill breeze and they set up in the shelter of a large rock. The sun still shone brightly but it was clear that a change in the weather was on the way. The solitary cloud had long since disappeared on its journey but its place had now been taken by a multitude of others following the same northerly path.

'This is fantastic Alexander. I have walked some of the best routes in the Alps but this is certainly their equal.'

It was true. The further they climbed the more peaks had come into view. It was an unforgettable experience. And they had it all to themselves. For, as far as they could see, no other walkers had followed their path and they had not met anyone travelling in the opposite direction. Perhaps it was just too early in the season. Whatever the reason it made their trek even more special.

One more hour, thought Alexander, and we will have cracked it. After the Saddle it will be mostly along the level, far above the tree line. A little exposed to the elements perhaps but easy walking. He remembered the views when he had reached the Saddle all those years before looking down on the Muller valley far below and out to the sea beyond. Amazing. Unforgettable. And now Sonja would soon share that experience. Just as these thoughts were receding

Alexander looked up again at the summit of Mount Kidd. But it was not the summit that drew his attention. It was the ominously dark layer of high cloud that was rapidly approaching from the south. It was a direction which had until now been hidden from their view by the barrier of mountains high above them. Clear blue sky interspersed with white cloud was now rapidly changing into something more sinister.

'I think that we should make a move,' Alexander calmly said to Sonja. 'I think that there's a change in the weather on the way. We should get a better idea when we reach the Saddle.' Alexander felt pleased that they had started so early and had made such good progress since he would not have wanted to have been caught on this side of the mountain in bad weather. Without delay they were on their way but Alexander was immediately surprised by the fact that their route took them not up but down. It was then that he remembered that indeed this was correct since they had to cross a shallow stream before steeply rising again to the Saddle.

What had so recently been an idyllic spring day was rapidly deteriorating into something closer to winter. He then remembered what his leaflet had clearly stated, *'Sudden cold storms bringing snow can affect this area even during the summer months.'* But he was not concerned. They were both well equipped and nobody could be more experienced than Sonja with her alpine pedigree. He was the weak link if there was one. The final climb to the Saddle was far harder than Alexander remembered it. The route was marked by steel stakes that had been bored into the bare smooth rock. He knew that there were sheer drops to the valley floor in the vicinity and that was why such care had been taken to mark the route so clearly.

The wind was now rising and the first sleet fall was making the rock slippery and somewhat precarious. Sonja was leading the way and Alexander would occasionally peer beyond her trying to catch a glimpse of the steel pylon that he knew marked the very summit of their route. Thirty minutes later they still had not reached their objective. How different it had been when climbed in brilliant sunshine all those years before. And then Alexander heard Sonja shout something indistinct but it sounded like, 'We've made it Alexander. It's the pylon.'

'Thank God for that,' thought Alexander. 'I'm about done. That was one hell of a climb up from the glacier.'

Alexander was soon standing beside Sonja. He had hoped that they would have been able to sit there for a while and take in the views. The sleet made the visibility very limited but they could still make out the valley floor far below. Alexander then looked to the south towards the sea and at first he could not believe his eyes. It was as if a solid wall was slowly but inexorably moving up the valley. From top to bottom. From side to side. It had that ominous brown white colour which he had seen many times before in his own country. It was the approach of winter snow but very different from anything that he had ever experienced.

'We had better get fully kitted up,' said Sonja showing her decisiveness once again. For the last few hours they had mainly toiled in sunshine and they had shed as many clothes as possible. In fact their bodies had been recently covered in sweat that had again dampened their inner layers of clothing. There was no time to change these for drier alternatives. They just had to put on as many warm layers under their waterproofs as possible before the storm finally broke upon them. It was a close run thing but they just managed it. They inspected each others kit and decided that they were well prepared for anything which nature could throw at them.

'Thank goodness we didn't get caught by this on the other side,' Alexander shouted to Sonja. 'We might have been in trouble then. As far as I can remember it's about four easy walking hours from here to an emergency shelter at Nelson's Bluff. If necessary we can stay there until this weather front passes. We might even make the Paradise Ridge hut tonight if the weather eases. How do you feel?'

'I'm fine Alexander. This is nothing unusual. Happens all the time in the Alps.'

Alexander was not so confident about his own experience in similar situations. To tell the truth he had none. But at least he knew the way. He knew that the path would be impossible to lose. He knew that it was on the level all the way right up to the emergency shelter. Put one foot in front of the other and it would be a piece of cake. Looking behind he said, 'Ready Sonja?' She did not reply but raised her hand in acknowledgement.

The snow and wind blasted straight into their faces as they headed due south. It was inconvenient but for the first half hour they made very good progress. But the next hour was particularly bad. The forward movement of the two bowed figures was becoming more laboured as the track became indistinct in the ever deepening and drifting snow. The wind remained directly into their faces further impeding their already slow advance. Alexander looked at his watch but even at their current restricted rate of progress he estimated that they could still make the emergency shelter at Nelson's Bluff in just over two more hours.

At that very moment he heard a muffled cry directly from behind. He stopped, and turning with care so as not to lose his balance on the narrow icy track, he looked back expecting to see the outline of the woman that he had come to love. The path was completely empty of any human shape or form. For a brief moment he could not take it in, so much was this whole experience becoming like an uncalled for nightmare. And then he saw her, crouched on her haunches, slightly to one side of the track, leaning against a rock.

At first Sonja felt a sense of embarrassment, that she, the experienced alpinist should be sitting in the snow whilst her far less experienced companion stood above her. She knew that she wanted to rise to her feet but she also knew that the script for the day had been irrevocably rewritten. There was something distinctly odd about the angle of her boot in relation to her lower leg. There was no pain as such since feeling had long since departed from her extremities in the bitter cold.

'I think I have a problem Alexander,' she said with commendable understatement.

'Indeed I believe you do,' Alexander responded in a like manner.

'I believe my ankle may be broken or very badly sprained. My foot slipped on that stupid bloody rock and over I went.'

'Let me help you off with your rucksack.'

Taking the weight with both hands he eased the straps from her shoulders and placed the rucksack carefully on the path. Slipping his own rucksack to the ground he then knelt and proceeded to inspect the foot with the air of an experienced medical practitioner. In reality he knew, and Sonja knew, that he did not have the faintest idea what to do. Why was he so completely useless, just when Sonja needed him most? Sonja looked at him briefly and knowingly and reaching into her pack she retrieved two plastic rucksack stiffeners and a large crepe bandage. She then proceeded to wrap the bandage in an expert way around the outside of her boot using the stiffeners as temporary splints. Over, under, around. Over, under, and around. She wrapped it until the job was done. Alexander was going to ask why she did not remove her boot and directly strap her ankle but dared not say anything since it would only amplify his ignorance. Why didn't he study first aid when he was younger? His only consolation was that whatever he might know was unlikely to be better than a trained nurse like Sonja.

'Let me help you try and stand,' he said and bending down he lifted her firmly but gently onto her one good foot. As he supported her she carefully placed the injured one onto the hardened snow and although he could not see her face he could feel her body tense with pain.

'I think I still have a problem,' she said, her voice indistinct in the forceful wind. He held her firmly against him and with uncharacteristic decisiveness he heard himself say,

'We have to find shelter until this storm passes Sonja. There's no way we can get through to the Nelson's Bluff emergency shelter like this.'

And then he remembered. The memory was indistinct at first but then fragmentary piece by fragmentary piece it all came back to him. Retained deep in the recesses of his mind for future unspecified use.

'When I walked this track twenty years ago I'm sure that there was an emergency bivouac somewhere near where we are now. It's a huge rock with a distinct overhang, a virtual cave. We'll be safe there.'

He carefully sat Sonja down again and unzipping his rucksack he rummaged in one of the numerous polythene bin bags that he used to keep his belongings dry. For the very first time in his whole tramping experience he actually found what he was looking for at the first attempt. It was an old 1982 guide to the tramping tracks of New Zealand. He fumbled through the pages as the wind tried to rip them away one by one. And there on page thirty five he at last found what he was looking for, *'About three kilometres from the Nelson's Bluff shelter a sign marks the start of the Devil's Track, which leads steeply to the floor of the Muller valley. Another two kilometres further on and you will see a huge rock below the track which can be used as an emergency bivouac in extreme weather.'*

'I've found it Sonja. I've found it. We're going to be alright.'

'I'm cold,' Sonja said in a voice that he had not heard before. It was a quiet voice. A vulnerable voice. A shocked voice.

'You'll be okay Sonja. I've found our refuge for the night. It's very close to here and we will be warm and snug in no time.' Alexander looked once more at the instructions and uncertainty once more entered his mind. Have we passed the rock yet or not, he thought? He honestly did not know.

'It's no more than a kilometre from here. Along the flat all the way and then straight down the slope about one hundred metres. We'll take your sleeping bag and my survival bag but we'll have to leave the packs here for the present so that Te Puke and I can give you support.'

She rose and put her arm around his broad shoulders and he around her waist and precarious step by precarious step they made their way once more along the track. It's just like normal, he thought, just one step at a time.

The first hundred metres they passed confidently, the second more uncertainly and the third more wearily. Every step of the way Alexander peered through the snowstorm and down to his left looking anxiously for the huge rock which he had seen so clearly on that bright summers day some twenty years before. Had he been mistaken? Had he failed Sonja once again when it could not matter more? For another thirty minutes they staggered along like two Napoleonic soldiers on that fateful retreat from Moscow. Sonja did not complain. She did not comment that surely they should be there by now. She trusted him. She trusted in him like she had never had to trust anyone in her young life before.

At first it seemed to be just another indistinct piece of rock escarpment far below but slowly Alexander determined that it was indeed the outline of the sanctuary that he had been so desperately seeking. Just as he had remembered it, there it lay. Sitting like an impregnable fortress nearly one hundred metres below. How such an immense object could have reached the solitary position in which it now lay he could not say and at that very moment the answer was of absolutely no importance.

'There it is Sonja. There it is,' he said trying to sound calm and in control. 'The next bit is going to be a little tough,' he continued, as though the last hour of struggle had been a gentle stroll. 'There's no proper path from here on down and it looks very steep and slippery. We'll just have to scramble as best we can.' Sonja took a firm hold of Te Puke and taking the weight off her injured foot she tentatively manoeuvred her way down the initial part of the slope. Step by careful step, past boulders, scree and occasional grassy tufts which protruded through the windblown snow. On occasion her one sound foot would slip and neither her own nor Alexander's efforts could prevent her from dropping onto her rear, sometimes with a soft landing, sometimes onto a rocky outcrop which made her wince with pain. The wind had by now risen to a frenzy forcing the increasingly heavy snow horizontally along the mountainside in a blizzard like ferocity. For some minutes they lost sight of their refuge but they had no other option but to continue their descent. Alexander had no idea what to expect if and when they achieved their objective since he had only observed the rock from the path high above so many years before. Perhaps something had drastically changed about the place and that was why their potential bivouac was no longer mentioned in the newer track guides. However it was all too clear that Sonja was in considerable pain and that there would be no way for her to regain the track. It was clearly a journey of no return for her.

At last they drew close to the massive structure that had suddenly reappeared out of the gloom to their left. A smooth blank wall of rock rose straight from ground level for a clear ten metres with neither a single crack to shelter the smallest living creature. Sonja let herself down where she stood, her figure now caked with windblown snow.

'Stay here for a moment,' shouted Alexander. 'The overhang must be around the other side. I'll be back as soon as I can.'

She observed him disappear into the whiteness then drew her tightly rolled sleeping bag to her breast as a mother would shelter a child. She had confronted difficult situations a number of times in the past when traversing alpine passes. You don't venture into the Alps without being prepared for such events. But this was different. This she could see was taking the form of a rapidly descending spiral. She was alone on the mountain with a completely inexperienced companion. Sonja had always prided herself on her cool head in difficult situations and her friends were always impressed by her strength of character. But at some point she, or more correctly they, must have made a critical and fundamental mistake. She felt that she had followed all the basic rules of mountain craft but somewhere along the way nature had played a cruel trick on them. The previous balmy spring weather had changed with a rapidity with which she was not at all familiar and she had been seduced by the clear sunny weather of the previous three days. And now here they both were enveloped in a severe snowstorm more reminiscent of mid-winter in Siberia.

Well to be more correct, here she was since Alexander seemed to have departed this earth for all she could tell. It would have been quite amusing if it was not so serious how she came to be stranded on a mountainside with a man the same age as her father. In the playful banter that had passed between them on the track he had replied, 'Thanks Mum,' when she had given him some tramping advice that he felt that his easily bruised ego did not require. He was certainly rather stubborn and in her turn she had called him 'Grandpa' just to playfully annoy him. Thus their easy relationship had developed over the past few days. After what seemed an age, but was more likely a matter of a few minutes, Alexander appeared once again.

'I think that we will be fine here until the storm passes,' he said with a sure conviction. Lifting her to her feet he helped Sonja step by painful step around the side of the huge edifice until at last they came upon the overhang that he had been looking for. In fact it was more like a cave than an overhang since there was nearly room to stand up under the extensive protrusion. The sight that greeted Sonja was not likely to impress many but her experience allowed her to quickly identify a large number of positive factors about the place. To begin with it provided excellent shelter from the driving wind and snow that they had had to endure over the last two hours. Within a short time it would be theoretically possible for two fit mountaineers to build two protective snow walls, one to the left and one to the right, completely up to roof level. However, in her present condition her contribution to the task would be extremely limited whilst looking at Alexander it was clear that he was quite exhausted after having borne her weight for so long. In addition, before they could start he would have to return for their two rucksacks that they had left back on the track. Their survival was beginning to depend on someone taking clear and decisive action and so she broached the subject.

'How do you feel Alexander?'.

'Pretty buggered actually,' he replied in a jovial sort of way that never ceased to annoy her. Why couldn't he be serious for a change.

'But how about you. You're the one I'm worried about,' Alexander responded. 'I think we should get you into your sleeping bag as quickly as possible.'

'Oh I'll be okay now Alexander. Now that we have shelter.' Without further delay they carefully began to remove her jacket, over trousers and boots. The right boot proved to be the biggest problem since by now Sonja's ankle had swollen greatly. She unwrapped the crepe bandage and removed the splints that had proven such an effective temporary support. They did not want to risk cutting the leather to release her foot from her boot since she might well need them again in an absolute emergency. Slowly she eased her foot from the opening. The pain was clearly considerable but she clenched her teeth and did what had to be done. The jacket and trousers came off quite easily and as quickly as they could they zipped her into her sleeping bag until only her face was visible. Alexander then unrolled the orange survival bag that he had only recently bought in Mamoe and hesitated.

'What are you doing Alexander?' she said impatiently.

'I'm reading what's printed on the bag, *'Bush Survival in New Zealand: preplanning for the outdoors.'* I guess I've left it a bit late as usual,' he said and with that he opened the vivid orange polythene bag and proceeded to gently ease the envelope up and over her from her feet until it again nearly covered her face.

'At least this will keep you quiet for a while,' he said with good humour. 'I think I should go back and get the packs before it gets dark. I'm going out and I may be some time,' he continued and the historical reference was not entirely lost on Sonja.

'Why do you always make jokes Alexander? I don't like it. We are in a serious situation and all you do is make stupid jokes.'

Somewhat bruised by Sonja's harsh outburst Alexander said nothing. After ensuring that she was as comfortable as possible he disappeared once more into the wall of white driving snow and was immediately lost from her sight. Sonja lay there and quietly rebuked herself for speaking so unkindly to the companion who had so recently and so ably assisted her in her time of greatest need. Their differences in culture were certainly very great. Their points of compatibility so very small. And yet she felt that she could not have a better man to be with her now. Not even her former boyfriend Herman seemed right for the present situation and this came to her as quite a shock.

Conditions on the mountain continued to deteriorate and Alexander had some difficulty regaining the main track that they had left but a short time before. His equipment for spring or summer tramping was adequate, even good, but for mid-winter conditions such as he now faced they were distinctly lacking. The worn soles of his ancient boots continuously slipped on the snow and ice whilst his makeshift gloves, fashioned out of his thick woollen socks, were proving of limited value as they became caked with snow when he grappled for hand holds on the climb. He had carried his skiing gloves, which he had brought all the way from England, on the Ailsa Track where the weather had been mostly mild and fine. He had felt so stupid carrying them. Determined to reduce the weight of his pack on the Mamoe he had left them in store at the backpackers, along with his ridiculously inappropriate pyjamas and slippers. He had hidden from Sonja the fact that he lacked gloves in order to avoid another telling off but now he was regretting yet another example of his own inadequacy. After about twenty minutes he at last regained the track and it felt as if he had attained the peak of a nearby mountain. Heading back along the path from where they had come he eventually stumbled upon two mounds of snow that signified the location of the two packs they had abandoned some time before.

Even though he had attempted to reduce its weight his own rucksack was still unrealistically heavy and was filled with a miscellany of unnecessary items. Sunscreen, spare summer clothing, shoes, his favourite cereal, numerous guidebooks, and a map of the North Island. In fact he still had a proud collection of virtually everything that could be considered totally inappropriate for their present situation. Knocking the snow off his pack he lifted it with difficulty and swung it over his shoulders. Sonja's pack was of equal weight and not without problems he contrived to place one of the straps over his right shoulder so that he was able to take the full weight of her pack on his right hip. Two packs weighing a total of forty kilograms on a good trail is far too heavy. In the present conditions it was virtually impossible. It was clearly going to be a real trial of strength that would test his resolve to the limit. There was no way he could just take one pack. He didn't have the energy to make two trips. It was all or nothing.

Each step that he took had to be foreshortened since one false move would see him slip and tumble to God only knew where. If only he had thought to bring Sonja's woollen hat which lay with her in the bivouac. Without doubt, a true tramper and mountaineer, he was not and would never be. If only his teachers or parents had encouraged him to join the scouts he would have at least gained a basic knowledge of first aid and other outdoor skills. But that's life he thought. Full of potential paths, few that are actually trod. Te Puke was a rock. Without him Alexander knew that he could not have continued. And for the first time Alexander noticed the strange glow that emanated from Te Puke's head.

If Alexander thought that he had a problem on the relatively flat track it did not compare to the task he was faced with on reaching the point where he had to descend down to the rock shelter. There was no way he could carry two packs down the virtually sheer face at the same time. There was no way he felt like leaving one pack and returning for it. His strength was draining from him and already dusk had begun to descend upon the place and darkness would shortly follow. And so dropping his own pack to the snow he proceeded to replace it on his back with Sonja's. If in doubt, he thought, drag, and taking hold of his recumbent pack he proceeded to descend step by step down the sheer valley slope, dragging his own pack behind him like a corpse. Every so often it would snag on a rock outcrop and he would have to climb a few weary steps back up the slope to release it. He knew that his strength was rapidly ebbing away. His energy bleeding into the fallen snow. His outer body was chilled through to the core but deep inside he had a warmth which radiated outwards in the opposite direction to the woman so close at hand. He knew that he just had to succeed. Reinvigorated by this thought he made a final effort and reached the overhang entrance as the final light of the day left the place, seemingly for ever.

'Alexander?' Sonja called out with distinct relief in her voice.

'The very same,' he replied.

'Alexander, where have you been? I was becoming very worried about you. You've been gone well over an hour.'

'Honestly, there was no need to be worried Sonja. It was quite easy really.'

But Sonja could see, even in the dim light, his haggard frozen expression and without delay she said, 'Alexander, please pass my pack. You must have something hot to eat and drink as soon as possible. And get out of your jacket and trousers as quickly as you can and into your sleeping bag. I have a small gas burner at the bottom of my pack that should see us through for the time being. A mug of hot soup each should do us both wonders.'

From her reclined position she then proceeded to unpack her rucksack by torchlight, each group of items carefully arranged in different coloured polythene bags so that she was able to immediately identify what was in each. Alexander could only marvel at this state of affairs compared to his own lucky dip method of packing. His trance was sharply broken by Sonja saying,

'For goodness sake Alexander, get out of those frozen clothes and into your sleeping bag at once. You'll freeze to death.'

Further chastened Alexander quickly did as he was told and he wondered at the fact that he actually enjoyed her strident tones as much as her softer ones. She was indeed a woman in the fullest sense of the word. From her prone position in her sleeping bag Sonja soon had mugs of soup prepared for them both. They devoured the steaming liquid without a word and even savoured the somewhat musty bread rolls that Alexander had fortuitously found in his own reserves. Soon things didn't appear quite so bad. They had partial shelter from the snowstorm raging outside. They were dry and relatively warm. They had sufficient food between them to last a few days. Sonja's ankle, although clearly broken, was not a compound fracture, and the pain had subsided somewhat. And above everything else somebody would surely organise a search of the track when it was found that they were overdue.

It was at that very moment that Alexander had an empty hollow feeling in the pit of his stomach. The little colour that he had in his cheeks drained away completely. They had originally agreed to walk from the Isolation Pool hut straight to the end of the Mamoe track in one day. This meant that nobody would be expecting them to take the Scorpion's Tail route or to arrive at the Paradise Ridge hut. *'Isolation Pool hut to Mamoe Exit'* Alexander had clearly written for them both in the hut intentions book the previous afternoon. 'Isolation Pool hut to bloody Mamoe exit.' He had failed to change their routing in the intentions book. He had promised Sonja that he would change it the previous evening but he had failed to do so. Why he did not know. Was it the wine? Was it his notoriously bad memory? Was it his preoccupation with Sonja? Whatever the reason they were now completely on their own.

Their early departure that morning would not have been witnessed by any of the others in the hut who were as usual sleeping so soundly. Furthermore, as far as Alexander knew, Sonja and himself were the only two who were walking the Scorpion's Tail route that day. All of the others, including the Nevada Club, planned to take the direct route back to Mamoe after stopping for one night at the Paradise Ridge hut. But surely there would be an intentions book of some kind at the track exit shelter where their final entry would be found to be missing?

But Alexander knew in his heart that so many people failed to follow the correct procedures. Of the thousands who walked the major tracks every year it had been reported in the local newspaper that thirty five percent failed to make any entry in the intentions book of any kind. It was basically a chaotic system that left the responsibility up to the individual walkers. Since they were predominantly grown adults it was rightly felt that they were quite capable of making their own decisions. The attraction of New Zealand was that it still remained a place were freedom of thought and action took precedence over too much regulation. After all, the walking tracks were relatively well marked and their dangers were insignificant compared to the severe mountain climbs further north in the Aspiring and Cook national parks. Apart from two schoolboys who had died from hypothermia on the Mamoe some thirty five years before no serious accidents or deaths had occurred since. That sad event had resulted in the introduction of the intentions books but over time a certain degree of complacency had seeped back into the procedures. It was very likely that the absence of two unknown foreigners would not be noticed at all.

'Sonja. I have something very important to tell you.'

She lay quietly in her sleeping bag looking up at him. He seemed grave and there was an absence of his usual good humour.

'I forgot to write our revised routing in the Isolation Pool hut intentions book. Anyone who checks will think that we have already left the track by the direct Mamoe route. Nobody can know that we are here.'

Alexander looked at Sonja and waited for her peaceful expression to change. He waited for the justifiable anger and her confirmation of his own clear stupidity. Of how he had put her life in danger and how she wished that she had never relied on him. Of how she wished that she had never met him. But it did not come. She looked at him with an unchanged expression and simply said,

'You're not to blame Alexander. I should have checked the intentions book before we left and I failed to do so. I'm supposed to be the experienced one in our party and it was I who let you down. We're in this together now and that's all there is to it. We both made a simple mistake. We just have to get on with it. Together.'

....

Te Puke surveyed the scene before him with dismay. It was not meant to be like this. He had always judged that Alexander was the weak link in this little adventure and that he was the one that Te Puke must protect from the harmful spirits of the earth, water and sky. Nobody was meant to get hurt. It was just a matter of returning Te Puke to the heart of his homeland. But the gods had tricked him. Whilst he had been paying attention to Alexander they had attacked Alexander's weakness, Sonja. They knew that if they wounded Sonja then they also wounded Alexander. It was all so very clever. It wasn't even a rock that did the damage, but a slippery root that had propelled her foot sideways before she had a chance to react. But Te Puke would stay and fight. He would defend his master and his master's companion with all his strength.

....

At six thirty in the evening the telephone rang at Craig William's home. It was a call that he had been anticipating for some hours as he had watched the weather deteriorate rapidly throughout the afternoon.

'Craig. It's Frank. Look mate, we're going to have to do a sweep of the tracks from entry to exit at first light. We want your team to do the Mamoe Track right up to the Paradise Ridge hut, and then around the Scorpion's Tail route until you reach the Devil's Track descent. We've got another team led by Brett Allan going in from the Isolation Pool hut side and then down the Devil's Track. We've got trampers all over the place and no certain way of knowing where they are. Some are entering, some are leaving, some are staying put in the huts, and others are just turning around. It's a complete mess. It's just a precaution but the weather is foul up there and it caught us all by surprise. We thought that the front was going to pass way to the south but it suddenly turned north and gave us a real sucker punch.'

Craig had wanted to say 'Nothing should surprise us in these mountains Frank,' but he kept those thoughts to himself. He simply replied, 'Okay Frank, I'll be ready with my team and gear at five o clock in the morning. Ready and raring to go as usual. You know I love the fifty bucks'.

'Greedy bugger,' Frank laughed, 'It's money for old rope.'

And with that Craig replaced his ancient telephone receiver on the hook and went over to his backpack that was always in a state of perpetual readiness. Nevertheless, as usual, he did a double check of the contents since somebody's life, and it might well be his own, could depend on it. Craig had spent what was now a sizeable part of his life in Fiordland and he knew the area as well as anyone. When the telephone rang he had expected it to be with regard to some mountaineer or other getting into difficulty in the Darrens. But a sweep of the Mamoe Track in late spring was a unique situation in his experience. It must be bad up there. Nevertheless, even with the reported conditions he expected that his experienced team would be able to make the sweep to the Devil's Track and back in two days at the outside. Full winter kit was clearly called for and after making one final check he went around the corner to the bar for a quiet game of pool before an early night. He would not be drinking on this occasion. Thank goodness Sonja should be off the mountain by now and be well on her way to Stewart Island, Craig reflected to himself, as he drew back the cue and potted another red.

....

High on the mountainside Alexander and Sonja had settled down as best they could for the night. Sonja's broken ankle had swollen further but in the circumstances and with the help of a double dose of aspirin she felt reasonably comfortable. In his state of exhaustion there was no way Alexander could have built the snow wall, which they would need to construct to create a windproof sanctuary, before they settled down. Occasionally spindrift would enter their haven, whirl around and finally rest like fine white dust over their horizontal forms.

'Thank you Alexander,' Sonja said softly as she lay looking at him. 'Thank you for helping me to our sanctuary. Without your knowledge about this place I would have been in big trouble.'

Alexander could not quite hear what Sonja had said at first due to the howling of the wind outside but when he had deciphered her meaning he replied, 'No need for thanks Sonja. No need at all. I know very well that you would have done exactly the same for me if our situations had been reversed.' And they both knew that this was true.

'What do you think we should do next?' she continued.

'Try to sleep and rest until daybreak and hope that the weather clears tomorrow. There's nothing more we can do. If you need some help in the night or just want to talk, just give me a dig in the ribs. Sleep well Sonja'.

'Sleep well Alexander.'

But initially Alexander did not sleep well. He lay there and tried as hard as he could to explore all of the options that lay open to them. As far as he could see they could stay put for a day or two and hope that the weather would lift. He could then proceed alone to summon help for Sonja. However, he was beginning to be concerned about her. His normally self-assured and confident companion had become somewhat quiet and her complexion had taken on a translucent hue. She seemed reasonably warm but had mentioned that her stomach was unsettled. Alexander reasoned that the track might well be searched for stranded walkers but there was no reason to believe that anyone but themselves had been stranded. Since no one knew of their plight why should anyone risk their lives in such appalling conditions to search an empty track. All he could hope for was to wake up to a bright and clear sunny morning. And how they would both laugh over a beer or two in Billy Burke's about the fuss they had made about a minor accident on a track walked by scores of people every year. And how everyone would sign Sonja's plaster cast. With that thought a wave of exhaustion swept over Alexander and he immediately drifted into a much calmer world.

10. A Sky Raised on Broad Shoulders

Saturday 4th December 2004

At four fifteen the following morning Craig Williams had woken to the shrill sound of his alarm clock and as he lay there in the dark warmth he could hear the unabated howling of the storm outside. Rising wearily and looking out into the gloom through closely drawn curtains he could see occasional flakes of snow illuminated by the bedroom light. Snow settling in Mamoe in early December. Now he had seen everything. He prepared a bowl of steaming porridge topped with a couple of sliced bananas, followed by a large boiling mug of strong coffee. Then out he went into the breaking dawn, revved up his battered four-wheel drive, and headed off to pick up his team.

....

Alexander awoke from a particularly deep sleep and gradually made some sense of his unfamiliar surroundings. It was dark. It was dark and rather damp. It was dark and damp and a wind was howling outside of his draughty bunk room. But there was no bunk room. And then he recalled where he was and what he was doing there. He looked to his left and although he could not see her clearly he could just hear Sonja's soft and regular breathing. Thank goodness she had got some much needed rest Alexander thought. The hoped for break in the weather had clearly not happened, whilst a slow build-up of frozen spindrift over their recumbent forms during the night had given the place a ghostly appearance. His survival bag had at least kept Sonja dry. How strange, almost embarrassing, to have been carrying that orange coloured survival bag strapped to the outside of his rucksack during the hot weather of the last few days. It certainly didn't feel so strange now.

It immediately became clear to Alexander that his main task for the day would be building the snow walls as soon as the dawn broke. He felt in the dark for Sonja's gas burner that lay between them but could not find the lighter that she had used the night before. In adversity find your own solution he thought. Grappling blindly through his own pack he finally felt what he was looking for, namely his compact cooking set into which he had placed his box of matches to protect them from any rain water which might invade his pack. His hands quietly separated the small group of pots and pans and in the middle he could feel his matches. He could feel them quite clearly. A wet, sodden, box of matches. Alexander had lost count of how many lessons of bush craft he had learnt the hard way over the last few days. This must be number thirteen, he thought wryly. Never, but never, place your only box of matches in your cooking set if it is not thoroughly dry.

'You're a fool Stewart,' he said quietly to himself. 'What are you? A fool, that's what. A bloody great useless old fool.'

'Sorry?' he heard Sonja say, 'I didn't hear what you said.'

'Oh nothing', replied Alexander, 'I was just talking to myself. But how about you Sonja. How do you feel if it's not too stupid a question.'

'I think the British would say, 'Just fine thank you,' when what you really mean is 'I feel bloody awful'.'

'Sonja! Where did you learn such language? That's not what I expected to hear from an innocent girl like you,' he replied teasingly.

'It's just a word I picked up at Billy Burke's in Mamoe a few days ago. It's bad, no?'

'It's bad yes. But not so bad in the circumstances.'

'Actually I honestly feel real crook. That's another Kiwi word you know. It means sick or perhaps ill. I have learnt all sorts of useful new expressions in my travels so far.'

'I'll make some hot tea, that should perk you up,' Alexander continued.

'Perk? What is 'perk' Alexander?'

'Perk. Well perk is perk. You know, perk.'

'If I knew Alexander I would not ask!' Alexander could feel from her rather strident tone that Sonja was feeling much more like her old self.

'Well, as I understand it, it means to brighten up, to cheer up, or something along those lines.' And with that Alexander said, 'Could I borrow your lighter Sonja. I seem to have mislaid my matches.'

The light of dawn attempted to lift the gloom outside but failed miserably. The snowstorm had clearly not relented throughout the long night. Alexander could see that the snow outside had in fact drifted and any trace of their tracks of the previous day would have been completely obliterated.

....

Craig's three man mountain rescue team were soon into their stride following the course of the Eyre river up the valley through mountain beech hung heavy with snow. Normally they would have been airlifted directly to the Paradise Ridge hut helipad by the police helicopter but the atrocious weather conditions had grounded every type of aircraft for miles around. For three hours they climbed through forest until they breached the tree line just below the hut. The snow lay heavy and deep on the ground whilst the trees gave a false sense of calm compared to the conditions higher up the mountainside. Occasionally they passed small groups of cold and weary trampers making their way down the valley to the track entrance. One of them cheerily shouted,

'Hi'yall, my names Morton and I'm sure as hell glad to be out of here!'

'Have you seen a German girl named Sonja on the track?' Craig asked. 'She was walking with an old guy, by the name of Alexander.'

'Why sure. You know them? Well they left early yesterday morning and the day before they told me they were walking straight through to the end of the track. I wish we had done the same and we might have missed all of this trouble. But Nance wouldn't hear of it.'

'Well thanks. Take care now on your way out,' a relieved Craig responded.

With each further group they quickly determined if anybody they had met on the track had gone missing. The universal answer was happily in the negative. However there was still some confusion since some of the trampers were in the process of completing the track whilst others had been advised by the female warden of the Paradise Ridge hut to abandon their walk in the opposite direction until the weather conditions improved. Possibly for a day or two she thought.

When they finally arrived at the hut Craig and his team stopped for a quick brew up and briefly discussed the situation with the warden, Jill Peters. Since the storm had started she had been in continuous contact with Mamoe headquarters. They in turn had been in touch with all of the other huts in the region trying to tally the entries in the intentions books with the number who had signed off from their walks. Mamoe had given Jill accurate details of the number of hut tickets bought for each day at each location. Names had been matched with intentions and intentions with exits. A number of arrivals at the huts had failed to make entries in the books but these were being checked out name by name.

'As far as I can tell the entries tally,' Jill Peters said. 'We had eight direct exits but they should have been well clear of the mountain before the storm fully broke.' Jill Peters was an experienced and respected warden who had worked out of the huts during the summer months for several years. The work of a hut warden was not an easy number. Each day she would be out on the trail ensuring that it remained basically safe for trampers from all corners of the world. Earth slips had to be repaired, fallen trees cleared and tracks compacted and made good. The combination of sun, wind, rain and physical exertion had bronzed her face, arms and legs. She was indeed a very fit and tough little woman. Craig knew her well and invariably trusted her judgement.

'I'm sure that you're right Jill. But as you know better than most the system is certainly not infallible. We had still better check it out just to be on the safe side.'

'Well Craig, you're the boss on this one, but it's a bitch of a day up there.'

'Great training for a real situation, ay mates?'

'Bollocks,' said Al with a smile on his face. 'Craig's just after his fifty bucks call out money. Bloody masochist.'

Without further ado the three orange clad figures said their goodbyes and disappeared up the track where life was about to get, as their other team member Jim would often say, 'Kinda interesting.'

....

'What are you preparing Alexander?'

'Oriental rice and chicken soup'.

'But you had that yesterday morning.'

'No, that was chicken soup and oriental rice. I do try to vary it a bit.'

'Alexander Stewart, you are completely and absolutely hopeless,' Sonja said in a teasingly friendly tone.

'Yes, I am aren't I. But mostly harmless.'

Somehow the oriental rice and chicken soup didn't taste quite as bad as usual. In fact it was stated to be excellent by Sonja. Certainly his best effort to date.

'Pity we couldn't wash it down with a good white wine. Snow chilled white wine, as we did two nights ago,' Sonja continued.

'You certainly seem to have perked up,' Alexander said.

'Indeed, I am perked,' she replied.

Alexander smiled at her endearing command of the English language. Indeed she was perked. She was the perkiest woman that he had ever met. Her vibrant energy for life radiated from every single pore.

'Is there any sign of the storm lifting?' she asked, although she already knew the answer.

'Not as far as I can see,' he replied. 'In fact I think it has actually got worse. I had better start on the snow walls that you suggested. We have to keep the spindrift and wind out of this place if we are to spend another night here. There's not much else we can do at present until the storm passes.' Alexander reflected on the situation for a while and then said, 'Sonja. How do I make a snow wall? Do I just make big compacted blocks of snow and then just pile them up?'

'Think Eskimo Alexander. Think igloo.'

Alexander thought Eskimo for a while and visions of Eskimos cutting great slabs of frozen snow entered his mind. Cutting them with thin stainless steel blades that Sonja and he did not have.

'I guess it's back to the big compacted blocks of snow for us Sonja,' and with that he put on his warmest clothing, jacket and over trousers and exited the overhang and immediately started kneading the snow into blocks. Alexander had once read how great a volume of snow it took to make a much smaller volume of water. When he got out of his present predicament he decided that he would write a thesis on how much loose snow was required to make an infinitely small block.

'Snow blocks are off the menu today Sonja,' he called out. 'It's heaping and packing for me. It's snowman time.'

Minutes turned into an hour, an hour into hours but slowly, so slowly, a wall appeared. First to the right, and then to the left, of their small sanctuary. The feeling from his sock covered fingers soon departed. This was followed by his whole hands and then his feet. As he worked he remembered one time at his remote English boarding school, on a chill freezing February day, how he had played for the school under thirteen football team and froze in a similar way. The freezing had been bad enough but the pain when he warmed himself up close to the radiators in the changing room was far worse. Fingers and toes. Indescribable pain.

From time to time Sonja called out, 'That's enough Alexander. Come back in.' But he could see that if he could make a continuous barrier from ground to rock ceiling then they would indeed have their own snug igloo where they could ride out whatever nature threw at them. At long last he was satisfied with his work and on entering their newly formed haven Alexander felt inordinately proud of his efforts.

'Nothing to this mountain craft business Sonja. Or is it bush craft? Who cares.'

In the corner he could see the clear blue flame of the gas burner and smell the delightful odour of something from Sonja's food pack. He looked at her and within her eyes he could see a look of concern.

'You look terrible Alexander.'

'I know. I didn't have time to shave.'

'Alexander, don't joke. You know I don't like it. Seriously you look ghostly.'

'Ghastly, Sonja. The word's ghastly.'

'I know what I mean damn you. Ghostly. Like a ghost!'.

Since he had no way of seeing himself he could only take her word for it. His frozen fingers could not feel his frozen face and so he had no way of judging the fact. Perhaps, in his enthusiasm, he had failed to notice the slow draining of the blood from his extremities. But what other option was there? He was the only one who could make their newly found home safe. It had to be done. It had to be done for the woman he now knew he loved and would protect as long as he had a single breath in his body. Alexander had difficulty removing his socks from his hands and so Sonja carefully pulled them off until the blue coloured digits were fully revealed. She helped him remove his frozen jacket and over trousers as best she could and undid the zip of his sleeping bag.

'I think that you should get into your bag immediately so that you can warm yourself up. If I see you leave your bag again today you'll be for it.'

He nestled into his cocoon once more and she zipped it tight until all that showed were the moon shaped features of his face. Just eyes, nose and mouth.

'You look like a baby,' she said.

'I feel like a boysenberry ice cream,' he replied with an absence of his usual humour.

'A large helping of my special soup will soon put you right.'

'I'm cohabiting with an angel,' he replied.

Within a few minutes Sonja was feeding Alexander with spoonfuls of an undetermined hot and tasty liquid full of the very best organic goodness. She could not help smiling at this helpless creature lying obediently by her side, like a vast pupae. With those deep blue eyes. She had not noticed them before because she was somewhat embarrassed by direct eye contact with new acquaintances. Perhaps it was a shy part of her nature that she hid behind the shell of her outwardly confident and strident manner. But now she noticed those deep clear bottomless pools of blue.

'Don't forget yourself,' Alexander said. 'We must both keep up our energy for the Saturday night dance in Mamoe.'

Suddenly his jokes no longer irritated her. They no longer made her annoyed. It was strange. For suddenly she saw him in a different light. Or perhaps she saw him for the first time.

'Shut your face Alexander and eat up.'

'Be quiet is more correct Sonja.'

....

The climb to Nelson's Bluff was difficult at the best of times but in the present conditions it was a nightmare. Two hours had turned to four and the higher the three colleagues climbed the worse it got. The track had long since disappeared under two feet of powder snow but Craig instinctively knew the route which had been indelibly engraved in his memory. Somewhere to his right in the whiteout he knew there lay the frozen Lake Burchill. Their first target was to reach the emergency shelter on the bluff itself. After a further thirty minutes they finally breached the rise and the wind seemed to scream and roar at them. Leave my mountain. Leave my mountain. You have no right to be here. It tore at their clothing trying to rip it from bodies bathed in vapour and sweat.

They simultaneously burst into the triangular shaped emergency shelter and knelt on the bare wooden floor gasping for breath, oblivious to the continual banging of the door behind them. Back and forth. Back and forth.

'Shit,' was all Craig could utter.

'Fuck,' was the best Al could add.

Finally they closed the door and gathered their battered senses. A gas burner was lit and a pot of water soon boiled merrily away in the middle of the room providing some warmth and light to the bleak surroundings. They knew they had to reach the Devil's Track and return to the safety of the shelter before nightfall but they were already two hours behind schedule. The battery light on the emergency radio blinked intermittently in the corner of the shelter. On. Off. On. Off. Informing the world that all was well. All was well.

....

Notwithstanding the intake of the hot and delicious soup Alexander failed to show signs of improvement and his teeth began to chatter. Barely perceptible at first but then uncontrollably. Sonja observed him closely for some time and then said,

'We're going to have to lie together for a while until you recover.'

Without waiting for his response she unzipped his bag and moving closer unzipped her own. Taking care not to catch her injured foot she instructed Alexander to lie on his side in a part foetal position and doing the same she drew herself to his back like the elusive missing piece in a Christmas jigsaw puzzle. Pulling her sleeping bag over them both they lay there in a perfectly fitting form. He giving up his chill to her, and she her warmth to him.

'People will talk,' he said between the staccato chatter of his teeth.

'Shut your face Alexander.'

'Be quiet Alexander. Remember Sonja.'

'Shut your face.'

She lay there holding herself closely to a man she had known just a few short days. He was old enough to be her father and yet somehow for all his poor jokes, for all his uncalled for interruptions, she felt not the chill of his body but the warmth of his generous heart beating deep within him. Her relationship to him before this moment had been purely practical, functional. As with all her previous male walking companions. They enjoyed female company whilst she welcomed a walking partner on the sometimes remote and difficult tracks. When each track was completed she would go her way and they would go theirs.

After every trek the first thing she did was to telephone her parents to assure them she was fine and having a wonderful time. Even though her homesickness revealed itself to their knowing selves on occasion. They did not say anything. As the youngest and only girl in the family they worried deeply about her but they tried not to show it during their relatively short conversations. She was their only girl. But she had not been their only daughter. Many years ago, long before Sonja had been born there was another girl whom her parents named Esther. They loved this girl with all their hearts since she was the baby of the family that then consisted of three sons and Esther. But this jewel in their lives shone for such a short time. Day by day her young health faded. And then she was gone. They never really recovered from a shock so deep and profound. When Sonja arrived so late and unexpectedly into their lives they lived in a state of constant anxiety. They loved her like no other but they also knew that they had to let her strong spirit run free.

Alexander felt her warmth and a glow passed through him from head to toe. Their partially clothed bodies touched along their length but the feeling Alexander had was not, unusually for him, sexual in nature. It was a deep and profound innocent love. The woman he had never even kissed lay with him, embraced him, enveloped him. He savoured these moments like a condemned man savours his last few hours. He was fully aware that within a day or two, when they extracted themselves from this predicament, she would be gone from his life forever. They lay there giving each to each, one to one, like two abandoned orphans on the ocean of life, clinging to each other.

And as their warmth returned they slipped hand in hand into sleep. A deep delicious sleep.

....

Barely thirty minutes after they had entered the emergency shelter the three figures emerged and roping up they proceeded to force a path along the long narrow traverse far above the tree line. The strength of the wind and snow remained unabated and they had great difficulty maintaining their footing even with the help of their walking poles. Al made some shouted comment to the others but it was mercilessly blown away in the raging wind. For two solid hours they struggled under bluffs, over precipices, along ridges, through the milk white gloom. Visibility was down to about ten meters but still they continued until they at last came upon the sign that they had been looking for. It was the steel stake with the fluttering red pennant hammered into the track by Brett Allan's team at the junction with the Devils Track, just where it disappeared vertically downwards into the valley far below. It was down that track that Brett and his team would have descended. Apart from a few indistinct footprints rapidly disappearing in the snow it would have been difficult for anyone to have known that barely thirty minutes before three other men had set foot on this very spot. The pennant continued to flutter noisily as Craig shouted 'It's an all clear. Let's get the hell out of here.'

11. Far Beyond the Mountain Peaks

<u>Sunday 5th December 2004</u>

The snow continued to fall covering the huge rock structure and all that surrounded it. Down below two people slept deep in their own private dreams. The snow walls that Alexander had built at such personal cost the previous day continued to do their job and a sense of coziness permeated the bleak place. It was quiet in there and the storm that raged outside seemed so far away.

As the first light of day broke Sonja turned in her sleep and with a start was rudely awoken and reminded by an intense stabbing pain of exactly where she was. And yes, she did indeed have a broken ankle. She also felt a familiar nausea coming over her that she could not explain. Close beside her Alexander continued to sleep, his easy breathing giving her no cause for concern. Sonja turned and reaching for her gas burner she proceeded to prepare some boiling water for a mug of coffee for them both. Perhaps that would make her feel better and she was sure Alexander would appreciate it. The warmth of the blue flame momentarily lifted her spirits and as she waited for the water to boil she once more drew herself to his sleeping body to try to regain the feeling of peace and contentment which she had felt the night before. It felt to her at that moment the most natural thing in the world. She wanted to hold this most annoying man. The water began to show signs of boiling as individual bubbles formed on the bottom of the pan. Then suddenly, without warning, the flame spluttered and then completely died. Sonja knew immediately that the gas had finally run out. She also knew that they had no other source of heating their water or food. Unlike the huts there wasn't a scrap of wood of any kind in their bivouac. It must have been years since it had last been occupied.

'Wake up Alexander. Wake up,' she repeated as she gently shook him to rouse him from his deep slumber. 'You had better have a drink of coffee before the water gets cold. How are you feeling this morning?' He turned and she drew back somewhat embarrassed by their close proximity.

'I think I'm feeling much better.' he replied. 'But then those were an English king's famous last words.'

Sonja passed him his mug full of hot coffee and said, 'Make the most of it Alexander, it's the last hot drink or food we can have until Saturday's dance.'

'Hey come on Sonja, I tell the jokes, remember,' and they laughed. She could see that he was indeed feeling better. Alexander knew that the only reason they still had gas in the first place was that it was the remains of Sonja's previous walk where she had had to camp on the route.

They lay close together, warming each other, when Sonja suddenly asked,

'Do you believe in love at first sight Alexander?'

It seemed such a strange question to ask in their present predicament, struggling to survive in a hostile environment. But then perhaps, there could be no better time to ask such a question. Alexander looked at her. His first reaction was to make some sort of joke about their intimate situation. To ask her if she was making a proposal of marriage. But he could see from her expression that she had asked a serious question, and that a serious answer was required.

'You mean about Craig?' Alexander responded in order to confirm his initial understanding of the reason for her question.

'Yes, about Craig. A few days ago I thought I was in love with my long time boyfriend in Germany. And then Craig walked into my life and I can think of no one else. It is the strangest and most wonderful sensation. I think that I knew within a few minutes of our first meeting that I loved Craig. That I would marry him.'

'To answer your question Sonja, yes I do believe in love at first sight. It has happened to me two or three times in my life and I feel very fortunate to have experienced that sensation. But unfortunately the women that I fell in love with just never felt the same way about me. We usually became the best of friends but in all truth I have never met a woman who has truly fallen in love with me. Not even my former wife. It's just the way it is. But what about Craig? Do you know how he feels?'

'At first I felt that I was just one of the many girls in his life,' replied Sonja. 'I was even very rude to him because I didn't want to get hurt. But the wonderful thing is, he feels just the same about me. And I know that he is not just saying it.'

Alexander looked across at the young women that he had come to love and said,

'Well you must just go for it Sonja. Grasp the opportunity with both hands and don't let go. I'm certain that Craig will be a good partner for you. I knew it from the moment I first saw him. You clearly have so many common interests and I'm sure that he will be a fine father to your children. I just know that it will work out well for you both.'

'Thank you Alexander. Even though we have only known each other for a few days I sincerely trust your judgment. From the moment I first spoke to you.'

Alexander felt both happiness and sadness in equal measure. But he knew that happiness would soon outweigh the sadness. What could be better than to see a couple who truly loved each other. It radiated out like a beacon giving hope to all others on their own elusive quest.

And as they lay there they talked about so many things. It was as if Alexander was giving Sonja a master class in life. At least, a master class of life as he had personally experienced it. They talked about his marriage. They talked at great length about his love for Minnie. They talked about his work and travels. Sonja, in her turn, told him everything about herself, from her kindergarten right up to the present day. There were no barriers to their discussion. No intimate secrets concealed. It was if they were the only two people on the planet. Survivors of some great catastrophe.

Alexander was just turning his head to look out through the opening of their refuge when he heard Sonja gasp and reach down to hold her stomach. The sensation that she had on first waking had returned with a vengeance.

'Alexander. Now it's my turn to be unwell. If both of us were ill at the same time we would make a fine couple.'

It pleased him the way she said, 'We would make a fine couple,' but that feeling was rapidly replaced by a deep concern for her. She did indeed look ill and that dreadfully pale hue to her complexion had returned.

'You know,' she continued 'the hut wardens always tell us that they always drink the water in the huts and mountain streams but that they cannot directly recommend the same to us for legal reasons. And you know every hut has information warning about *giardia*. Well, I have a horrible feeling that I now know why,' and with that she rapidly rose onto her good foot and with Te Puke's support she hopped outside of their shelter to be violently sick.

Alexander made his way to her as quickly as he could but at first he was reluctant to touch her since he was powerless to help. What could he say, 'How do you feel?' Hardly helpful in the circumstances and it would probably only elicit a justified rebuke from Sonja. Braving the likely outburst he lent across and gently felt her forehead that was indeed showing clear signs of a high temperature. He told her get into her sleeping bag and to lie quietly. He dressed as quickly as he could, went outside and placed a clean handkerchief in the snow to make a cold compress. Returning he folded it carefully and gently laid it to her forehead. The sensation clearly gave her some temporary relief since she said 'Danke' and then was quiet.

Alexander had indeed read the *giardia* notices himself and he had memorised a great deal of the contents because he had been amused by the dire symptoms. Having travelled the world for twenty five years he considered himself, quite wrongly, to be largely immune from such dangers. He had therefore taken an uncharacteristically smug delight in the described symptoms. He had learnt that *giardia* was a parasite that lived in the intestine and that it was very infectious. The telltale signs were diarrhoea, stomach cramps, dehydration, nausea and weight loss. Perhaps Sonja had contracted *giardia* on one of her European walks and that was why she had been so ill on the plane? They said that it was very difficult to eradicate for good. Treatment was said to be simple and quick acting when the sufferer was prescribed certain drugs. But they had no drugs. Alexander felt so helpless. If it was *giardia* he knew that antibiotics were required. And soon.

Throughout the rest of the morning, afternoon and evening he watched over her but it was clear that her condition was deteriorating rapidly and a high fever was setting in. Occasionally she would raise herself from her stupor to be sick yet again and then recline letting out an occasional soft groan as she did so. She was clearly losing a lot of fluid and becoming very dehydrated. It was painful for Alexander to sit there and watch the one he loved suffer so. He felt so incredibly useless in her hour of need.

If anyone had reported them missing then surely some rescue party would have located them by now. But no, it was clear, that as Alexander had anticipated, nobody had cause for concern about them. And at that moment he again realised he had made yet another basic mistake. He swore inwardly to himself. He should have left a sign of some kind on the track directly above their refuge. If somebody had passed along the track then they would have seen it and would have raised the alarm. But no, he comforted himself, nobody would have passed along the track in this weather. Not even the abominable snowman would have been out in that storm.

But he just had to do something. He could not lie there any longer and watch her suffer and grow weaker before his eyes. Although his fingers and toes remained an unusual colour, somewhere between sepia and dark blue, he was feeling much better following his long rest of the night before.

'Sonja. It's Alexander. Can you hear me. I have to go and get help. I have to go and get help now. I will return as soon as I can. Do you understand?'

Sonja stirred a little and looking into her glazed eyes he saw what he thought were vague signs of acknowledgement. It was clear that by now that her condition was serious. He wrapped his sleeping bag around her own and after making her as comfortable as he could he put on his jacket, over trousers and boots. 'I love you Sonja,' he said quietly to himself. He was about to leave but he turned and knelt down beside her. Placing his lips to her forehead, he kissed her. Gently. Lovingly. Then he departed into the night.

12. Above the Tree Line

Monday 6th December 2004

    The time spent by the three men after they had returned to the Nelson's Bluff shelter could not be called comfortable. They had passed the night amiably enough making jokes at each others expense, playing cards, eating and consuming copious quantities of tea and coffee. They had slept well in an environment they were well accustomed to and at first light they left the shelter to descend to the Paradise Ridge hut below. Then after a planned short break for a drink and chat with Jill it would be back to Mamoe and their normal working lives. The descent was no easier than the previous ascent, possibly more difficult, and the storm that was due to have passed by now sat stubbornly over the mountains. The three men had certainly earned their call out money on this occasion and none could recall conditions such as this at this particular time of year. However, a few glasses of beer and the odd whisky in Billy Burke's that night would soon make their experience but a distant memory to be filed away with all the others.

                        ....

    Alexander once more made his way up the sheer slope to their original path. Turning to his left he felt his way like a blind man, the brave Te Puke at his side, relying on vague memories of that sunny day some twenty years before. By now it was four o clock in the morning and it was colder than he had ever experienced. He knew that he should have waited until the dawn but also knew that he would never have forgiven himself if something had happened to Sonja. He could clearly see in his mind's eye his objective, the emergency shelter sitting in splendid isolation on Nelson's Bluff. He also remembered the short climb he had made to the adjoining mountaintop with its panoramic views over the mountain range opposite. Up the broad sweep of the valley below, and out to the sea in the far distance. He could also recall that the track would not rise or fall markedly and that if he kept his concentration he would not lose the way. For some reason, which he could not directly explain, the path seemed to be demarcated in some way, even in the darkness. Sonja's torch was unfortunately proving of little use, its fragile beam offering little penetration through the driven snow. It was agonisingly slow progress but he could not afford to make one slip since it would surely prove fatal. Even though he had his hood pulled as tightly closed as possible the snow bit hard into his eyes so that he had to adopt a continuous squint.

Somehow, all of the time he was moving, he did not feel the cold and his storm proof jacket was proving to be an absolutely indispensable lifesaver. After two hours the semi-dawn broke but his objective seemed as unattainable as ever. Had he missed the Bluff? Should he have struck up to his right already or was it further yet? For some reason he suddenly remembered watching the film Dr Zhivago and seeing Omar Sharif shuffling along a single railway line between two platforms. Clothes caked in snow, icicles hanging from his frozen beard, asking falteringly, *'Is this Kuryagin?'* or a similar place name. He felt that he must look exactly the same but he had nobody to ask to confirm that it was so.

....

Far below Jill Peters was preparing large mugs of steaming hot chocolate for the men who had so recently arrived at her door. 'Don't forget to wipe your feet,' she had shouted sarcastically from her small kitchen as the weary threesome had appeared. 'We don't want any untidy day trippers in here.'

She could see by their eyes what they had been through but nobody made any comment. After removing their outer clothing and boots they sat down and drew close to the warmth radiating from the crackling log stove. They talked about many things. The solitude and beauty of the mountains. Their family and friends, present and departed. About how there were suddenly more Irish bars in Mamoe than there were Irishmen but what good value they were. They all enjoyed their short rest and were about to leave when the crackle of the small loudspeaker on the wall opposite caught them all by surprise. So much so that they had to look at each other twice to make sure that they had not imagined it.

'Hello! Can anybody hear me!' shouted an indistinct voice through the static. 'May Day, May Day or some bloody thing,' the voice continued as Jill rushed across the room to pick up the receiver.

'Receiving loud and clear. Receiving loud and clear. Please identify yourself. Who is speaking please? Over.'

The voice at the other end went momentarily silent, as if in shock, and then slowly and determinedly said, 'My name is Alexander Stewart. I'm at the Nelson's Bluff emergency shelter. I need help. I'm sorry, we need help.'

Craig looked at the others and said to Jill, 'Ask him to confirm. We were there only three hours ago.'

'Please confirm that you are at the Nelson's Bluff shelter. Please confirm. Over'.

'Confirm. Confirm. My companion had an accident two days ago and we had to shelter from the snowstorm at the rock bivouac halfway between the Scorpion's Tail Saddle and the Nelson's Bluff shelter. I believe she has a broken ankle. She is now very ill with a fever and vomiting. I think it's *giardia*. I'm deeply concerned for her. We need help quickly.'

'Alexander. What is your companion's name? Over.'

'Sonja. Sonja Schneider.'

'OK Alexander. I have three mountain rescue men with me here at this moment. Are you yourself OK? Are you OK? Over.'

'Never felt better,' he replied. This was followed by a long rasping cough that indicated exactly the opposite.

'I'm sorry Alexander but we have to ask some short questions to help us formulate a rescue plan. What is your companion's age, nationality and overall condition. Over.'

'She's twenty something years old. Nationality, German. Probable broken ankle. Probable *giardia* or similar symptoms. Dehydrating fast.'

'And you Alexander. What about yourself. Over.'

'I did this route twenty years ago. Forty nine years old. British. Totally knackered but apart from frozen hands and feet, not too bad in the circumstances. Well not too good actually. But I'm OK.'

'Hold on Alexander I'll be back to you in thirty seconds. Repeat, thirty seconds.' The four quickly discussed the options and then Craig picked up the receiver and said firmly, 'Alexander. It's Craig here. Craig Williams. Mountain rescue. We met the other day in Billy Burke's. Look mate we're coming up to get you as soon as we can.

Stay where you are. Repeat. Stay where you are in the shelter. We'll be with you in about three hours. Over.'

There was hesitation at the other end until they heard, 'Sorry Craig. I've got a very sick companion back there. I've been gone too long already. I'm going back. Repeat. I'm going back. I gave Sonja my word. Over.'

'Look Alexander mate,' said Craig unsuccessfully trying to hold his language under control, 'You sound buggered with clear indications of hypothermia and frostbite. You won't make it back mate. Repeat. You won't make it back. I don't want to carry your fucking old body off this mountain. Is that clear? I'm ordering you to stay in the shelter! Over.'

A silence descended over the warden's hut as they waited for a response. The few seconds that passed seemed like minutes. Then a voice said quietly, 'I'm sorry mate. I'm sorry. I promised Sonja. That's how it is.' Then silence. Just silence.

'Alexander!' No response. 'Alexander!' No response. 'Alexander mate where the fuck are you?'

Craig slammed down the receiver and sat down angrily to put his boots on regretting his harsh words. He had thought it might work but it seemed that they had had the opposite effect. But within himself he knew by the sound of Alexander's voice that nothing would have stopped him returning to Sonja. And he knew that he would have done exactly the same himself.

The three rapidly put on their clothing until Al said, 'Christ, just what we need a fucking old guy stuck on the mountain in a snowstorm!'

'Al. I'm nearly fifty you know,' said Jim.

'Just like I said, a fucking old man,' Al immediately responded.

'Jill, you know the routine' said Craig. 'Contact the services in Mamoe. Tell them we've got an emergency and give them the details. There's no way we're going to get a chopper up there today so it looks as if it's up to us.'

'Why the hell didn't Brett's team check the rock bivouac out for heavens sake,' said Al angrily.

'Be fair Al,' said Craig. 'Remember nobody had been reported missing and who would know about the rock shelter?'

'A bloody old Pom knew, that's who Craig,' said Jim.

'How did he know about the emergency bivouac at the hanging rock?' continued Al. 'We haven't marked it on the maps for years now to discourage camping at unauthorised locations.'

'He said he did the track twenty years ago,' Jim responded. 'When the biv was referred to in the guide. He must have remembered it. You see Al, we old guys are fucking smart.' The two looked at each other, eye to eye, until both gave a grin.

'Jill. Check the intentions lists again,' said Craig.

Jill Peters scrolled down the lists that she had written down and there they were. Leaping out at them from the page. Alexander Stewart and Sonja Schneider. Mamoe Track. 2nd December 2004. *'Isolation Pool hut to Mamoe exit.'* Jill had barely finished reading out the information when they were gone. Climbing once more the path to Nelson's Bluff. Climbing with a new urgency. Climbing with optimism shaded by doubt.

....

Sonja lay in the semi-darkness. Still and alone. She had an indistinct memory that Alexander had left her the night before but she could not recall his exact words or intentions. She lay in her own wretched misery knowing only that her future, even her life, lay in another's hands. A man she had known for a few short days and yet who now seemed to her like a lifelong friend. No, not friend, she thought. It was more than that. She felt extremely weak and had had difficulty moving about the floor of the shelter as she searched for her torch. Now gone. She looked at the luminous dial of her watch and determined that if Alexander had left her in the early morning then he would have now been gone about seven hours. Seven long hours in the storm outside. Perhaps he had reached the emergency shelter that he had mentioned and was at this very moment warming himself by a log fire and drinking the shelters small stock of tea or coffee. That would be the sensible thing to do. The textbook way. Wait for his rescuers. But somehow she instinctively knew he would return. Somehow she knew that the deep stubborn streak within him would not allow him to remain there. He would return to their shelter whatever the conditions. Or perish in the attempt.

'Bloody Alexander. Bloody, bloody, Alexander.' And then she wept. At that very moment she knew beyond doubt that she loved this man.

What sort of love it was she could not truly tell. It felt like the love for her very own father. It felt as if she knew him better than her own father. But now he had gone and she might never have the chance to say, 'I love you Alexander.' And before he could reply she would have taken his body to her own in a long embrace. A pure and innocent embrace.

....

Alexander sat down for a moment on the bare wooden bench that extended along the length of the shelter. He wearily surveyed his refuge which was barely illuminated by natural light filtering through snow caked windows. There were no chairs, tables, bunks, gas stoves or anything of note. Just a bare wooden floor. It was indeed just an emergency shelter. It was then that his eye fell upon a padlocked cupboard recessed into the wall at the far end of the structure. He rose and as he approached he could just make out the words 'Emergency Cache' and in smaller words below 'No unauthorised entry!' This was certainly an emergency but how on earth was he going to gain access to whatever lay behind the door. There was nothing for it. He would just have to find some way to force the padlock. And at that moment he felt Te Puke in his hands. Faithful Te Puke. Te Puke who had been his loyal companion over the last few days. But wood against steel? It was no match. His first attempts were repulsed and the lock stood firm, totally unmoved. Alexander became extremely angry but anger alone would not advance his cause.

It was then that he remembered a Maori war challenge that he had seen some time before. And for the very first time he remembered that Te Puke was not just an old walking stick. Te Puke was a weapon. Te Puke was a real fighting weapon. But somehow Alexander inwardly sensed that he could not harness that power without due respect. And with one leg advanced he raised Te Puke above his head and began his challenge to his enemy. His eyes rolled, his tongue extended, he began to shout out words of a language of which he had no knowledge. Just hazily remembered words. The Haka? That's right it was called the Haka. Louder and louder Alexander sang until with a stunning blow he brought the glowing head of Te Puke down with a force that he did not know that he possessed, onto the head of his enemy. Faced with this formidable foe the lock simply gave way and spiralled through the air until it came to rest in the far corner of the shelter. Defeated. Alexander was jubilant but for some reason he self-consciously looked behind him to make sure that nobody had witnessed his momentary madness. There was nothing there but shadows.

The cupboard space was smaller than Alexander had expected but it was clearly a real treasure trove. Stacked neatly on internal shelves he could see a number of small gas canisters, burners, matches, candles, pans and so on. In another section there were freeze dried meals and soups of various kinds, biscuits, chocolate, coffee and nuts. In yet another were two compact sleeping bags and other survival material. But the real prize was the first aid kit. When Alexander opened it up he was overjoyed to see that it contained a large number of different medicines and tablets. He had no idea what they were for but he knew that Sonja would. Hopefully they would include some antibiotics or whatever it was that she urgently needed. A veritable gold mine for the unfortunate. Alexander rapidly proceeded to load his rucksack with the most essential items. He felt sure that their rescuers would reach them within a few hours, a day at the outside. So without further delay he hoisted his pack onto his back and strode through the door and outside into the raging storm.

During the first few hundred metres of his return journey Alexander had been jubilant and was buoyed along by the knowledge that the outside world at least knew of Sonja's plight and that help was, if not directly at hand, on its way. Within a matter of hours the rescuers should have got through to them with all the help that they would need. And then he thought of Sonja lying there cold and alone. Had she understood his words when he departed or did she lie there accusing him of abandoning her to her fate? The thought spurred him on and he shouted into the raging storm, 'I'm coming Sonja, I'm coming,' but no one would hear. Just the answering roar of the wind in the treetops far below.

As time passed his steps became shorter and more uncertain, his vision less clear, and his strength less apparent. On one occasion he thought he could make out the rock edifice down below but it was just a cruel illusion. His hands and feet were now unknown to the rest of his body as he shuffled along the track like a vagrant on the winter highway. 'One step at a time Alexander,' he repeated over and over again as his own private mantra. 'Just one step at a time.'

Te Puke was a tower of strength for Alexander. Without his faithful companion's aid he knew that he would not have had the will to continue. At one point something very strange happened. It may have been the delusions of a man whose grip on reality had finally left him but Alexander suddenly felt his hands forced vertically above him. The head of Te Puke glowed white hot and a bolt of light seemed to project itself high onto the hidden white slopes high above them. It was as if a laser beam was being trained onto some fixed spot. It seemed like hours but it was no doubt just a few seconds that Alexander was transfixed by something entirely beyond his control. And then the glow died down to its more usual blue green and Te Puke once more seemed just like a normal stick helping a weary traveler on his way. But Alexander sensed that some hidden danger had been averted. Exactly what he could not tell.

Two further hours passed. And then at last, through the glaze of his frozen eyelids he looked down and there it was, the rock, their haven. He looked away and back again to make absolutely sure that this time his mind had not played him tricks. 'Kuryagin,' he cried. 'Kuryagin,' and down he went, falling, rolling, warm tears running down his cheeks. Pain meant nothing to him. Only one thing mattered. Sonja. His Sonja. At last the giant rock towered above him. But on reaching the opening in the snow wall that he had built just a short while before he hesitated, fearing what he might find inside. He could not bear the images that had invaded his thoughts over the last hour. They were all so real. Bracing himself he at last stumbled through the entrance looking like a terrible Ngati Mamoe warrior bent on vengeance.

……………………………………

The three men once more bent their backs to the task in hand but this time they did so with renewed urgency. Two people desperately needed their help and that was their job. That was what they had trained for. That was what they were paid for. The track to Nelson's Bluff had been made clearer by their previous exertions and at last there seemed to be a slight lessening in the wind and in the intensity of the snowfall. Three hours after starting out from the Paradise Ridge hut they again reached the Bluff and quickly confirmed that the emergency shelter was empty.

'We'd better have a quick brew and something to eat,' said Al. Craig desperately wanted to continue along the path in search of Sonja but he knew that Al was right. They had to do things according to the book. Three more hungry and dehydrated people on this mountain wouldn't help anyone. They closed the door and Jim quickly had two gas burners roaring way giving heat and light to the room.

'He found the emergency cache,' said Al. 'Must've had an ice axe or something to crack that lock.' They did a brief tally of the contents and they could see that most of the food, gas and medicines had been taken. The bivouac and spare sleeping bags remained.

'At least they must have some decent kit with them to leave the bags,' said Jim. 'That's one good sign.'

The three of them sat on the bench and silently consumed the scalding hot tea and porridge that Jim had prepared for them. Heaps of brown sugar layered the porridge, just as they all liked it. The break had done them good and they felt the fatigue of their rapid climb receding.

'Well come on you lazy sods,' said Craig jovially. 'This is not a holiday you know.'

In unison Al and Jim replied 'Bollocks,' but they were already up on their feet kitting up.

'I think that we should rope up again on the next leg,' said Craig. 'I'm a bit worried about all this powder.' And with that they struck off to their left and immediately started to make good progress along the level traverse. 'Two hours should do it,' shouted Al as they went on stride for stride. Craig was leading out the first stretch and he could see quite clearly what at first seemed like distinct steps in the snow but very soon these turned into a continuous trail which indicated the weary shuffle of the man they had spoken to.

'Mad bugger,' Craig said to himself. 'Mad old bugger.' As he continued around each corner in the track he half expected to see the shape of a body lying prone in the snow. A lifeless figure. It was a sight that he had seen a number of times before in these mountains and each time he prayed that it would be the last. As the time went by 'Mad old bugger' changed to 'Tough old bastard. Tough old pommie bastard.' But still the trail led on.

It all happened so quickly and so silently that they would talk about it for years afterwards. There was no dramatic rumble from above, no sharp cracking sound, just a caressing whoosh as if a snow train had passed silently by. But they all knew what it was. And it nearly had their names engraved on it. It was an avalanche. Powder. White, enveloping and suffocating. They stood still in their tracks. Visibility was down to about twenty metres and they didn't see a thing. But somewhere close at hand they knew that thousands of tons of powder would have crossed their path in an instant, making its way down to the valley below.

Craig stood for a moment and thought of Sonja. How Sonja was in desperate need. How he had the means to help her. How in a few seconds he would make a decision that could mean the difference between life and death. And he knew what that decision would be.

'We're going back to the shelter,' he shouted at the two men behind. There was no need for explanation. They understood far better than most how difficult that decision had been. But they knew that it was the right decision. And that was why Craig was team leader. They adjusted their ropes and without further ado Al led them back along the path that they had so recently trod. Craig followed the other two, his emotions in turmoil, detached from his surroundings.

13. A Land of Ice and Snow

Tuesday 7th December 2004

Sonja was initially startled by the white apparition, with a half demented appearance, which had suddenly appeared in the confined opening of their shelter. But then she was up with her walking stick in hand, hobbling painfully across to this thing whose only recognisable feature were those deep blue eyes gazing from a sea of frozen white.

'Alex-an-der! Alex-an-der! I knew that you would return. I knew you would.' And gathering her composure she said, 'We must take those frozen clothes off immediately.' And he with his frozen fingers and she with her broken ankle grappled with his zips and buttons ineffectually until they laughed and laughed. And cried and cried with overwhelming relief. Later, and not without difficulty, they at last achieved their task. Alexander just lay there in his thermals on the earth floor, motionless, exhausted.

'In the bag Alexander. In my bag immediately Alexander. While it's still warm.'

And he dutifully did what he was told. It was not easy for him. His whole body felt like ice, solid and immovable. His hands and feet had no feeling. He could not close his fingers to grip the opening of the bag but somehow, inch by inch, he drew it up around him until he was enveloped by the echo of Sonja's warmth and fragrance.

'My piano playing days are over,' said Alexander, looking dispassionately at his blackened fingers.

'You don't play the piano. I know your silly jokes by now. Can't you be serious about anything?'

'I'll have to think about that one,' replied Alexander, giving her question his full attention. Had the sum total of his life been just one catalogue of nervous jokes. He hoped not.

'Oh Alexander. What a find!' Sonja exclaimed as she opened his rucksack. And without delay she had one of the gas burners casting shadows on the place that they now called home. In her excitement and relief she had briefly forgotten her nausea but soon it came welling up to the surface again. She checked the medicines that he had brought one by one with her expert eye and at last there it was. The very antibiotic that she was looking for, Metronidazole. Thank

God for that she thought and pouring part of the warming water into her mug she immediately downed the specified number of tablets, and an extra one for luck. Adding the concentrated beef soup mix to the now bubbling water she suddenly felt the cold for the first time since Alexander's return. This was no time for modesty and she quickly slipped inside of her bag alongside the still form of Alexander. It was only now that she realised the full seriousness of his condition. He was just frozen through, from top to bottom. She knew she had do something radical and quick. It was then that she remembered the notice in the hut of a previous track. At the time she had found it amusing since it was not what she had been taught in Germany. The notice read..... *'If not treated promptly hypothermia may lead to stupor, unconsciousness and eventually death. If they are severely cold leave their legs and arms alone. Gently remove the clothing from the upper body and have a naked person get in also. If two sleeping bags can be joined place a naked person on either side and make sure all are kept well covered. Rewarming will not occur simply by placing the victim in a sleeping bag by themselves.'*

Alexander was barely aware of her presence. He vaguely felt his thermal vest being removed and somehow it didn't seem right. What was Sonja trying to do, kill him? And then he felt her body. Her naked body. Enveloping him. Warming him. Imperceptibly he felt the glow of her body. Slowly she gave up her fever to him. And he gave up his icy chill to her. There could be no fairer exchange. They embraced as one, face to face, looking into the bottomless depths of each others eyes.

'You're beautiful you know Sonja. You're the most beautiful young woman in the whole world.'

'Be quiet,' she replied as she held his body closer in her naked embrace.

....

For the very first time Te Puke understood it all. How could he have been so stupid when all the signs had been shown to him over the last few days. No ordinary man could have battled the storm like Alexander had. There were times when even Te Puke had faltered but Alexander just kept on fighting. More than once the fatigue had driven him to his knees but up he got time and time again. Just like a champion prize fighter. And what had he said just before we left the

Nelson's Bluff emergency shelter for the last time? 'We have to get back to the sacred rock Te Puke. We just have to. We have to go home.' How did he know that the rock was the most sacred place for our people? He must have instinctively known. Something deep within him had revealed to him the truth of truths.

It was now clear to Te Puke that Alexander was one of them. He was family, he was *whanau*. And Rita knew all the time didn't she. For years she used to say, 'Our cousin is coming one day Te Puke.' And I just thought that she was getting old. It must have been that Tane. He was a bit of a lad and a damn fine rugby player. Toured the old country back in the early nineteen hundreds with the very first All Blacks. The Indomitables they called them. Or was it the Indefatigables? Whatever it was they showed the home nations a thing or two about the great game. Undefeated throughout their tour of those strange lands. Thrashed the lot of them and became heroes over there. And when they came home what a party. We had all felt so proud. Tane was a real ladies man and the rumour was that he had met a young woman there of some standing. But her folks wouldn't hear of a marriage and that was that. Name of Montgomery. There were also rumours of a child. Tane never did marry and there was always a certain sadness about him. He should by right have been chief but he passed it by. No one ever knew why. And so from his mother's Montgomery side of the family Alexander was part Ngati Mamoe. Maybe only one eighth. Maybe only one sixteenth. But he was one of them! Te Puke lay by his master. His leader. His chief.

....

'You know her, don't you mate?' said Al, looking towards the figure of Craig who was sitting on the bench, uncharacteristically slumped forward, head in his hands.

'Sorry, did you say something Al?'

'You know this Sonja girl,' Al repeated.

'Yes, I know her.'

There was silence for a minute or two, and then at last Craig said, 'Yes I know her alright. The best thing to happen to me in my whole life and I'm sitting here doing stuff all.'

'Don't be so hard on yourself mate. You know that there's nothing we can do until later tonight when it freezes up again. It would have been madness to have gone further in those conditions.'

Craig knew that what Al said was right. But he had this gnawing feeling that he should have gone on. He should have sent the other two back and gone on by himself. Stuff the consequences. So he would never have been allowed to be part of mountain rescue again, never mind team leader. But what did that matter. The only thing that mattered was Sonja.

....

'Help is on its way Sonja. I got through to the Paradise Ridge hut on the emergency radio. It was Craig.'

Craig. He had told her that he was in the mountain rescue service but this was bizarre. The man she had slept with, the man that she undoubtedly loved, the man that she would undoubtedly marry, was close at hand. She was going to be alright. They were going to be alright. For a brief moment she felt embarrassed to have got herself into such a predicament. Would he severely scold her for being so stupid? Breaking her ankle on a gentle stroll in the mountains. Failing to make a revised entry in the intentions book. She knew that he would not. It was just one of those things.

'What did he say Alexander?'

'Not much. He just said that I should get back to you to make sure that you were alright.'

Sonja knew instinctively that this was a lie. And anyway Alexander couldn't tell a convincing lie if he tried. She knew from her own experience that any mountain rescue team would have told him to stay put. But he had come back. For her.

'I think that they will be here in a few hours Sonja. They'll know what to do. How do you feel now?'

'Much better already Alexander. Much better, thanks to you. I should never have let you go.'

'You didn't have much choice at the time. You were barely conscious and things didn't look too good. I couldn't have just sat here and watched you suffer. I honestly feared for your life. And anyway, you would have done the same. I just know it.'

And she did know it. She would have done just the same.

'You're the best thing that has happened to me in a long long time Sonja. You know that I have fallen in love with you, don't you?'

'Yes, I think that I do,' she replied tenderly.

'And you know that I also love you as if you were my own daughter. The daughter that I have never really known.'

'I know that too. But I could never replace your daughter.'

'But you have allowed me to feel for the very first time what I have missed. As far as I am concerned you will always be a daughter to me.'

'We've certainly been through a lot together over the past few days Alexander. Enough adventures to last us both a lifetime. Somehow I feel that the bond between us will never be broken.'

Alexander turned his head to look at her more closely. He knew it was true.

14. Smoke Rising in a Clear Blue Sky

<u>Wednesday 8th December 2004</u>

The wristwatch alarms of three sleeping men sounded simultaneously. Four o'clock in the morning. It was time to move. This time they would not be turning back. It was still a dangerous option but they were confident they could force the path. They roped up again and as they emerged from the shelter it was clear that the storm was now abating. They had known nothing like it before but soon the Great Storm would be just a tale that the locals would tell to visiting strangers sitting around log fires open mouthed. Before long the wind had dropped and the clouds had cleared completely. The stars shone in their southern brilliance in a moonless sky.

After an hour they reached the furthest point of their advance of the previous day. They warily scanned the white slopes above them for the slightest sign of danger. But the extreme cold had temporarily fixed the powder in place and they agreed as a team that it would be a justifiable risk to cross the avalanche danger zone that presented itself directly in their path. Playing out the rope as quickly as possible they individually crossed to the relative safety of the other side. And with that they ploughed on into the new dawn.

....

'You know I'm not going to make it Sonja,' said Alexander without emotion.

'Don't talk nonsense and open your mouth.' Spoonful by spoonful Sonja fed her patient the steaming liquid. She cradled him with her free arm and body so that he could more easily swallow the life giving elixir. Occasionally she would take a spoonful herself, the first hot food that she had had for what seemed like a lifetime. It tasted like food fit only for the gods.

'It's no big deal Sonja. It's just life. People come into this world and leave it every single second of the day.'

'I told you Alexander, be quiet! I don't want to hear any more of your rambling.'

'I was working as a theatre orderly at the time,' said Alexander oblivious to her command. 'It was just a temporary job after university. Not much to it really. Wheeling patients from the theatre entrance into the operating room, adjusting lights, cleaning up and so on. One of the surgeons was doing hip replacements that day. We must have done three or four in a morning. It was just routine. But it was different that time. An elderly lady arrived from the ward and as usual I had a friendly chat with her to put her at her ease. But she said to me, *'I'm not going to make it you know.'* I playfully scoffed at her and explained that it was just a routine operation. *'I'm not worried about myself,'* she continued. *'it's my grandchildren. That's who I worry about. About how they will take it.'* I tried to reassure her again and before long it was time to wheel her in for the anaesthetist to do his work. I thought no more of it. The next morning I arrived at work and they told me she had gone, passed away. The operation had been successful but she never came around. Just faded away. It made an impact on me. Made me think.'

'Shut up! Shut up Alexander. I don't want you to talk this way. Help will soon be here.' But where are they, she silently thought to herself. They should have been here hours ago. And with that Sonja collapsed onto his chest, sobbing uncontrollably, her tears making warm rivulets over his bare shoulders.

'I failed Minnie,' continued Alexander. 'I failed her. When she needed me most I wasn't there. I could have got to her if I had really tried. Flown to Canada. Skipped across one of the longest borders in the world. I just let her down and now it's too late.'

'You did your very best Alexander. Nobody could have done more. It would not have helped her if you had ended up in a US jail for a few years. And when we get out of this mess I promise with all my heart that I will help you. With all my heart. We'll get you and Minnie back together again.'

Alexander looked into her eyes. 'Sonja. Promise that you will find Minnie and tell her how much I truly loved her. Promise me.'

'I promise,' said Sonja. She realised for the very first time that his life was ebbing away before her eyes.

Alexander could not understand why his throat felt so dry. He could barely croak out his words. A long remembered melody came into his head. No, not just melody. It was an aria. Was it Puccini? *La Fanciulla del West*? He could not be sure. It just seemed appropriate.

His cracked lips moved, and the words came slowly at first, each one making its own tortuous path.

Ch'ella mi creda, libero e lontano,

He did not know their meaning

dopra una nova via, di redenzione,

Sonja held him tightly as if she held his very life by a single gossamer thread

Aspettera ch'io torni, E passeranno i gioni, ed io non tomero,

The words came more easily now

Minnie, della mia vita mio solo fiore,

It was if some great burden had been lifted

Minnie, che m'hai voluto tanto bene, Ah. Tu della mia vita mio solo fior.

Minnie would live on in his place.

'Don't cry Sonja. Life's far too short to be sad. We just travelled a short distance together on the track of life. Fourteen short days with you. Fourteen days. More than any man deserves in a single lifetime.'

....

As Craig descended towards the rock, about fifty metres distant, he saw a solitary figure emerge unsteadily from the huge overhang. The air was now still. The sky was pure blue. A sound, at first indistinct, and then rising gradually to a crescendo, emanated from deep within the naked female form who stood motionless before him. Arms uplifted to the heavens. It was a sound that Craig had prayed that he would never hear again. It was the cry of a wounded fallow deer. Standing proud and erect. Informing all the world what injustice had come to pass. It was the sound of life. It was the sound of death. It was the sound of a million universes colliding.

And far to the west of Stewart Island the earth god roared deep beneath the sea and distant mountains trembled. Imperceptibly at first, the great rock began to turn on its axis. The concave overhang, which had been Sonja and Alexander's sole refuge for the last few days, moved closer to embrace the earth. Two thousand tons of mass moving with slow precision. And then, finally, the rock gently kissed the sacred soil and moved no more, entombing forever all that lay within. Te Puke of One Thousand Battles lay beside the still body of his master. They had done their duty. They were once more in the land of shadows. They had returned home.

……………………………………

A shaft of sunlight broke through a leaden sky and played its way along the tree line of the Southern Alps. A solitary Haast eagle soared high in the quiet air until at last it disappeared from view among the mountain tops. And then, far below, a bellbird sang. As clear as a raindrop, as pure as the morning dew.

The Writer's Diary

A contemporary diary account of the creation of 'Track'.

Trevor Cree

1. Where to Now?

Wednesday 3rd November 2004

Where to now? My suitcase was packed. The books and reference material I required for the mission lay along my hallway in a neat row. My diary stated that that very day I was due to fly from London to Rome for briefing at the UN Food and Agriculture Organization (FAO). On Saturday it was Rome to Dubai, and then on to Kabul. But I would not be going.

The advice posted on the UK Foreign Office website for the past few months could not have been clearer.

......*"We strongly advise against all but essential travel to Kabul and against all travel to other parts of Afghanistan. The security situation in Afghanistan remains serious and the threat to Westerners from terrorist or criminal violence, including kidnappings, remains high. There have been a number of attacks against the UN, NGOs, ISAF, coalition forces and individuals"*.......

But it was a risk that I had been prepared to take. After all I had spent thirty years working in some pretty difficult places: North Korea, Vietnam, Sudan, Liberia, Sierra Leone, Iran, Iraq, Syria and so on. And anyway the money would have been particularly useful since consultancy opportunities for an agricultural engineer were few and far between. Just as they should be in a rapidly developing world.

And so when I was first contacted by the FAO on the 20 August 2004 about the short-term mission to Afghanistan I said yes. Yes I would be interested in a mission which coincided with my particular area of expertise. Compared to Iraq the situation in Afghanistan had been comparatively tranquil for months. Elections were due in October 2004 and notwithstanding the warlord problem the country appeared to be emerging from a longstanding nightmare.

It was a rush job as usual. I don't know why but that invariably seems to be the way it is with UN assignments nowadays. Tentative start date 5th September 2004 they said. Fifteen short days to have another compulsory medical, update vaccinations, update UN personal history form, dust off and update the Will, obtain an Afghan visa somehow, book flights, locate Afghan information sources on the internet and so on.

"Had I taken the UN Basic Security in the Field (Staff Safety, Health and Welfare) test? Since I had been working for FAO in Malaysia in 2003 I should have taken one", the email stated.

No. Not a clue what they were talking about. Now only ten days to the specified departure date and counting and so FAO say they will send me a CD-ROM by DHL and I must pass the test before I can be cleared to go to Afghanistan or anywhere else for that matter. Bermuda? Sorry, rules are rules. One or two days later the CD-ROM arrived. Well not quite. I wasn't in and so the package was returned to the DHL depot somewhere close to Novigrad. Yes they could post this urgent package through my letter box if I left a note outside my door providing written authority. Tomorrow or was it the next day. And so I did so. When the neatly packaged CD-ROM finally arrived I read the introduction on the back with interest.

"The continuing rise of conflict situations together with conditions of general insecurity and criminal activities, continues to place staff of international organisations at greater and greater risk. This alarming trend means that increased awareness and focus is required for security planning and training. This course will help you understand the basic security concepts and techniques - to help ensure your safety, health and welfare."

Very true. But what's new? Have you stayed in the Rooster Hotel in Monrovia in 79, an apartment in Albania with gunshots going off through the sultry night in 98, or in a grass hut in a refugee camp in the Sudan in 81? Been there, done that. But hey. Why so uptight. Relax. Just place the CD-ROM in your Bill Gates haven of peace and tranquillity and complete the test.

But we have a problem Houston. Since 1984 I had been using various forms of Apple computer, starting with the original Macintosh until now I had two iBooks. Old tangerine and blue models of course. Money's too tight to mention. I well remember lugging my old Macintosh up the plane steps in Yemen in 89 whilst my wealthier World Bank colleagues laughed at me as they lugged their equally ridiculous, but marginally smaller, PC computers up the same steps. But how did I become a heretic and not a follower of the one true faith. Simple really. MSDOS. Younger people will not have experienced the ancient days when in order to enter the Microsoft brother and sisterhood you had to study the

Great Book for months on end. And that was just to turn the computer on! And then behold a new faith arose in the west. Macintosh. I had read that Apple had a promotion whereby you handed over a fifty pounds refundable deposit and they let you take the computer home for the weekend. No instruction, nothing. Just a simple floppy disc guide. I took it home, plugged it in, and away I went. Write a letter, cut and paste, no problem. Simple.

There was no turning back after that. After all I was in the business of writing reports. The following Monday I went into the computer shop, wrote out a cheque for two thousand two hundred pounds and walked out a very happy customer. But the Great One was displeased.

"The Macintosh is just a toy and cannot be used for for serious work" he said. MSDOS is the one true faith. And lo, the multitude did believe the Great One and the magazines ridiculed the people of Mac. One or two years later the Great One brought out the Windows operating system that was virtually identical to the Macintosh product. Funny that.

But I digress. Microsoft format CD-ROM and Apple iBook just do not get on. And so I took the disc to a friend who was a true follower and plugged it in. After all I had to complete the test otherwise there would be no UN work in the future. Let's be positive. The screen came alive with accompanying strangulated *Chinglish* voice providing a laboriously slow commentary. After about thirty minutes I was becoming seriously deflated. From the various modules that must be passed it looked as though it could take three weeks to complete. And the really great thing about the CD-ROM was that I could not save the work that I had already done and the tests that I had already completed. Three weeks at the machine without food and water. And what if the computer crashed just as I was reaching the end and had not completed the final test. Suicide would clearly have been the only option. And so I put it on hold and planned to complete the security test at the very last minute when I was certain that I was actually going to Afghanistan. After all in this line of work the only certainty is when you are walking up the steps of the plane and the door closes.

On the 30th August 2004 I received an email which stated that:

"Due to the present security situation, the security clearance for your proposed mission has not been granted."

This did not surprise me since a day or so earlier a suicide bomber had killed himself and a few innocent people in the Chicken Street market area of Kabul. The relief was enormous. Not the Afghanistan security situation with its bombs and bullets. No. The relief was that I would not have to face that infernal CD-ROM for a while. The email went on to ask if I would be available for a revised mission towards the end of October 2004. Indeed I would, I replied.

2. Afghanistan Here I Come. Or Not.

Wednesday 3rd November 2004

On the 15th October 2004 I received an outline travel schedule which required me to be in Rome on the 31st October. No mention of the dreaded CD-ROM security test. Perhaps they had forgotten and if I was lucky I could quietly let it drop. I was due to continue my part-time green keeping job at the golf club until Wednesday the 27th October and so my time for actual project preparation was very limited. Fortunately the mission start date was subsequently delayed until the 3rd November once FAO realised that they were actually on holiday on the 1st November.

I had read somewhere that a visa for Afghanistan was not required and so I asked FAO to clarify the situation. However it turned out that I did need one and that I would have to apply for it myself in London. Time was now rapidly running out since the Afghan Embassy website stated that a visa would take two to five days to process. By now it was Tuesday 26th October and so I planned to submit my passport and application form on the following Thursday, hoping that I could collect the visa on the following Monday at the latest. Thursday the 28th October came bright and clear and taking the train to London I finally arrived at the Afghan Embassy at about 11.00am. There were no helpful notices anywhere and so I just joined a queue of Afghans. Long slow queues are just an accepted part of the visa application process but fortunately after about five minutes a kindly Afghan told me that he thought that I was in the wrong place. I was actually in the returning Afghan refugee queue! Where I needed to be was upstairs, he said. And indeed he was right. After handing in my application to the helpful visa officer I asked how long it would take. If it was going to take five days all my travel plans would go out of the proverbial window. *"Come back in an hour"* she replied. *"There's a nice vegetarian restaurant around the corner."* At times like that your spirits lift and somehow Afghanistan didn't seem such a bad place after all.

I returned home from London at about four in the afternoon and turned on my iBook computer to check if there were any messages from FAO. Since my internet homepage is the BBC website it rapidly became clear to me that events in Afghanistan had moved on. With distinctly black humour I had previously said to my friends that if they saw me on television dressed in an orange suit they would know that things were not going as well as I had hoped. The news report stated that three UN employees, Angelito Nayan, Annetta Flanigan and Shqipe Habibi, had been kidnapped in broad daylight in the middle of Kabul. UN employees working for the overall welfare of Afghanistan had never been directly targeted before and so this was a new and disturbing development. A nationwide presidential election had just been successfully contested with a high turnout and with minimal disturbance. It had seemed like Afghanistan was moving on. But clearly some people were not prepared to let it do so.

I immediately sent an email to FAO requesting clarification on the security situation expecting that, as before, the mission would be postponed for some days or weeks until it could be determined if this was just a one-off event or the start of an Iraq type scenario where regular kidnappings and executions were the norm. They said that they would check it out but could I complete my CD-ROM security test and fax the final test result to them. And so it was back to the dreaded test. Three hours and twelve minutes. Three hours and twelve minutes! The only thing missing was a questionnaire for your kidnapper to fill in which they could forward to the UN market research department. That's how long it took. And what did I gain from this ordeal. Absolutely nothing. If it had crashed before I had reached the end of the tests I would have politely told FAO where they could put their project. I'm sure that I would not have been the first. The disc must have cost tens of thousands of dollars to produce and I'm sure that everyone at UN Headquarters in New York is absolutely delighted with the end result. However, a simple twenty point checklist or a concise booklet would have been far more effective. Nevertheless I continued to make preparations for my departure to Afghanistan. I still could not see how an organisation which purportedly placed staff safety as a very high priority would send people into such an uncertain situation.

On Sunday 31st October 2004 the first video of the three hostages was shown on an Arabic television station and relayed around the world. The situation was bad. Very bad. The kidnappers threatened to execute the UN hostages by Wednesday 3rd November unless the authorities agreed to three main demands including, the withdrawal of foreign forces from Afghanistan, cessation of UN operations in Afghanistan, and the release of Taliban and al-Qaeda prisoners. You don't have to be a political genius to see that none of these demands could be agreed to.

Seeing the hostages on television really made an impact on me. There but for the grace of God go I, I thought. But it was the UN spokesman in Kabul who really made me angry. *"We continue UN operations as before"*, he said. No temporary suspension of activities. Nothing. I certainly did not expect the UN to give in to the kidnappers demands and withdraw from Afghanistan. It had to stay the course. But it seemed to me that the UN were playing Russian roulette with the lives of three of the very best. It reminded me of a track on the Pink Floyd album, Dark Side of the Moon:

Forward they cried,
From the rear,
As the front rank died.

So much for the Staff Safety, Health and Welfare CD-ROM that I had just successfully completed. It was now crystal clear to me how much support I could expect to receive from the UN in Afghanistan should I need it in a similar situation. A big fat zero. I informed them that I was still prepared to go but only after another eight week postponement by which time the situation would be much clearer for everyone. Even if the hostages were released unharmed time would still be required for things to settle down. Clearly I wouldn't be much use confined to a UN compound in Kabul for the duration of my three week stay.

I was due to fly out to Rome on the 3rd November and FAO were closed on Monday the 1st November. But I had to inform them of my position as soon as possible. So on the Monday I wrote an email to FAO which outlined the situation and which stated that I anticipated that the UN would suspend their new project activities in Afghanistan until the situation became clearer. I stated that I would not be prepared to work in Afghanistan within the following eight weeks. I felt that I could not wait until I arrived in Rome on the 3rd November to inform them about my safety reservations since money would already have been spent on my airfares and accommodation. If they wished me to go to Rome later to discuss alternative ways forward for the project then I was quite prepared to do so.

On Tuesday the 2nd November 2004 I expected a flurry of emails. Perhaps even one sympathising with my view of the changed security environment in Afghanistan and how best the project situation could be resolved. But no. Dead silence. My bags remained packed and ready to go. Then late in the day I received a short terse email from the FAO stating that my contract had been terminated. I can only guess that FAO considered it particularly inconvenient that I had deigned to pull out of the Afghan mission at short notice. Perhaps they considered it was their sole responsibility to tell me whether or not I should travel to Afghanistan. I don't honestly know. Clearly it was not the done thing for me to make adult decisions for myself. In contrast I felt that it would have also been particularly inconvenient for me if my head was to be separated from my body by the space of a few feet.

Do I feel that I have let the Afghan people down? The answer is both yes and no. It is disappointing that the project did not proceed on schedule, but at a time when all UN staff in Kabul were restricted to their secure compounds what good could I do. I was still prepared to go to Afghanistan when the situation resolved itself but it would have been foolish for anyone to place themselves in a situation where there was such uncertainty. And so the question for me is, *Where to Now?*

3. California Dreaming

Thursday 4th November 2004

So where to now for an unemployed consultant agricultural engineer and part-time green keeper? A grey squirrel is busy in my garden hoarding food for the coming winter. At least it knows what it is doing. There's the possibility of a job green keeping in March 2005 and so perhaps I should do the same as the squirrel and hibernate through the winter. Prospects, one may conclude, do not look good. Last summer I applied, without great enthusiasm, for many permanent jobs. Van driving and shelf stacking at Tesco come to mind. Failed the leaflet psychometric test and didn't even make the interview phase for either. What is the world coming to? Companies complain to the government that there is a shortage of workers and yet they don't give thousands of ordinary people a chance. Since I failed the first psychometric test I asked a Cambridge University veterinarian friend of mine to fill in the second. Just for fun. She failed to make the grade also! And B&Q were no better. I'm not sure if it has changed it's policy but at one point you could only apply to B&Q online. I've worked with computers for over twenty years and have run my own website for seven years. Even I could not handle the application process and so what chance for the great *illiterati* who leave school unable to spell their name properly. But that's OK Luv, just spell it as you like.

The predictable ranting of someone rapidly approaching grumpy old man status? Too old to accommodate change? But it's not change for the sake of change we need. We've had far too much of that. We've spent billions going around in circles. We need progress. We need to rebuild a civilised society. Today I just happened to turn on the television shortly before noon where I caught the final ten minutes of a documentary programme. I couldn't tell you whether it was for schools, the Open University or for what. However, it was about the founding of the UK welfare state directly after the Second World War and covered the period 1946 to 1951. Britain was devastated and bankrupt. Nevertheless enlightened people had already formulated a plan to introduce a public welfare system which covered health, education and housing with the objective of banishing disease, ignorance and poverty. It would be too harsh to call them propaganda but the clips from the public information films of the time illustrated clearly and concisely how the then Labour government planned to deal with the problems of the day. They were works of art and I'm sure film makers of today could learn a great deal from them. They certainly made a positive impact on me. I wanted to be part of that brave new world. Barbara Castle (of *"I said to Harold"* [Wilson the Prime Minister], *"I told Harold"* fame) was shown, and although she was never one of my favourites, you could see her sincerity and the satisfaction she had gained from being directly involved in that process. For the last twenty years politicians of all persuasions have promised the earth whilst presiding over an inexorable decline in the quality of life within this country. It's starting to remind me of Pyongyang. We can do better. We really have to do better.

But I digress. I have to admit that Plan B had been in my mind for some time. It was a book that I had started in New Zealand a few years ago. Was it 1998? I'm not honestly sure. The partially completed manuscript, if that is not too grand a description, had sat there taunting me for nearly six years. Every few months I would pick it up and read a few pages until I would come across another piece of complete drivel. I've always found writing hard. Very hard. Lucky if I could complete three pages of a report in a morning. Yet report writing has been my life, the necessary end product of all my work in the field. But after all the toil I did seem to produce something which people found very readable. At least most of the time.

It all started, as happens, when a woman literally walked into my life. A young woman named T. I first saw her striding through the bush towards the Lake Howden hut on the Routeburn Track. Clearly she made an immediate impression on me. Love at first sight they usually call it. The event which happens so rarely in our lives, and for some never at all. Or was it just infatuation at first sight? We became friends, walked another track together, and than parted forever. All over in the matter of a few short days. There was absolutely no indication that she felt the same way about me. After all I was probably the same age as her father! That might be fine for Woody Allen and Rupert Murdoch but I was a few million short in the finance department.

But the encounter inspired me. It inspired me to write the outline of a love story against the backdrop of the spectacular scenery of the Southern Alps. The words just flowed as I travelled on the Inter-City and Newmans buses along the routes of the South Island. It must have been somewhat disconcerting for the people who sat next to me to see this idiot scribbling away in an old notebook whilst New Zealand flowed past the window. And sometimes, I admit, certain passages I wrote moved me near to tears. But until this moment I have been unable to finish or even progress the book. Had fate, in the form of Afghanistan, presented me with the opportunity to do so? After all there was no better time than November to travel to New Zealand. The airfares were relatively inexpensive prior to the Christmas and New Year rush. It would be quieter in Spring and the snow would still be clearly evident on the mountains. The book was set in late spring and so there would be no better time to gather the background material I required to strengthen the storyline. I was easily persuaded.

And so I did it. I picked up the telephone and called Trailfinders. I had travelled with them a number of times before and had been very impressed with their efficient and friendly service. In a matter of twenty minutes I had my flight to Auckland booked and my bank account relieved of nearly seven hundred pounds. London to Los Angeles, one night stopover, Los Angeles to Auckland. Departure Tuesday 9th November 2004. Absolutely bonkers. Totally irresponsible. But it felt really great.

4. Long Days Journey Into Night

Saturday 6th November 2004

No good news on the Kabul hostages yet except that it appears that they are still alive. The deadline for the civilised world to give into the kidnappers demands has moved from last Wednesday to yesterday and now until tonight.

It might appear that dipping into my bank account to spend a few weeks in New Zealand is no problem to an international consultant. In fact, the New Zealand venture could be described as the last throw of the proverbial dice. I'm gambling that I have one book in me which might actually sell at a reasonable profit. What did I hear on the radio the other day? Was it that eight thousand English language books are published each month or was it each year? I hope that it wasn't every week! However my plan is not completely based on a fantasy since six years ago I actually wrote over sixty pages of the story. The few friends that I have revealed my unsound scheme to asked why can't I finish writing the book in England. There is no sound argument against that proposal except to say that I've had it laying on my desk for years now, and nothing has happened. I just don't feel it. Very occasionally I would pick it up to read but simply put it away again without adding a word. I didn't feel inspired like I did on those long bus journeys in NZ. I'm hoping to recapture that feeling by travelling to New Zealand. I need to get it out of my system once and for all. Succeed or fail.

It's really strange how things happen. Today I was nonchalantly looking through my original handwritten scripts and what do I find. Fourteen A4 pages that I had forgotten all about for six long years. They cover the first meeting between two of the main characters, Alexander and Sonja. This is great. This is brilliant. Perhaps it's an omen of some kind. I had already identified that I must start writing this particular passage as soon as possible once I reached New Zealand but there it already was. The sooner I start transcribing that section onto my iBook the better. Before I fly off I'll have to check that I don't have any more nuggets, or fools gold, hidden away somewhere else.

Monday 8th November 2004

Tomorrow morning at eleven I leave for Heathrow airport. A friend of mine is taking me to the airport and I hope to return the complement when he goes to Australia in the New Year. I had already prepared for Afghanistan and so packing was a real breeze. At least I hope it has been. I've managed to pair it all down to my rucksack and a laptop computer case. It certainly beats the last time I travelled back from New Zealand with an overweight suitcase, rucksack and golf clubs.

Long distance travel has never been one of my favourite pastimes, particularly in economy. One moment the crew are informing you about the dangers of deep vein thrombosis and the next that regulations state that you must not congregate near the toilets to stretch your legs. As Homer Simpson would say, *"Doh!"* This time I will have to have my fingerprint and a photograph taken at US immigration. I had vowed not to go via the US to NZ again since I am very much opposed to the inexorable creep of Big Brother. But the alternatives of Hong Kong, Kuala Lumpur or Singapore did not appeal this time. I hope that I have the determination to resist the introduction of identity cards in the UK. Here we have a government that can't even be bothered to reintroduce passport checks on people leaving the country and yet wants to number its own citizens like prisoners in the gulag. You don't have to be mad but it certainly does help.

The good news is that not only did I write up the fourteen new pages that I had found in my old notebook but I also located another four pages elsewhere. Overall this condensed down to about twelve computer pages worth of script. And I have to immodestly say that it's not bad. It was an interesting experience since on many occasions I could remember the phrase which was to come next. Much of what I had written was based on actual experience and the smaller of the two entries reminded me of another young women who I had completely forgotten about. I certainly didn't have that embarrassed feeling about what I had written since it seemed to flow pretty well. Whether anyone else will agree with me it's difficult to tell. The storyline revolves around two separate tracks and at the moment I've got into a bit of a muddle since I've taken location scenarios from one and placed them in the other and vice versa. I think that I can sort it out by introducing my Cascade Saddle experience into the story and have the two main characters continue along the Routeburn and not back by the Rees Track as they had originally planned. In reality the Routeburn is completely separate from the other two and so that is where the fictional aspect comes into the story. I'm sure people who know the walks will be able to work it out, but not without a certain difficulty.

Still no final outcome to the Kabul hostage situation yet. The kidnapper deadlines keeps passing and they state that they have reduced their demands to a total of three. They're not even demanding that US troops withdraw from the country now. It would therefore appear that a ransom is very high on the list although this hasn't been revealed. In some ways that could be a good thing but if the UN and authorities give in then it will just lead to open season on kidnapping for financial reward. Of course, denials will be made that any ransom was ever given but everybody will know. Whatever the outcome it will not take away the sheer terror and misery that the innocent hostages are being subjected to at the moment. If I had gone ahead with the FAO mission I would have arrived in Afghanistan yesterday with the security situation still totally unresolved. At least I would have had my CD-ROM with me for protection!

Tuesday 9th November 2004

I'm now sitting in Terminal 1, Heathrow, adjacent to Gate 50 from where my flight to Los Angeles will depart in just over one hour. There was the normal heavy congestion on the M25, it seemed for no apparent reason. Fortunately I had allowed plenty of time for the journey. The check-in went very smoothly. I had asked Trailfinders to request an aisle seat but they said that British Airways had closed the seating allocation and that I should ask at check-in. The BA girl was very pleasant but said that I would have to ask again at the boarding gate. Fingers crossed. The freedom to get up as and when I like is pretty important since you just don't have to bother anybody when they are sleeping. As I boarded the plane I was given an aisle seat. Hallelujah! The news from Afghanistan has deteriorated with the kidnappers now threatening to kill the Kosovan girl, a muslim herself, if their demands are not at least partially met.

I have just read the part of the draft where Alexander first meets M, Hoop and Sonja. It reads pretty well but I now realise that I must replace the descriptive passages by dialogue. For example, instead of stating that Alexander told Sonja about his boarding school experience I should actually write his words. This may take quite a lot of effort but I hope that it will solve a few problems. I think that this particular passage will be a very good section to start working on. Another thing that has become apparent to me during this reading process is how many incidents actually happened, not always in the order or location stated, but at some time I certainly did experience them. The incident at the swimming hole where a girl I had completely forgotten about went for a swim, for example.

Wednesday 10th November 2004

It's seven thirty in the morning and I have just finished a full American breakfast at the Hilton LAX. I've stayed here a few times in the past because it's neat and tidy, and has proven to be very efficient. I have yet to make the transition from holiday maker mode to pauper mode since I really do have to minimise my daily expenditure. I can justify the current hotel cost to myself because flying straight to Auckland in economy is just not a healthy or, for that matter, a sane option. Alternative hotels where I have stayed in L.A. in the past are not much cheaper and certainly not as good.

I haven't flown British Airways economy for some time but it is clear that they are determined to achieve the very top rating for deep vein thrombosis. Second place is clearly for losers. At five feet eight inches and thirteen stone I do not consider myself of above average stature. Simply average. I'm not exactly sure how wide the seats were but if I hold my breath I can just slide neatly between the armrests with absolutely no space to spare. The screen for the in-flight entertainment is located in the back of the seat in front of me. When my fellow traveller reclines his seat the screen very conveniently rests on my nose, a thoughtful facility for the visually impaired. I hypothesise that if the person in the very front of my cabin rapidly reclined his seat it would force twenty five seats behind him to fall down like a pack of cards crushing all of the passengers in-situ. It would be the most significant British Airways air accident in many years. Sheer carnage. Such is the way of the modern world. Forget 1984. This is 2004. In the Economy Plus section (*Cattle Plus*) I also noticed that the company have placed some large black and white photographs on the bulkhead illustrating a group happy travellers in what would appear to be the 1960's era. They are sitting in comfortably wide seats with ample leg room. What are they trying to do, take the proverbial Michael.

My Qantas flight from Los Angeles to Auckland is not until eight thirty this evening. On previous occasions I have taken a city tour, visited Universal Studios or something similar. However, in order to reduce costs I am happy to stay close to my room and hopefully do some background work on my book. I might also take in one or two in-house movies. I've never been in my comfort zone in Los Angeles but I could say the same about any city, London, or even Auckland. I'm just the product of a countryside upbringing and I don't feel totally at ease among all the high rise, concrete and tarmac.

The USA Today paper, which was slid under my door in the early hours, has some good coverage on the battle for Falujah. It lists the deaths of four soldiers, including Army Specialist Quoc Binh Tran, 26, from Mission Viejo, California. In 1975 I was in-transit in Bangkok on the point of starting my very first six month mission in a developing country, namely Malaysia. The lobby of the hotel where I was staying was full of American GIs and their Vietnamese girlfriends who had just pulled out of Vietnam in an undignified manner. It was therefore very poignant to see the Vietnamese name of the soldier who died in Iraq and to personally note that tragedy had once again visited his individual family group. However much one may question the United States motives I am very clear that communism in its practical implementation was and still is evil and that fundamentalism is also evil. The much used phrase *"For evil to succeed it only requires the good to do nothing"* has much truth in it. The monotonous bleating of Claire Short and her friends makes me very angry. A good two year dose of voluntary service overseas might do her some good but I'm not sure that Africa would take her. The USA Today paper just happened to cover the recent flare-up in Ivory Coast where nine French *'peacekeepers'* were killed by the country's minuscule airforce. The French retaliated by completely destroying the planes and thereby propelled the country into further chaos. The French are now busy evacuating thirteen hundred French and foreign nationals from the capital Abidjan. *"Sorry Claire. Please speak up since I did not hear you. What was that you said about colonisation?"*

5. We Are Sailing

Sunday 14th November 2004

I've just awoken after a night on the floor at my pal Martin's temporary pad in downtown Auckland. It's a very neat studio apartment situated right at the bottom of Queen Street. Very modern and extremely well equipped. The central location is very convenient apart from the unfortunate fact that it is situated directly opposite at least two very noisy night clubs. Luckily I slept well until about four in the morning when the booming music and and loud clientele milling around outside woke me from my slumber. But there we go. Certainly I can't complain since it cost me nothing and helped me conserve my budget. Well that's the theory.

In fact I've spent quite a lot of money since I arrived in Auckland on Friday morning. The Qantas experience from Los Angeles was favourable with enjoyable food and attentive, friendly staff. The flight even arrived on schedule. However the seats were as uncomfortable as ever and I never really got any sleep. If they want to get any Al Qaeda suspects to talk all they have to do is book them economy from London to Auckland. *"Yes, I'll tell you what you want to know but please please upgrade me to business class first."*

Martin was there to meet me at the airport with a game of golf with Charles conveniently arranged at eleven. They'll do anything to beat me and I guess a few days of sleep deprivation was another particularly cunning plan. After a forty minute catnap and there I was teeing up at the North Shore Golf Club on a beautiful Spring day. Joel, a seventeen year old playing off four, joined us and it was a pleasure to watch and learn. We all had a close and competitive game. Charles did not disappoint us when he threw a tantrum and his club at the sixteenth after missing a putt. This was not a problem except for the fact that he was my partner and we might just have salvaged something from the hole. *Doh!* That evening we went with Charles and his wife to a really great Italian restaurant in Takapuna. A couple of bottles of fine Italian wine with excellent food and atmosphere rounded off a great first day in NZ. I have to admit that I did sneak in a couple of much needed hours of sleep before going out to eat.

The following day, Saturday, Martin and I moved out of Charle's home and unloaded our gear at the rental apartment in Queen's Street. We then went to have a look at Martin's two bedroom Scene One property. Unfortunately it was not due to be finished for another two or so weeks and therefore Martin was kicking his heels in Auckland, frustrated at not being able to spend time furnishing the place and enjoying the apartment for a while before returning to the UK. Nevertheless it will be a great investment since the panoramic outlook over Auckland harbour is second to none. Naturally, Martin suggested that we had time to fit in another game of golf that afternoon and so we stopped by the tourist office and picked up a list of Auckland clubs. The course at Howick looked to have a fantastic location on a peninsula and was moderately priced. Yes we could play, and yes we could qualify for a twilight game. Twenty well spent dollars. The course was undulating and very tight with tree lined fairways. Martin pipped me at the eighteenth when my three foot putt lipped out. Nevertheless, a great game and a lot of fun. Another enjoyable dinner at the Indian restaurant down at Viaduct Basin. Saturday night Auckland was full of gaggles of girls heading this way and that looking for a fun time. Martin was naturally keen to explore more but not being in the teenage bird pulling age bracket I just fancied crashing out.

My golf game is holding up but this hasn't helped progress my 'bestselling' novel by one sentence! Martin tried to persuade me to stay on for a week, since clearly he would be very happy to have an on-call golf playing and drinking partner. However, if I carried on at this rate it would take me four weeks to get to Queenstown and by then I would be broke. And so I decided to head to Napier on the Tuesday, providing I could get a seat on the bus, and then on south a couple of days later. I still feel extremely positive about the whole writing venture. The fact that I am continuing to write this diary is a real achievement because I have never kept a diary in my life, at least not for more than a few days. Perhaps in years to come it will bring back a few memories.

I think that it is particularly fortunate that I am no longer married and don't have a live-in partner. You can hardly say *"I'm just off to New Zealand darling to finish a novel. No, I know that we don't have any money, and yes I know that I've never written anything worthwhile before, but I'm going. It's something I just have to do. Goodbye."* And it would certainly not just be a friendly *"Au Revoir"* from my partner, but *"Get out of my life. For good."* And so I am fortunate to have this great sense of freedom. My selfish whim does not impinge on anyone else's private space. Martin has just said, *"Well yeah, you're writing a book about somebody who has been backpacking in New Zealand. Well as if that has never been done before!"* It's nice to have the support of friends when you most need it.

"But I'll get by with a little help from my friends, Oh I'll get high with a little help from my friends." But of course he's right.

Tuesday 16th November 2004

I've just completed my four day backpacker induction course at Martin's temporary apartment in Queen's Street. I slept on some sofa cushions laid on the floor in the lounge. It proved to be very uncomfortable, particularly noisy into the early hours and very hot. Sleep was intermittent and unsatisfactory. I can therefore conclude that the intensive backpacker hostel training programme was a great success and I am well prepared for what lies ahead!

It's ten o'clock in the morning and I'm now happily sitting on a Newmans bus heading for Napier, via Taupo. Whilst sitting here I think that I have been able to resolve one of the problem areas in my book, namely how to seamlessly join up two parts of the story which I had already written some six years before. I will now insert the Cascade Saddle walk between the existing Kepler Track and Routeburn track hybrid passages. I will have the vast majority, or all, of the other walkers take the easier path which in reality follows the Rees River back to a pick-up point for Queenstown. Some may have planned to take the Cascade Track but change their minds when the weather changes for the worse. However, the night before Sonja and Alexander will be looking at the map and Alexander will tell Sonja how twenty years before he had walked the Cascade Saddle on his own. He will describe it as a brute of a trek but with spectacular scenery to match. Although their original intention was to follow the easier Rees River route they both became excited about doing the Cascade Saddle and staying an unplanned night at the Falls Hut on the Routeburn. Alexander is shown to be a bit apprehensive because after all he was now twenty years older and certainly not as fit as he had been. But the weather was so wonderful with clear skies and little wind. A rare occurrence in Fiordland in Spring. And after all it would give him an extra day in Sonja's company. There would be no warden in their current hut but Alexander says that he will write their changed programme in the intentions book the next morning. However, the combination of drinking the majority of the wine and his suspect memory mean that he will forget to do so. And he would only realise this fact over an hour into their walk the next day. Because he estimates that it would take eight to nine hours they leave the hut at six o'clock in the morning when all the others are still tucked up in their sleeping bags. Nobody will realise that they have taken the Cascade Saddle. I can use my Cascade Saddle experience to describe the stream crossings, indistinct route marked by stone cairns, the severely rising track which takes them above the glacier on the other side of valley. As they approach the highest point the weather rapidly changes. However, they still feel no danger because the track will remain level after the Saddle and there is virtually no more climbing to contend with. Within four hours they will be proudly enjoying a steaming mug of coffee and a good meal at the Routeburn Falls hut and will be revelling in their achievement. That is before they fall victim to Sonja's accident. I think that this solution will work well.

Wednesday 17th November 2004

The journey down from Auckland yesterday reminded me how much I love this country. It is a long standing affair. Looking out of the coach window onto rounded hills of springtime grass as we passed through the Waikato following that mighty meandering river. Then down to Taupo through extensive pine forests with steam rising from hidden vents and boiling streams. The relaxed and often humorous commentary of the driver, mature in years, who points out various historical or geographical landmarks. And breaking out around one last corner to be met by panoramic views of Hawkes Bay, with it's turquoise and dark blue sea below. And there, Napier, sitting citadel like upon it's rock.

It was some thirty years before that I fell in love with Carole in that place. I had left university the year or two before and had been unable to find suitable employment or was I perhaps uncertain what I really wanted to do. And so I found myself joining the Peninsular and Oriental line (P & O) as Eighth Engineer on a wild reefer named Taupo. Somehow I must have thought that a naval life might suit me since my father had spent twenty two happy years in the Royal Navy. I soon found out that it did not but I certainly did not regret the experience. After first berthing in Auckland to unload some general cargo we proceeded down to Lyttelton to do much the same. Then it was back to Napier to load frozen lamb, beef and venison, as well as chilled fruit, mainly apples, all bound for Bermuda and the UK. We had to lay off Napier for a few hours watching the distant sparkling lights along Marine Parade until at last we entered the port. I was on watch from eight to twelve deep down in the bowels of the engine room but as usual a party had started in the officers mess.

The word would soon get around town that a ship was in port and girls were never a problem. Nurses, teachers, whatever. Everyone liked to party. Shortly before I was due to go off watch my fellow eighth engineer, Mick, brought one of the girls down into the engine room to have a look around. I was immediately smitten. It is the strangest of things, love at first sight. Does anyone have an explanation for it? I really don't think so. The next day we were all invited back to Carole's house in Cameron Road, minus Mick who was on duty. Carole and I talked and the romantic feelings were clearly mutual. Mick and I had got on very well and I felt that I could not have a relationship with Carole without telling him about the depths of my feelings for her. It seemed the gentlemanly thing to do. And so Carole and I went down into the engine room, reversing the roles of the previous night. I explained the situation and I think that he would have had every right to have punched me on the nose. But he didn't. The next morning I woke up lying next to Carole. I subsequently left the country with true love in my heart and as rapidly as I could I left my roots in the UK and caught a plane back to New Zealand to start a new life. But by the time I returned Carole had moved on in the romantic and literal sense. We remained good friends and the other people in the Cameron Road villa somehow adopted me. I still have very fond memories of them all, Dave and Jo, Dave's brother Mick, Manfred and Sally, Murray and Jenny, Mark and his Carol, and not forgetting Johnny, a bubbly Maori girl. The influence of Pink Floyd and Dark Side of the Moon, Santana's Abraxis, Cat Stevens disturbing the neighbours. Those records have stayed with me for a lifetime. Cameron Road was a special experience.

The three UN hostages in Afghanistan are still being held. The kidnappers are reducing their demands but they may still do something dramatic, especially after it has been officially confirmed that Margaret Hassan was executed in Iraq.

6. Heading South

Friday 19th November 2004

I'm writing this entry sitting at a specially designated area for computer work on the Cook Straits Ferry, Ahura. As much as I love the crossing it does take rather a long time and I have seen the sights many times before. I've already had something to eat on the ferry and I have to say that for maintaining consistent standards for the last thirty years the company deserves some sort of award. By consistent I mean consistently bad. It would seem that the 'closed shop' has still got a firm grip on what should be a premier tourist experience.

Earlier today I left Napier at nine fifteen and took the Inter-City coach to Wellington, via Palmerston North. I had a bit of a hangover after drinking one too many Kilkennys at Billy Burkes in Taradale with my brother and his wife. Not forgetting the glass or two of red wine with dinner. As it turns out I have decided to change the name of the Irish pub in Pelorus to Billy Burkes. It has a nice ring to it. I've also realised that I will have to walk the tracks again on which the story is based. The Kepler and Routeburn should be fine but I'm not so sure about the Cascade Saddle. It took me to my limit the last time and on this occasion it's earlier in the year and there may be snow about. Last year a man was killed after he slipped close to the Saddle. However, if the weather forecast looks good I would love to do it again in the same direction. I'm sure that it would help me build on my existing descriptive passages.

On Wednesday and Thursday morning I had two good sessions on my book. On Wednesday I built on the story after the visit to the swimming hole on the Kepler. On Thursday I took Sonja and Alexander from the hut up the Cascade Saddle route until they very nearly joined up with my existing storyline. A paragraph or two should do it. Another idea with respect to the storyline is to use my Afghanistan experience as the reason why Alexander decided to go backpacking in New Zealand at the very last minute. This may allow the incorporation of his inept packing scene. He may be able to describe the reasons why he was in NZ to Sonja at a suitable point in the story when they are alone together. She can then recount her own trials and tribulations of her flight to New Zealand. Possibly at the Routeburn Falls hut or perhaps later in their rock refuge.

I have already lost some financial discipline since I have booked a hotel in Picton and not a backpackers. My excuse is that I have had a long day and will not arrive in Picton until eight thirty. Secondly I feel that my computer will be safer. Both reasons are pretty feeble. I have already booked my bus from Picton to Nelson tomorrow although I have failed to give Sandy any notice of my arrival. If she can't put me up that's no problem since I'll stay in a backpackers and try to travel down to Franz Josef the next day. I'll certainly catch up with her on my return north. Sam has already telephoned Barry to let him know that I will be passing through Nelson but it looks as if I will miss him because it will be the weekend and he will be back in Napier.

Saturday 20th November 2004

Last night I began to feel that it was taking me far too long to get down to the Queenstown area where I anticipated that I would really be able to make progress on the book. But after a good nights sleep at the Picton Beachcomber I woke seeing things in a different light. After all, before I left the UK, I resolved not to make this a rushed process. I have to, as they say, *"chill out"* a bit and relax into it. The analogy came to me that it is like climbing Mount Everest. I have completed the plane journey from London to Katmandu and I am now on the long trek into base camp. Along the way I hope to get acclimatised. One never knows what new thoughts, ideas and experiences will occur along the way and which could contribute to the storyline. If Queenstown is to be my base camp then Te Anau will be my advanced base camp for the assaults on the Kepler and the Routeburn Tracks. It all sounds overly dramatic, which it certainly is, but it helps me visualise how I am going to approach the job in hand. I'm a little concerned about where I can safely store my computer on a day to day basis. It's not so much it's value but the amount of material that I have on it, my website data, book, past reports etc. It's the inconvenience of it all. I have left a back-up of my book and diary on disc in Napier and I think my website is on a Zip drive in the UK. I suppose that's like driving in a piton in a rock face in case of a fall. I'm sure that there must be a left luggage lock-up facility in Queenstown, but you never know? You might ask why did I bother to bring the computer south in the first place? Why not just use pen and paper as before? I think that the main reason is that I really want to have the book put to bed before I leave the south. I don't think that I could face typing up my writings in Napier or the UK only to find that there were big holes in the story. I think that it would prove very difficult to raise the necessary motivation to get writing again, as I previously found in the UK over the last few years. No, it's got to be a single solo push to the summit or fail in the attempt.

Saturday 20th November 2004

I'm sitting in Le Cafe in Picton looking out onto a view which would make any estate agent tremble with pleasure. It's a million dollar view if ever there was one. Queen Charlotte Sound stretching into the distance, clear blue sky with tree clad slopes rising steeply from the waters edge. Unbeatable location, a cafe with excellent decor and feel, but lousy service. It's not so much the service since the girls are very pleasant. But I came in here for breakfast and it looks as if I am going to get lunch. As I look around I can count only ten other people. The chef, who I can see through the counter opening, is dressed dramatically in black and is wearing a red bandana. Swarthy in appearance, stocky in stature. He is clearly a perfectionist and loves his job. It's just that he's in the wrong job. Perhaps he would have been better working in the British Library painstakingly translating ancient hieroglyphs or a monk writing early religious manuscripts.

But here's the rub. When my breakfast finally came it was a culinary sensation. I can honestly say that it was the best breakfast that I have ever had in New Zealand, and possibly anywhere. Top quality bacon crisp and dry, fried mushrooms, eggs, tomatoes, sliced potatoes and fried bread, all presented beautifully on a large white plate. It was one of those unrepeatable experiences. If I went there tomorrow I would probably not enjoy it as much. So what does this story say about me, or even Le Cafe. On the face of it it looks as if I have a problem relaxing and get stressed very easily. There is indeed truth in this. But it is the uncertainty of the waiting process which caused that stress, not the actual time it took to get served. Too many past experiences of an order being forgotten, past frustrations locked in the memory. If the cafe management had placed a little sign on each table saying *"Master Chef at Work, please be patient while your order is individually prepared"*, then everyone would no doubt have enjoyed the Le Cafe experience more. After finishing my breakfast I just had to let the chef know how highly I rated it. I think everyone loves their good work being recognised.

I caught the one o'clock bus from Picton to Nelson. The driver had earlier told me that I could put my rucksack in the bus's storage compartment and whilst I was waiting a young women walked up in a slightly puzzled way. I asked if she was going to Nelson, which she confirmed, and I said that she could also put her pack on the bus. I think that she was a bit suspicious of my motives since I am a pretty dangerous looking dude. I think she was quite right to be suspicious of strangers. However, after a short while she came up to me and we started talking. Her name, it later turned out, was S and she was from Canada and had been in the country a few weeks. We talked a lot on the bus and I found her very attractive and pleasant company. I guess she must have been in her late thirties or early forties, but it is difficult to say. She was hoping to work on an organic farm near Takaka for a few days in exchange for free lodging. Another time and another place it would have been nice to travel together. Who knows, we may meet up again further south. That evening, in the Trafalgar Square backpacker I was sitting having a quiet beer and it turned out that two of the three people sitting at the table came from within twelve miles of Steyning. One from Storrington and one from Brighton. Small world.

Monday 22nd November 2004

Yesterday I travelled down from Nelson to Franz Josef Glacier. The journey was as spectacular as ever, particularly the coastline between Westport and Greymouth. The coach is such a relaxing way to travel, it's powerful engine just seems to hum along, even up the severest inclines. I hadn't booked a place to stay in Franz Josef and so when we arrived in Hokitika for the afternoon break I went off in search of the tourist information centre. Fortunately it was still open and they were able to book me a place in one of the dormitories at Glow Worm Cottages. This turned out to be a lucky break since it was highly rated in the backpackers guide. When we finally arrived I checked in and went straight to the four bunk dorm. I opened the sliding door and said a friendly *"Hi"* to the two men inside, one who lay on the top bunk and the other on the bottom bunk who was watching the television. Absolutely no response. I think that I would have felt more welcome if I had walked into an Al Qaeda secret cell! I diplomatically tried to start some form of communication but it was clear that they were not interested. Well this should be a fun stopover, I thought. I was pretty tired after the long journey and so after a quick shower I walked into the village centre to look for something to eat. Clearly I had yet to reach the backpacker cooking stage. I had a really enjoyable meal which was quite expensive but I managed to rationalise this by saying that when I arrived in Wanaka I would start cooking for myself. After all I had already made the transition from hotel to backpacker dorm.

The backpacker dorm was really well equipped with shower, toilet, microwave, a two ring gas stove, pots and pans, knives and forks, toaster, and not forgetting the television. Each bunk had it's own clean duvet, pillows and bottom sheet. Backpackers had clearly changed for the better over the years. During the night the guy in the bunk over mine managed to drop down two unidentifiable objects. Well it was actually three as I found his underpants the next morning, in addition to his book and his money purse. I had already identified him as a particular nationality, since although I have met a few good ones on my backpacking travels on the whole they can be a noisy, arrogant and selfish bunch. However, the next morning he turned out to be extremely amiable in direct contrast to the night before. I believe that he was a computer programmer from California. What is it with some people? Fortunately such people in backpackers are the exception rather than the rule.

I was waiting for the Inter-City bus to Wanaka and Queenstown this morning and I was uncertain as to where the bus was going to leave from, this side of the road or the other. Things sometimes operate differently in New Zealand. I asked an Irish girl backpacker who was also sitting close by but she was also uncertain. When the bus finally arrived it turned up on the other side facing north, directly opposite from the direction anticipated. It pays to keep your wits about you. During a brief chat before the bus arrived, F, the Irish girl had told me she was a nurse. At the first tea break I took the opportunity to ask her what she would do if someone broke their ankle in the mountains. I explained that I was writing a story without going into detail. She basically told me that the foot should be raised and if possible it should be kept immobile. It might also be possible to construct a splint to help this process. This seems to indicate that Alexander may have to carry Sonja on his back by improvising a backpack like sling to carry her rather than have them walk side by side along the path. Thanks F. A pretty girl taking six months off to see Australia and New Zealand between jobs.

7. He Who Dares Rodney.

Thursday 25th November 2004 (Wanaka)

I have just spent my third night at the Mountain View Backpacker in Wanaka. As far as facilities go it doesn't rate that highly, not enough toilet and cooking facilities. However, the staff are good, the atmosphere friendly, and it's only a short walk from the centre of town. On Tuesday morning I was sitting in a cafe having a latte when I felt my chair rocking gently as though one leg was shorter than the others. It was the same sort of queasy feeling one has after having one too many drinks the night before. It was then that I noticed that the cars outside were rocking backwards and forwards and for the first time I realised that we were in an earthquake. The cafe rattled and rolled for a bit but nobody rushed outside. It was a great experience to witness. It later turned out that it was 7.2 on the Richter scale but was quite a way south west of the South Island. The only other time that I have been in an earthquake was some twenty years ago in Jordan. I was staying in a good hotel and the water in my wash basin started slopping from side to side. Strange I thought.

Since Tuesday it has rained quite a lot but the great thing is that the snow has come down to the tree line and it gives me a visual impression of how conditions would be for Sonja and Alexander. The Routeburn had yet to open last week because of the winter snow and this extra drop will no doubt have kept it closed. However at the moment this is no problem because I have been happy holed up in Wanaka for a few days. At this time of year it is relatively quiet and still retains that village atmosphere. I have found a wonderful library which is very modern and yet intimate. There is an ideal workplace where I can set up my computer. One of the staff came up and said that, like myself, she was a longtime Apple user. Another non-believer in the Great One. I have made very solid progress on the book during the two four hour stints that I have spent in the library. It is certainly not easy but when I re-read what I have written I am sufficiently satisfied. It's going in the right direction. It was only last night that I realised again that what I am trying to do is serious. It's not just a matter of making a bit of progress on the book, having a great holiday, and then jetting back home. I really do have to give this book my best shot since there are not many other options open to me on the job front. At least I must stick with it until I have completed every part of the storyline. I have no idea how many pages it will be but that doesn't matter. It will be as long or short as necessary, either a long short story, or a short long story!

Sunday 28th November 2004 (Te Anau)

Well 'Alexander Stewart' had made his bookings for both the Kepler and Routeburn tracks. The Routeburn only opened yesterday and so the timing could not have been better. I start on the Kepler on Wednesday and finish on Friday 3rd December. Unfortunately the Routeburn didn't have any places for the 5th and only one for the 6th, so I plumped to go on the 4th December. This means that I won't have a whole days rest between the two walks and so it will/could be a bit of a struggle, especially if I pick up any blisters on the Kepler. However, the six day straight through trek will be fairly realistic of Alexander and Sonja's Pelorus adventure. Hopefully this will give me a particularly good feel for the fatigue that they will have both felt.

I had a really productive time in Wanaka spending at least three to four hours per day at the library. Slow progress but I feel that I am improving and expanding on the storyline all the time. I may well stay a few days in Wanaka on the way back north since the backpacker was very friendly and the library was perfect. It was a strange coincidence that a Danish girl, M, with a very strong Irish accent, confided to me that she was feeling homesick. Shades of Sonja! I don't know if I radiate that sort of confessional persona or it's simply that I look like some sort of father figure. But I certainly don't mind the trust put in me. Her thirtieth birthday was due in a day or two and I guess that it was quite a milestone and perhaps she was reflecting on her life to date. Another sweet girl, N, a Canadian, said that before she started her ten month trek throughout South-East Asia she had hoped that it might have helped her understand life a bit better, but it had not. I unhelpfully said that even at my age I hadn't sorted my life out and therefore couldn't really assist her on that one. So homesickness and the purpose of life. Two interesting questions.

Te Anau is as pleasant as ever at this time of year. Relatively quiet, which is I'm sure how the locals like it. However, this must be about the only time of year, namely summer, when the shops can make any reasonable income. As Jetje would say, *"Life is difficult!"* Happened to share my bunk room with an English guy named A, and three girls, one Dutch and two German. They are very special people, backpackers, and this is something that I have always recognised. Very tolerant, resourceful, inquisitive and with very pleasant characters. Of course, you run into the occasional pain but not very often. Andy is a fireman, late thirties, who like myself keeps coming back to New Zealand. He can't quite make the decision whether or not to move here permanently, and perhaps may not. He's off to do the Milford Track tomorrow and by coincidence we will be on the Routeburn at the same time. Nice guy and have shared a couple of pints together.

Wednesday 1st December 2004

I am now sitting in the Luxmore Hut on my first day of walking the Kepler Track. The weather forecast was bad but in fact it was a beautiful day for walking, neither too hot or too cold. Yesterday the track between Luxmore Hut and Iris Burn Hut was officially closed because of snow and therefore I have been very lucky to have the opportunity to make the alpine crossing. To have had to turn around and head back to Te Anau would have been very disappointing. The walk up was beautiful and better than I remembered it the last time that I was here with T. Perhaps I was too busy trying to keep up with her pace or too concentrated on doing the right thing on our first day alone together? The track from the Control Gate start to Bark Bay follows the lake shore. There was a stillness about the place even though there was plenty of birdsong. Forget your New York shrinks, just send the patient on a walk here for two hours. The floor of the beech forest was carpeted with a light green sphagnum moss and this made everything very special. On leaving Bark Bay the stillness became even more pronounced since there was no longer the sound of waves lapping against the shore. The climb through the forest was steady and relentless. I stopped to rest a number of times and to take on water. Wonderful refreshing water. Had it ever tasted so good. As the track climbed higher and higher the forest floor covering changed to ferns and higher still the trees were covered with mystical pale green and white lichen. Once I had passed the limestone bluff I thought that I had just about cracked it but it took far longer than I had imagined to break out of the forest and into the alpine tussock grass above one thousand metres. I was basically at my limit and virtually running on empty when I passed that very clearly demarcated line. It is very reassuring that the climb demands quite a considerable effort and cannot be achieved by just anybody, even though it is only officially classified as a moderate walk. It is certainly hard enough for me with a loaded pack.

I had a few more ideas about the storyline on the climb. One is that Alexander is into tree hugging and at various times on the climb he places his hands against some mighty standing beech or on an enormous sawn trunk crossing the path and just stands there deep in contemplation for a few seconds. I certainly did this on a couple of occasions. Sonja thinks that this is all rather odd but Alexander explains that part of his ancestry originated in Ireland where trees used to be very sacred objects. And also his Maori friend, Rita, told him to talk to the tree spirits to ask their permission to enter their domain. I'm not sure if this is the first time I thought about including A and P's Maori friend Rita into the story but hopefully it adds another more spiritual dimension.

Another idea that I had is to actually produce the book on my computer in PDF format and possibly sell the first part of the book online. I may even give the first chapters away online for free as a teaser in order to market it more widely and hopefully word of mouth on the internet will increase demand to buy the whole printed book. I could create a specific website for this, possibly, pelorus.com, advertise on my agmachine.com website, or in outdoor magazines. If people wished to read the complete book then they would have to buy a hard copy although a secure PDF payment system would eliminate printing costs. However, I like the idea of people holding a hard copy of the book in their hands better. Each copy would be personally signed by myself and would have a unique identification number, making it very personal to the purchaser. Payment over the internet could prove to be a problem although I could get some help on that one. An even better option would be to use the Amazon.com route since this would take out all the security and set-up problems. I would first have to sort out the unique book registration number (ISBN?) or whatever it is called. A website for the book could allow people to send their comments (whoops!), add photographs, exchange track experiences and so forth. It could actually create a community, perhaps a blog.

The idea that Alexander may have an estranged daughter Minnie, possibly named after Minnie Driver, from a failed and bitter marriage may have possibilities. Perhaps his former wife lives overseas and this makes contact difficult apart from occasional photos, letters and cards. The USA might be a good option since custody laws are quite strict and his daughter might not have been able to visit him in the United Kingdom. Perhaps Alexander finally comes to see Sonya, not as a potential lover and partner, but as the embodiment of the father/daughter relationship which he never had. This would allow the love relationship between Sonja and Craig to be developed, which would be far more plausible. Perhaps after the first walk Sonja goes first to Wanaka to catch up with some friends, returns to Pelorus where her affair with Craig really starts, and then travels on to Milford and subsequently meets up with Alexander in Te Anau. Craig tries to persuade Sonja not to go on the Pelorus track but to stay with him but she decides to keep her word to Alexander, of whom she has grown quite fond. Craig admires her willingness to keep to commitments. All this could be done in say three to four days. Perhaps during that period Alexander stays in a backpacker in Te Anau and this gives me a chance to describe some of the characters who stay at backpackers and backpacker life in general.

7a. He Who Dares Rodney (cont'd).

Sunday 5th December 2004

It's about seven o'clock in the morning and I am sitting in the freezing cold at Lake McKenzie Hut on the Routeburn Track. I've already had a warming breakfast of Thai chicken curry and hot tea. There is snow low down in the surrounding mountains and fortunately the sky is pretty clear at the moment. Yesterday evening it snowed quite heavily at the hut level and the warden said that he didn't rate our chances of going over very highly. However just before dusk the sky cleared just like magic and the magnificent snow covered mountains came into view. I had seen them before but I think it staggered a few of the people to see what had been previously hidden from them. Hopefully it should be a really great crossing over to the Routeburn Falls Hut. It was so cold in the bunk room last night that I wore two pairs of socks, thermal underwear and long sleeved shirt on in my sleeping bag with the hood drawn tightly closed. Fortunately I was really warm. The only disappointing thing was that the usual suspects made a very noisy late entrance and talked loudly for some time. What's wrong with these people, it seems to be so common. Without giving a clue about who I was talking about I asked a guy named Steve, who had worked at a Queenstown backpacker hostel for a year, who the worst behaved backpacker nation was. He confirmed my own experiences as have others since. God really screwed up on that one.

Going back in time a bit it was on the 2nd December that I started the Kepler Track and as previously noted I reached the Luxmore Hut *"running on empty"*. In fact just above the tree line both legs seized up so that I walked like the tin man in the Wizard of Oz, or whatever that Judy Garland film was called. The muscles at the back of my thighs just knotted up. I guessed it was just some kind of cramp but thrombosis did cross my mind. After all I had not done any preparation for the walk apart from wearing my boots rather a lot.

On the morning of the 3rd December we awaited the hut warden's decision on the Kepler alpine section. It had been closed by snow the day before and it would have been very disappointing to have had to walk back down again after expending so much effort. My objective of researching the walk for my book would have been over before it had barely begun. The warden simply announced that a storm was due in the afternoon with rain, sleet, snow and winds gusting to 120 km per hour on the tops. If we wanted to go across we had to go now. And so there was a general stampede out of the door. It is a long hard climb up from the hut to the turn off for the Mount Luxmore summit itself and for me it was a real struggle. It was already blowing hard and sleeting. At least I had had the experience of doing the track with T some years before but that was in bright sunshine with clear blue skies, and very little wind. The first target was the first emergency shelter. From below you could see the track winding its way inexorably up until it disappeared from view around a corner. I guessed that that point was the top of the first climb. Wrong! At least when I looked back I could see a number of other trampers way down below and that made me feel much better, but them no doubt worse. Conditions were now getting very unpleasant. On the way up I had been passed by a young Irish couple who seemed to be going very well. However, when I finally arrived at the first emergency shelter they were both very cold, wet and shivering. They were just totally ill-equipped for the track in those conditions. They wisely decided to turn around and they said that their aim was to carry on straight back to Te Anau. That would have been a dreadfully long walk and they certainly will not forget their Kepler Track experience for a very long time.

There were also four girls in the shelter, three from Singapore and one from Malaysia. I had briefly made their acquaintance since we had travelled to the start of the track together the previous day. Two were particularly poorly equipped for the alpine conditions and were shivering. I said they should change into warmer clothes and offered one girl a pair of thick woolly socks for her hands. One of them was giggling and shivering and I was concerned about hypothermia since it brings on rather strange behaviour. The party had a definite leader who seemed to be in charge but she seemed to think that everything was fine. She was being quite stupid. I therefore politely insisted that I would walk behind them until the second emergency shelter which was located some two hours distance. When we started again the conditions deteriorated quickly and they were moving so slowly. A young Austrian, Martin, who I had briefly spoken to the night before, caught us up. He was obviously very experienced and well equipped and so I told him about my concerns. He said that he would wait at the next shelter and he could provide them with some spare clothing if necessary. The lead girl kept taking photographs of the group oblivious to the potential danger. The weather continued to deteriorate with howling wind and snow along the ridge line. The group made the next shelter but if the weather had deteriorated further into thick snow then they would certainly have been in trouble. As they waited at the shelter it became noticeably colder and the snowfall more prevalent. This was all marvellous material for the book.

Another idea for the story is that Alexander receives his walking stick Te Puke from Rita the Maori. She tells him it is a very special item, perhaps owned by male ancestors, but she wants to give it to him. Alexander is afraid to take such a special object and says that he is afraid that he might lose it. Rita says not to worry because Te Puke will find his way home. He is also worried that he might break it but Rita assures him that he can never break Te Puke. All the time Alexander has Te Puke it tries to get away or causes him problems. If Alexander leans him against a rock he will slip down onto the path so that Alexander has to bend down with a heavy pack on his back to pick Te Puke up. Also Alexander is careful not to put him down close to a stream in case Te Puke falls in and escapes that way down the stream into a river and into a lake or the sea. At the same time Te Puke saves Alexander a number of times on the path when he would otherwise have fallen. These ideas have come from direct experience of my own when Te Puke (the actual name I gave to my own walking stick) kept slipping down from where I put him. I should also try to develop the Rita and Maori aspects of the book more fully with the Storm God fighting Te Puke.

The walk from Lake McKenzie Hut to the Routeburn Falls Hut was as good as ever, if not better. The climb up from the McKenzie Hut was beautiful with the mountains in clear view and with snow down to the tree line. The view down to the hut was impressive but the hut looked so vulnerable under the steep mountainside. Beautiful grotto like walk through the trees on the lower slopes with moss all over their twisted shapes. Along the main traverse I was able to see right down to the sea and the peaks of the mountains on the other side of the Hollyford river were visible through the cloud. Below me huge clouds drifted down the valley like great ocean liners. It was very strange to be above them. The 'rock' of my book still looks as impressive as ever and I was pleased to confirm that there was no track down to it. In addition it did not look as if the shelter had been used for a very long time since the overhung floor was covered in grass. Hopefully it had not been visited since I climbed down to it a number of years ago. It was also good to be able to confirm that the Deadmans Track is located between the rock and the Harris Saddle since this fits in perfectly with the storyline. Also the emergency shelter at the Harris Saddle clearly has two padlocked cupboards which may contain some emergency equipment. I hope that it is more than on the Kepler shelters which only contained a single shovel! The snow was falling quite steadily at the top which certainly added to the atmosphere.

The walk down from the Harris Saddle to the Routeburn Falls Hut was very dramatic and entailed walking along quite narrow ledges. Lake Harris was larger and more impressive than I remembered it. The track also crossed an area of very deep snow which would have been up to my chest if a path had not been cut. At the beginning of this section an overturned notice read *Safe* but it was only after I reached the other side that the notice for walkers in the other direction stated that there was a danger of avalanches! Overall I held up very well and yesterday and todays walk were well within my capacity. The Meindl boots have been fantastic and I have no blisters to talk of, a major change from my previous tramping experiences. My kit has been good and I have certainly needed all of it, leggings, waterproof jacket, woollen hat, gloves. The gloves only just made the journey from the UK since I thought that I would be walking in sunshine. Strangely various muscles ached at different times rather than the problem concentrating on one area. There is no doubt in my mind that repeating both the Kepler and Routeburn Tracks has firmed up a lot of ideas and has been really worthwhile research time. For example, seeing the rucksacks of the Singapore girls caked in snow as they climbed in a small group above me was very visual and so many other observations have made an impact on my thoughts. I am now planning two nights in a single room in Queenstown which will hopefully be bliss. I then have to decide whether or not to return to Wanaka since the library and lake/mountain scenery provide me with a great environment to continue writing the book. I'm not yet clear how long I will stay in New Zealand but I know that I must try to finish the story once and for all before I leave.

The idea of having back to back books appeals to me with "Pelorus" starting at the opposite end from "Where to Now", the diary of my writing efforts. I think a great deal will depend on how interesting "Where to Now" will be for readers, but only time will tell. Perhaps having a record of how and when ideas arose will be quite interesting since they can be directly related to the book. I have no doubt that my decision to travel to New Zealand was the right one even if it still seems quite irresponsible. He who dares Rodney.

8. Staying In The Zone

Thursday 9th December 2004

It's six fifteen in the morning and I have just spent my third night at the Hippo Lodge in Queenstown. Fortunately I was able to book their only single room and so I have had three wonderful nights of sleep. Beautiful, beautiful sleep. No more of that tossing and turning on hard mattresses in track huts. The truth is that roughing it does not really suit me, and neither does it suit most foreign backpackers who walk the famous tracks. Two nights and three days walking is usually enough for most. But today I have to move out of my haven of peace and tranquility and into a four bed dormitory. Oh well, back to reality!

The relevant point about my current stay in Hippo Lodge is that it is associated with one of the characters in my book. She is the person dressed in black and yellow horizontally striped leotards who I first met on the Routeburn, who was making her first trek and who told me she planned to open a backpackers. She was a lovely women. The character has always been named M.... but I couldn't remember if that was her real name or not. And so to spare the innocent yesterday I changed her name to Kathy! Hippo Lodge has a million dollar view of Lake Wakitipu and is now certainly worth that amount on the open market. So things have certainly worked out well for M. The Lodge is well away from the noise of Queenstown and so it is a very good place to relax. However, the climb up the hill from town tests any hardy tramper and I certainly wouldn't have wanted to undertake that walk with my rucksack and computer bag.

Saturday 11th December 2004

Tomorrow is my fifty sixth birthday. When I walked the Routeburn track with M and T I can well recall that I had my birthday at Routeburn Falls hut. I only told M about my birthday during that days walk, or just after, and of course she had to announce it to a full hut that night and I had to endure an embarrassing "Happy Birthday to You" from about thirty to forty people. At least it made the anniversary particularly memorable. And now with my book I have the chance to get my own back on M! Revenge is sweet. Only joking.

Progress on Pelorus has been slow but solid. A significant problem is finding a place to quietly work at a time which suits me, which is usually early in the morning. The Queenstown library doesn't open until ten o'clock and so there is a lot of dead time before that which is difficult to make productive use of. I don't like to show my computer around at the backpackers too much since, although the vast majority are great people, it only needs one bad sort. Writing longhand is another option but that necessitates transcribing everything onto the computer at a later date. Not a very efficient process. The main components of the ending of Pelorus were written all those years ago although I have subsequently refined and improved parts significantly. The start of the book was a real mess before I arrived in New Zealand this time but I reverted to my original start point with Alexander sitting at the Lake McKenzie hut and it works again. The middle part, between the "Kepler Track" walk and the "Pelorus Track" walk was always problematical. The concept of Alexander himself falling in love with Sonja is quite feasible but the age difference does not ring true from Sonja's perspective. And so a love affair between Craig and Sonja is much more realistic whilst Alexander comes to understand that his love for Sonja is more like the love between father and daughter. The daughter that he has hardly seen since the break up of his marriage. Instead of Sonja just going to Milford Sound I am now giving her more time to go to Queenstown to meet up with some relatives for a day, return to Pelorus to begin her affair with Craig, and only then on to Milford Sound followed by her meeting with Alexander in Te Anau. In the meantime Alexander will have to reconcile himself to the idea that a love match with Sonja is out of the question.

Backpacker life is really special. Or more accurately the backpackers themselves. There is a constant flow of young people in and out, most only staying at one place for a night or two. Unlike a hotel or motel conversations between various people can be started at will and information about where and where not to go, what and what not to do, is the main currency. People from all nationalities interact very well and friendships are often formed which can last for a few days tramp or even longer. There is no obligation to stay with someone if you do not wish to and so it gives everyone a great sense of freedom. As I have noticed before, travelling alone has many advantages because you can always meet up with someone with similar interests. This is particularly useful for single girls. It might appear somewhat dangerous for a single girl to travel alone but in fact it is not, if she has the smallest amount of common sense.

Sunday 12th December 2004

"Happy Birthday to me. Happy Birthday to me!" Well I guess that is some kind of landmark for my personal obituary, fifty six instead of fifty five. Not that I am being morbid about it at all. I think that my feelings will be no more or no less even if I reach ninety three. Liz will be happy today because we are once again the same age. I woke up in my small four bed dorm refreshed after a good nights sleep. I just hope that I didn't snore and disturb my room mates, an Australian man, American and Austrian girls, all I guess in their early twenties. All the "A's". It was interesting to briefly look around the room whilst I lay there deciding whether or not to get up. Complete strangers sleeping peacefully in the same room. I didn't even know their names and probably never will. The two girls lay like chrysalis waiting for their hibernation to finish. This is very special. It doesn't often happen in other adult situations. I hope that it doesn't change. It would only take one serious incident and it would. Another loss of human trust. Like unlocked doors. Like conversing with a child who innocently asks you a question.

Today I will travel to Kinloch Lodge, a backpacker geographically close to Glenorchy, but which actually requires a circuitous route via gravel road around the top end of the lake, perhaps fifteen to twenty kilometres. I have arranged that they will pick me up at Glenorchy wharf by boat, a much shorter five minute trip across the lake. Twenty dollars for the privilege. I feel that it is a good time to take a break from Queenstown just to keep my thoughts fresh. A few days in the comparative peace and quiet of Kinloch Lodge and the Glenorchy area. Hopefully I may find some quiet space to write.

Yesterdays effort in the library was limited to two hours because on Saturday they are only open from ten thirty to twelve thirty. However it was a very productive period. I think that I managed to make the cementing of Craig and Sonja's relationship quite realistic. A brief passage which didn't require going into the gymnastics of love making. It is very satisfying creating the various pieces of the jigsaw and fitting them into place. The number of hours that I can spend writing each day is limited by my creative energy. After two or three hours I feel quite tired and you have to be the opposite to write and to actually enjoy doing so. Another very limiting factor is that, apart from the library, I have nowhere to separate myself from other people. I feel a bit self-conscious, even a pseudo, if I start using my computer in the backpackers. At least with longhand people just think that you are writing a journal.

The whole Pelorus book writing project is clearly *"off the wall"*. Can I imagine going in to see my bank manager and asking for a loan of two to three thousand pounds to write a short story, novel or, wait for it, novella. I guess a novella is for somebody who is not good enough to write a short story but too lazy to write a novel. That seems to fit. However, it really doesn't matter since a book should simply be as long as the story, no longer, no shorter. And so the bank manager starts. *"What experience do you have of writing fiction?"* None. *"How many first novels are actually published?"* Next to none. *"How many novels which are actually published make any money?"* Next to none. *"What are your alternative employment prospects."* Next to none. *"What savings do you have?"* Less than none. *"Well thank you very much Mr Cree. Please close the door quietly as you leave."*

I have now arrived at Kinloch Lodge. Thorough interrogation of the Austrian girl revealed that I did not snore last night. There is still hope for me yet. Secondly the shuttle bus company informed me that when I arrived in Glenorchy another company, Backpacker Express, would take me by road to the Lodge, and not by boat. However, when I arrived in Glenorchy I was given a lifebelt and was whisked across to the Lodge in a jet boat at a total cost of ten dollars. Good on yer, Backpacker Express. The Lodge is very peaceful and the four bed bunk room well appointed. The Lodge has a restaurant, a bar and backpacker lounge and cooking facilities. I am hoping that I will be very happy here during my short stay. At present I am the only one in my room but what fate does the next few hours hold? The Dunedin snoring club? Wellington ballet on tour? Greta, Mette and Sweta from Sweden? Who can say. Glenorchy Gay Club? Get me out of here.

The time is five eighteen precisely. This is a good example of the limits of my writing energy. I have nearly two hours until the barbecue starts and yet I know that I don't feel like writing or even editing what I have already written. I have the room all to myself, have a power plug at hand, and a comfortable sofa to sit on. But any words will have to wait until tomorrow morning when I guess my room will be full of sleeping guests until ten, and the more public rooms, such as the dining area, full of people going about their business. As Jetje would say theatrically, "Life is difficult!"

Tuesday 14th December 2004.

Kinloch Lodge is absolutely wonderful. A nearby place is called Paradise then this must be called Heaven. It has such a relaxing atmosphere and yet everything is to hand, even an incredibly well stocked television room full of videos and DVD's. The owners are extremely friendly and that friendliness transfers itself effortlessly to their guests. Just five minutes walk from the Lodge a shingle bank protrudes into Lake Wakitipu. From that point you can take in a three hundred and sixty degree panorama of the most breathtaking scenery anywhere in the world. On a clear sunny day like today, that is. On Monday, my birthday, I had a very nicely prepared barbecue and then rather overindulged on the red wine. Only three glasses but I felt hungover the next day. The label was Oxford Landing but it felt like Hard Landing to me. Nevertheless it was a great place and a great way to spend my birthday. Hard to beat.

Yesterday morning the weather was quite good but not great. I decided that it would do me good to go for a walk and I had read that the Glacier Burn short walk was nearby. The distance along the gravel road to the start of the track was further than I anticipated but it was really enjoyable. A group of beef cattle had escaped from their field and without any intention on my part I managed to herd them along the road for at least two kilometres! A bull on the other side of the fence seemed somewhat put out by my activity. Fortunately half of the cattle jumped over a fence on the opposite side of the road whilst the remainder made a dash past me back to where they had come from. The Glacier Burn track was well marked with orange triangles nailed to trees every so often. It was initially a very stiff climb and my initial reaction was that I would just walk up a short distance and then return to the Lodge. However, the further I rose the more determined I became to reach the tree line and the end of the walk. It was a charming little trek and finally I broke out into the valley bowl surrounded by high cliffs. A notice at the beginning of the walk gave warning of potential avalanches in winter and spring further up the mountain and so that was good enough for me. On my way down I came across a small group of tuis who appeared to be in the middle of courtship. Not only did they sing but they sang in concert. I managed to spot one tui with his/her feathers all puffed up, a male I guess. As I descended further the wind got up and the tall beech trees were swaying visibly. I was a bit concerned that a piece of deadwood could come crashing down on yours truly at any time. By the time I finally reached the road again the weather had changed dramatically and I was pleased that I had brought my full waterproofs, even though it was only threatening rain. Further up the valley, towards the Routeburn Track, it was clearly tipping down. Luckily for me the wind was on my back the whole way home.

Since I have been here I have made some good progress on the book. The opportunities and facilities to write are not great but I am satisfied with my solution for the Alexander/Sonja relationship. I have also managed to fit Minnie into the story which allows the original Puccini aria finish to work. I think that when I return to Queenstown I should make a hard copy of what I have written to date. I have already identified a shop where I can print directly off my Mac disc. It is difficult to get an accurate feel for the balance of the whole story at present but overall I think that it is pretty good. I would like to build up the character of Te Puke more and perhaps one more section on Craig. I hope that making a hard copy will help this process. I am not sure whether or not to start redrafting from the very beginning again or try to improve parts section by section. Section by section has worked quite well to date. I am still hoping to complete the fundamentals of the book by Christmas whilst I am still in the south and "in the zone." I guess that the final editing will take much longer than I would like, perhaps up to one month. Hopefully I can do most of this work at A and P's in Napier, and perhaps some at Sandy's bach in Stephen's Bay. Clearly time spent carefully refining the book is essential, even if it will be quite frustrating and certainly not easy.

9. Heaven Is Close To Paradise

Wednesday 15th December 2004

I am now back in my single room in Hippo Lodge for the next three days. It is only a small room but the bed is really comfortable and I don't have to be concerned about other people, or they about me. I was extremely lucky at Kinloch Lodge because for two of the three nights I had a four bed bunk room all to myself. Kinloch really is a gem and I hope that they can sort out the transport to and from the Lodge to make it easier for independent backpackers to stay there. The Backpacker Express transfers that I had, by jet boat and fast launch, would certainly do it. I would thoroughly recommend Kinloch Lodge to anyone. Heaven is indeed close to Paradise.

This morning I managed to do a little more writing in my room and I added some improvements to the first day and second day on the Pelorus Track. I now have Morton's snoring causing a partial evacuation of his bunk room and that fits in quite well. It's good to be back in Queenstown since I will be able to make full use of the library over the next two days. My mind is drifting more towards walking the Dart/Rees and over the Cascade Saddle to Aspiring Hut again since fate seems to have returned me to Queenstown with a sufficient number of days available to make the crossing and still get back to Queenstown in time for my Christmas booking at Hippo Lodge. And so I will have from the 18th until the 23rd December at my disposal, six days. I'll just have to keep a very close eye on the weather. I'll also take the opportunity whilst I am in Queenstown to make a hard copy of Pelorus, if possible.

A few days ago I finished reading my second book, Mr Nice, the autobiography of the marijuana smuggler Howard Marks. Extremely well written and an excellent read. How he remembered all those facts is staggering although I suppose that he had a number of years in jail to do so! The first book was Touching the Void by Joe Simpson. Another riveting read about survival in the mountains against the odds. The great thing about staying in backpackers, away from the demon television, is that it encourages you to both communicate and read. Both very beneficial activities for all. It was too late for me to go down town to buy another book. I was thinking that it might be appropriate to re-read The Hobbit, which I must have last read over thirty years ago. The backpacker had a few old paperbacks in the office and I went looking for The Grapes of Wrath by John Steinbeck. I had seen it there last week. It had now been taken and so the best of the remaining bunch seemed to be The Magus by John Fowles. The foreword was particularly interesting for me in my present situation. He writes that he originally started working on The Magus in the early 1950s and that it was finally published in 1966. The significantly revised version, which I am reading, was published in 1977. This knowledge is both encouraging and disconcerting. It is encouraging because it illustrates just how difficult it is to create good prose and that even the best writers often have a battle. They just don't sit down and magic flows from the pen. Secondly, even after he had had great success with The Magus he basically rewrote significant sections some eleven years later. I find this encouraging since even if I don't produce a perfect outcome with the first draft there is still room to improve on it over time. It even gave me an idea that readers of the book could send in their revised sentences, paragraphs, chapters and even the whole book, perhaps submitted to a blog. In ten years time the book, or even a range of different books, would be reprinted with the best contributions included. It would be an extension to the BBC End of Story idea.

The disconcerting part is that the future is pretty bleak after I complete this Pelorus project. I could do some more work on my agmachine.com website at home to try to generate more income but that is very tiresome and I don't hold out much hope of success. The other options of green keeping at the golf club, or stacking shelves at Tescos (application twice rejected) and so forth are very depressing. Consultancy work doesn't solve the self-fulfilment requirement any more although it does make a very positive contribution to income. But then again assignments are now rather rare. I am drawn between finishing my work on the book as soon as realistically possible and returning home to an uncertain future and a cold winter, or remaining on in New Zealand to see if I can find a solution to the career dilemma. I fear that if I return home with the book still in draft form then it will never be finished to my satisfaction. Renting out my house and writing whilst continually travelling is a remote option. I think that I love my home comforts too much, or at least the knowledge that I can return home at any time.

I now begin to have doubts about the Cascade Saddle walk since perhaps I should put all of my efforts into writing before the Christmas deadline that I have set myself. This would mean returning to Wanaka and going to the library which has excellent facilities and an atmosphere conducive to work. I guess that I am afraid that as soon as I go north again, to Nelson or Napier, I will lose the passion which up to now I have been able to sustain in the south.

Friday 17th December 2004

Yesterday morning I had a very good four hour stint at the Queenstown library. I was able to write one of the last remaining pieces in the jigsaw and start reading and editing my book from the very beginning. Overall I am very satisfied with the end result, at least as far as I have got, namely about page fifty. It is very difficult for me to gauge how good the book is because I can clearly picture locations, events and characters which my writing might not convey sufficiently well to the reader. I'll just have to ask one or two people to give me really honest feedback, if it's not asking too much for them to read what could be a poor offering. At the moment I have Sandy and my brother, Alec, in mind. Nevertheless, whatever the final outcome, I am quite proud that I have managed to complete the overall project to my own satisfaction. The first objective of my trip to New Zealand has therefore been achieved and I have kept to the task well.

I took the opportunity to look inside the dust covers of some books by New Zealand authors in Whitcoulls. It would appear that the company Reed, although small, is one of the biggest publishers in the country and their titles include Whale Rider. Could do a lot worse. It would also appear that Harper Collins in New Zealand do have a facility for authors to submit a synopsis and the first three chapters of their books for review. Both of these options may be worth investigating further once I return north. If I receive no positive feedback then the self-publish option will still be there.

Last night I went to see the film *Hero* by Zhang Yimou. I remember what a great impression his first big film, *Wild Sorghum*, had on me visually. Unfortunately there was just too much balletic sword fighting for me and a confusing storyline. However, I'm glad that I went to see it. I believe that to make a film of my storyline would not cost huge amounts because the set is already in place, namely the Kepler, Routeburn and Cascade Saddle tracks, and Queenstown, Wanaka and Te Anau. The scenery should be one of the main stars of the film. The music would also be fundamentally important but whether or not it is an original score or appropriate tracks by various artists, I'm not so sure. The Puccini aria at the end is important and I can visualise the camera slowly scanning up from the rock to the mountains beyond. Who says I don't have a positive attitude! Think big. Think Hollywood!

Saturday 18th December 2004

I finished reading the last thirty or so pages of Pelorus last night. There are a number of inconsistencies that I have yet to correct. For example, I still have Sonja falling in love with Alexander, as in the original version. The routing of the trek still needs clarifying as does why Sonja and Alexander are the only ones who walk their route and why Craig and Co. should need to make sure that it's clear of trampers. Perhaps I can write that later trampers turn back from both directions because of the wardens eight thirty warnings or because they simply turn around based on their own assessment of the weather. The warden warning is tricky since he/she would check the intentions book and make a note of Alexander's and Sonja's plans and realise they could be in trouble. I will therefore have to emphasise that there was no warden at their last hut. I can also write that there is confusion about intentions because people are arriving to walk the track whilst others are turning back. Also there is no mention of Te Puke later in the book. In fact it is stated that Alexander left Te Puke behind after the first walk. That aspect has to be corrected and developed further.

I will also have to develop a conversation between Sonja and Alexander where she asks him does he believe in love at first sight, namely her feelings for Craig. She says that she can discuss it with him since he is a much older man. This will occur after he returns to his sleeping bag after building the snow wall, and has recovered sufficiently. The discussion is clearly difficult for him since he loves Sonja himself. I could relocate the paragraph about the changes that occur when young people travel away from home for extended periods for the first time.

It's now afternoon in Queenstown and its been a pretty miserable rainy day and I am sitting in my backpacker waiting for a three thirty bus to Wanaka. This morning I spent one hour in the library and used that time reading my hard copy from the very first page for about thirty pages. For some reason I felt quite tired but even so the book seemed particularly hard going and the writing laboured. This is the first time that I have felt that I would not be able to produce an acceptable read, even if I could never produce high quality fiction. This initial conclusion, although not final, is quite depressing. I suppose that most books have to set the scene and introduce the characters in the opening pages. I undertook this mornings exercise in order to get a feel for the Harper Collins three chapter assessment for an author's work. Would the opening chapters capture my attention or just make me yawn. I'm not sure. Perhaps I am too close to it all to assess it objectively. It will need the honest opinions of others before I will finally know. However over the next week I must work hard on the book at Wanaka library to correct all the most obvious imperfections.

10. Queenstown Blues

Sunday 19th December 2004

The journey from Queenstown to Wanaka by the Atomic Shuttle was very scenic with snow down to relatively low levels. I had a Craig Williams migraine type headache for the whole afternoon and didn't feel too bright. In the evening the weather started to clear. I had an interesting talk with an attractive girl from Brighton, L, who was just on her last few days of a six week trip to New Zealand. She was a graphic designer, shades of Julian, who had recently broken with her boyfriend and had hoped that the trip might clarify her direction for the future. She had clearly enjoyed New Zealand but had not identified a solution for herself. Young people seeking to resolve a few major issues in their lives seems to be a recurring theme, although clearly this objective is clearly not restricted by age.

I went to bed last night still feeling very down, particularly about the quality of my book, and was in the state of mind which basically says, get on the bus north. I realised that if I did there was a good chance that I would lose the motivation for writing. That would be a disaster because the whole reason to be in New Zealand revolves around finishing Pelorus, for better or for worse. I went to bed quite late for me, about ten o'clock. I still had a bit of a headache but I was hoping to settle down for a good nights sleep. Wrong. At about twelve o'clock a tightly knit group of mixed nationalities took their noise from the distant lounge to the rooms close to mine. Banging doors, loud talking, and disturbance just continued for hours whilst I was reluctant to play the old man and politely ask them to shut up. What really gets me is how selfish and self-centred people can be. I've now bought some ear plugs for tonight!

My depression about the book has been lifted by the Wanaka morning sunshine and the whole ambiance of the place. It must be my spiritual home but only time would reveal whether or not the reality of living here for an extended period would change that view. Probably. My gloom about Pelorus was partially lifted by a passage in The Magus which I believe was based on John Fowles own writing experiences. After all it would appear that it took him a long time to establish himself as a successful writer and I'm sure he must have had many instances of disappointment with his work. The relevant piece starts on page fifty seven:

"And there was the poetry. I had begun to write poems about the island, about Greece, that seemed to me philosophically profound and technically exciting. I dreamt more and more of literary success. I spent hours staring at the wall of my room, imagining reviews, letters written to me by celebrated poets, fame and praise and still more fame.......But then, one bleak March, the scales dropped from my eyes. I read the Greek poems and saw them for what they were: undergraduate pieces, without rhythm, without structure, their banalities of perception clumsily concealed under an impasto of lush rhetoric. In horror I turned to other poems I had written - at Oxford, in East Anglia. They were no better; even worse. The truth rushed down on me like a burying avalanche. I was not a poet.........Taking all the poems I had ever written, page by slow page, I tore each one into tiny fragments, till my fingers ached."

Making today a rest day from the book has had a very positive effect on my outlook. I now look forward to getting to the library tomorrow and starting on the revisions and additions. At least I know that the facilities for using a computer at the library are excellent.

Tuesday 21st December 2004

Yesterday I went to the Wanaka library at ten o'clock needing a good day to rebuild my confidence and to get the book back on track. It is quite a noisy place with a number of little children running about and lowered tones are not compulsory, that's for sure. Perhaps that's one of the beauties of the place. However, nearly five hours later I emerged having had my most concentrated session to date and I feel that I have made a number of small but significant improvements to the first thirty or so pages. I think that it is essential to get and retain the readers interest early on otherwise they may give up after a few pages. Just as I would. Today I am hoping to develop the description of backpacking and the backpackers themselves. How they drift into and out of the backpacker hostels like flotsam and jetsam on the sea shore, washing in and out with the tide. Some stay for days, some for a week or two and some stay forever. Another important word change is to use wooden staff instead of stick or pole for Te Puke. It sounds stronger and more appropriate.

Sunday evening I went to see the film Wimbledon at the Paradiso cinema in Wanaka. It is special place since the seats are secondhand sofas and armchairs. There is a long intermission during the film so that people can have a cooked meal, a beer or whatever. The film was very easy viewing and I enjoyed it very much. Last night I went to see an obscure film entitled Coffee and Cigarettes. It was a series of about eleven short stories which all revolved around people at tables smoking cigarettes or drinking coffee, and on more than one occasion, tea. I think that the objective of the first part of the film was to see how many people left and of the remainder how many shot themselves to release themselves from their misery. I'm open to thought provoking films but this seemed to me to be just ad libbed rubbish. It got slightly better towards the end with a piece by Kate Winslett, and another by Alfred Molina and Steve Coogan.

It is different not having any daily objectives like most backpackers, whether it is to go sky-diving, bungy jumping or track walking. What are you doing today? I'm going to the library for two to five hours. Oh. Yes. Well. Nevertheless the backpackers have given me a good base from which to work and you always meet some very nice people to talk to, particularly the girls who travel independently.

Friday, 24th December 2004

The four days that I spent in Wanaka were very productive as far as writing was concerned. I managed to put in some very solid hours ranging from three to five, and that was very encouraging, and also very necessary. On Wednesday I basically finished the book for the first time as far as being able to read it continuously from the first page to the last. There are a few paragraphs to be added here and there, and the character of Te Puke needs to be developed more strongly. It may be that I will continue to expand the content over the next few weeks as new ideas and themes come to mind. I was able to get another hard copy made in Queenstown yesterday and I am hoping to start another read through today. Looking at the first page in The Cow yesterday didn't give me much encouragement but perhaps I was just tired. A bit of both I think, tiredness and reality. Nevertheless, at the end of the day, I stuck to the task well and whatever the outcome I have managed to complete a fairly readable story. I now have to transform that into a very good read.

I am now in Queenstown for the next three days and then it is the long haul back to the north. I must have been in the Fiordland area for nearly a month now and there is no doubt that it was very beneficial since it has provided me with the correct surroundings for writing this particular book. Lazing on a Nelson beach in the sunshine would certainly not have felt right. I think that it will be a very quiet Christmas which I don't mind at all. A number of the backpackers are in the same position and they make very pleasant and friendly company. Queenstown for Christmas ranks pretty highly among any location in the world.

Martin has asked if I would help him sell his apartment in Auckland and he will pay my expenses plus a bit more for doing so. This could certainly be an option for January and might be a way to recoup some of my costs, if successful. The other day a New Zealander, who was sharing the same bunk room, suggested I might consider working for Lonely Planet writing guide books for them. I'm not sure that it would be ideal but it certainly never occurred to me before. Lonely Planet Series for the over sixties! Wheelchair access is very good at this backpacker and hearing aids are widely available!

11. It's Christmas Time

Saturday 25th December 2004

Christmas Day in Queenstown! This morning I got up just before eight whilst everyone else was tucked away in their beds awaiting the first shock of their hangovers. I took the gondola up to the lookout above Queenstown. The sky was clear blue and the view absolutely magnificent. I was the first one to go up when it opened at nine and so it was just a perfect situation. Well worth the eighteen dollars for the trip. After that I just wandered around Queenstown in the warm sunshine and checked my email and the news on the internet. I guess it is now approximately six weeks since I left home and it has been a really great trip. The three thousand dollars that I already had in my BNZ account has helped to reduce the feeling that I am spending money that I don't really have. However, now I have just started to dip into my travellers cheques and that is not so good.

Yesterday I had a great spell on the book and worked from about ten until three in the quiet of the backpacker lounge. My negative feelings of yesterday about the opening of the book have been significantly lifted since I have been able to rework some passages and remove many of the words, sentences and phrases which didn't seem right. It is really encouraging that I can still improve the script and have not yet hit a terminal brick wall. I think that the storyline just grows as I think of new ideas and themes to add to the overall structure. However, I have hit a major snag with respect to my title, Pelorus. Unfortunately today I did a search on the internet and found out that a Pelorus Track already exists, near Nelson. I already knew that Pelorus Sound existed, and perhaps a small settlement of Pelorus, but the existence of an actual Pelorus Track has really thrown me. Clearly I cannot use that title now, which I loved, but will have to identify an alternative title, possibly a place name in Fiordland.

I had a look on my detailed map of Fiordland and Pluvius is a possibility since there is a Mount Pluvius in the general area where I am locating the fictitious track. Other possibilities are Resolution, Fortitude, Perseverance, Steadfast, and Integrity. All of these could be used as the name of the settlement and of the track itself. However, this afternoon I did a book search on Amazon using the title "The Track" and it didn't immediately throw up a book with that name. The only way to make sure is to go to a library which hopefully has access to a database of all books in print. Overall "The Track" is not at all bad since it is very relevant to the book and quite short and pithy. Another option for a title is of course "Te Puke" but this would require the character of Te Puke to be developed much more. I read on a map that Puke means "hill" in Maori and so that has some relevance.

With respect to self-publishing I have found a US website which might be worth investigating although the UK equivalent would appear to be much safer and the testimonials were good. As far as I remember the author only gets about fifteen percent of the sale price and so that is very low. You would have to sell thousands to make any reasonable money on a ten pound book price. The largest New Zealand publisher is Reed whilst Harper Collins have a system whereby you can submit three chapters and a synopsis.

A vague idea of pyramid selling came to mind whereby I could sell ten copies to one person for say seventy five pounds and then they could sell their spare nine copies for ninety pounds giving them a profit of fifteen pounds. Clearly this doesn't work as laid out but using some incentive system or chain letter to end up with one thousand people selling your book via the internet is worth further investigation. Another thought is to try to sell the book through the New Zealand backpackers since there are a large number of them and they have a steady stream of backpackers and trampers from all over the world passing through them. Perhaps the backpacker owner would receive one pound out of the ten pound sale price. And then there is the e-book option which costs far less to produce and could be a very good way to test the demand. If demand is great then it would be possible to move to publishing in the hard copy format with numbered copies and signature. But above all I must produce a first class read before I can consider the marketing aspect.

Sunday 26th December 2004

This morning I was able to continue revising the first draft and I have now reached the point when Alexander and Sonja spend their first night in the rock bivouac. It was a good session and I continue to make improvements. I think that there will be definite advantages in relating the fictional tracks to real tracks since this will enable people to visit the locations where events occurred. Similar to Lord of the Rings locations. The rock bivouac is a very good example whilst much of my track descriptions relate to actual parts of the Kepler, Routeburn and Cascade Saddle tracks.

By consulting this diary it would appear that I arrived in Wanaka on the 22nd November and so I have been in the Southern Lakes area for over one month. There is no doubt that this was a very good decision but now I feel confident that I can move north again without missing out on something fundamental. I feel confident that I can work well at A and P's in Taradale since I can have the study to myself for the whole day long. I might even find Sandy's bach suitable for a few days but I know that she will soon have visitors and I will have to move out anyway. I think that I will provide Sandy with a synopsis and give her the first three chapters to read. If she wishes to read more then of course she can. I think that honest feedback will be valuable even though I still have to develop and improve many passages.

Whatever the outcome I know that I will publish this book in some form or other once I am happy with the final product. If I can find out how to produce PDFs, and possibly encryption, then perhaps I could sell the e-books directly myself thereby allowing me to retain a greater percentage of what is after all my own creation. How this would fit in with the Amazon.com outlet I will have to investigate further. I certainly feel that this last six weeks has been extremely productive and positive. I set myself a challenge and I believe that I have risen to that challenge. Perhaps I have more than one book in me but that will greatly depend on the feedback that I receive from readers. At the end of the day, if John Fowles can take nearly two decades to revise a book then so can I. Well I guess the great reaper will harvest me well before then. And so it's goodbye to the south. Hopefully it will not be too long before I return here again.

Monday 27th December 2004

At four o'clock this afternoon I arrived once more at the Glow Worm backpacker in Franz Josef on the West Coast. The weather all the way from Queenstown over the Haast Pass to my final destination could not have been better with clear blue skies. It was good to see the mountain peaks since I don't think that I have had such a clear crossing in the past. It was certainly a long but interesting journey.

On the bus I got to talk to a middle aged English women, P, who seems to be at some sort of crossroads in her life, but perhaps that is too strong an interpretation. She plans to take a year off in New Zealand and Australia before subsequently heading off for South America. She didn't seem to be the long-term backpacking type and I gained the impression that it was a bit of desperate remedy to try to solve some issues in her life. In my backpacker room were two girls, aged about twenty five, one Australian and one English, who both went to university in England (Durham and Nottingham). It would appear that both have very good and well paid jobs in Sydney, one in a recruitment agency for legal staff and the other as a personal assistant for an established legal company. However, the former wishes to have a complete change and study marketing, whilst the latter wants to leave and get into the publishing industry. She had already spent a year studying publishing but even that was not enough to get a foot in the door. These three examples encountered in one day have given me the idea that they are all seeking fulfilment and in some ways that is analogous to "The Track." Basically backpackers are physically walking the tracks, or are travelling the routes through different countries, but basically their real purpose is to seek fulfilment, direction, or at least a purpose to their lives. The metaphorical track. I think that this theme will be worth exploring further and perhaps should play a greater role in my book.

12. Homeward Bound I Wish I Was

Tuesday 28th December 2004

Todays journey from Franz Josef to Nelson took ten hours. Although I did the same journey on the way south this time it appeared to be much longer and was very wearing. Last night the weather in Franz Josef cleared giving wonderful views of the snow capped mountains nearby. The weather deteriorated throughout the day and this certainly changed the mood. The Punakaiki coastline looked grey and sombre when usually it is a stunning blue with wind born sea spray. Fortunately my place at the Trafalgar Square backpacker was still available on arrival and unusually Nelson was extremely quiet. I had expected the place to be packed but perhaps that will occur over and after the New Year. I shared my room with a thirty year old New Zealander who had never stayed in a backpacker before. He was a bit unnerving since at one moment he was on the New Zealand America's Cup team, then he used to be a professional cyclist having drugs injected into his bum, and so forth. He just seemed so different from the usual backpacker type and it was a bit unnerving. He went out and never returned until dawn. I didn't sleep that well because I guess that I didn't feel at ease.

Wednesday 29th December 2004

At eight twenty this morning I took the bus from Nelson to Stephen's Bay to catch up with my long time friend Sandy. She has a beautiful bach overlooking the bay which has been in her family for years. By the time I arrived it had started raining and it basically hasn't stopped all day. After a short trip into Motueka to get some much needed cash to carry me through the New Year holiday period we returned home.

I had asked Sandy if she would read the first twenty pages of my book. She was to give me an absolutely honest opinion since anything else would not be worthwhile. I was extremely apprehensive since if it was very poor then that would be very disappointing after all the time and effort that I have put into the task over the past few weeks. As she was reading I was thinking about all of the weak passages, the clumsy use of language, and whether or not she would give up after a few pages. Her initial reaction was that it was good but that a lot of professional editing would be required to sharpen it up. She said that she was going to read the whole book and when I went to bed at nine thirty I left her to it. I'll just have to see what she says in the morning.

Thursday 30th December 2004

I had an extremely good nights sleep. No doubt this was due to the fact that I had my own room again, felt very relaxed, and was particularly tired from all the long distance travelling. At breakfast Sandy told me that she had reached page thirty five of my book and that she still thought that it was good. I had hoped that she might have read to the finish but at least the first indication from her reactions is that there is still some reason to hope. I lay in bed last night and realised that I still have a lot of work to do and instead of being ninety percent finished I am probably only seventy five percent finished. Hopefully the writing environment will be good in Napier for the final push. Sandy has now gone off to Nelson for the day and that has left me with the peace and quiet to do some more writing. I will probably have a go at the section where Sonja asks Alexander if he believes in love at first sight.

It's now one thirty in the afternoon and I've had a good session editing the last thirty pages of the book. I have included the love at first sight passage although I will have to make sure that it does not clash with a piece that I included elsewhere. There are still inconsistencies but overall it moves along quickly and, from my biased perspective, it is quite gripping. As I finished the last page the word Mamoe presented itself as a possible name for both the track and the main town of the story. The Mamoe Track and the town of Mamoe. It reads quite easily. Mamoe is particularly relevant since it is the name of one of the historic tribes of the area, the Ngati Mamoe. It therefore fits well into the storyline and provides some historical foundation to the tale. I think that this solution could be a possibility. The other very positive change that I have made is instead of Alexander saying that Sonja and he "just passed in the night," based on ships passing in the night, I have now written that Sonja and he "just passed on the track of life." This sounds very relevant to the storyline and is a good fit for the hoped for book title of "The Track."

Saturday 1st January 2005

Well the New Year has arrived. Last night Sandy invited some friends over for a drink and we had a very relaxed time. Other neighbours had a small firework display on the street outside at about eleven o'clock and later, Paul, one of Sandy's neighbours let off his own box of fireworks. The highlight was one particular firework which he had inadvertently placed on it's side and which then proceeded to shoot it's banging, bright flaming display horizontally along the cul-de-sac. It was the best individual event, as far as excitement and audience participation (dodging exocet missiles), that I have seen for a long time!

Two nights ago I woke up at four o'clock in the morning to go to the toilet. I then had this idea of naming the alternative track which Alexander and Sonja take as the Scorpian's Tail Route. Until now I have had a problem with the fact that most of the trampers must follow one route and Alexander and Sonja follow another. I could not have them all going the same way otherwise the story does not work because if the other trampers left the hut after Alexander and Sonja then they would not get through to the end of the track because of the severity of the snow storm. I now have Alexander and Sonja following the original Maori greenstone hunters and European gold prospector route which is no longer widely known, only to local tramping clubs who wish to keep a few top trails to themselves. The Scorpian's Tail describes the curving route and the potential danger of that route.

Sunday 2nd January 2005

Today I woke up at six o'clock to a golden dawn. The hills to the east of Nelson were sharply silhouetted by a beautiful sky and within minutes the brilliant sun rose above the horizon. Last night Sandy finished my book and overall her conclusion was that it was *"good", possibly "very good"*. I can't quite remember her exact words but the main thing is she didn't think that it was a complete disaster. This is extremely encouraging since I don't think that I could have had anyone better to be the first to read my first complete draft. I think that she would have told me if she didn't think that it was any good, perhaps diplomatically, but she would have indicated as much. Her initial reaction confirms that this whole project has been justified and that I haven't been deluding myself. That is not to say that the book will sell, just that I can happily give it to friends without making a complete fool of myself.

The stay at Stephens Bay has been very relaxing and the comfortable bed has allowed me to recharge my batteries. On Friday we drove over to Golden Bay and the weather was wonderful. It is a very special area and I think that I could happily live there for an extended period, if I had the money. Yesterday we walked over to Kateriteri via the coastal path and had fish and chips for lunch. Very beautiful and not too crowded. The recent bad weather may have kept people away.

Later this morning Sandy will take me to Motueka and I will start heading towards Picton and the crossing back to the North Island. I have been out of touch with my email lately and so that will take a bit of catching up, particularly deleting the spam. Ideally I would like to go to Waverley in the next few days to see Merce and Brenda. A lot will depend on whether or not Martin wants me to start selling his apartment. I hope that that process will not upset my drive to write. I'll just have to make sure that it doesn't.

Tuesday 4th January 2004

On Sunday I managed to get a stand-by seat on the seven o'clock Lynx fast ferry to Wellington. Luckily I was able to book a single room at the Cambridge Hotel which is a backpacker that I have stayed at once before in my travels. It was a very long hike from the ferry terminal to the backpacker, certainly further than I thought. It was clean and comfortable and fortunately they have an all night reception since I arrived very late. By chance I woke quite early, about six forty five, and therefore decided to try to get a bus either to Napier, or to Waverley. All the places on the Napier bus were taken but fortunately I was able to get on an eight o'clock bus to Waverley via Bulls. I would have quite liked to have spent a day in Wellington but I was short of clean shirts and I felt pretty scruffy. The journey to Waverley was very pleasant and not too long.

I telephoned Merce and Brenda from Bulls and luckily they were at home and my unannounced arrival was not too much of a shock for them. They were very pleased to see me and and in fact Merce, who is ninety one, told me that when I left the last time she thought that she would never see me again. You don't get off that lightly Merce! I have always loved their little cottage. It is very homely and welcoming, and if I could have located a similar one when I was house hunting in NZ I would have been very pleased. Last night we had an excellent dinner of silverside, home grown new potatoes, broad beans and carrots, followed by the Big Sun's lemon meringue pie.

13. The End of a Journey

Thursday 6th January 2005

This morning, at about three, I woke up and thought of the following synopsis for the book cover:

"Each year the major walking tracks of New Zealand act as a magnet to thousands of people from every corner of the world. Sometimes their paths interact in unexpected ways and strangers may become friends, lovers and even victims in a landscape which can show it's many faces within a single day. Set against the backdrop of the majestic Southern Alps Track follows the story of three such people and the relic of an earlier era, Te Puke. Te Puke of One Thousand Battles. And the enemy that they all face is the power of nature itself. [Some will survive. Others will not.]"

Overall I don't think that it is a bad start and perhaps after further refinement something along these lines will be acceptable. It has to be short and descriptive but it also has to immediately engender in people a desire to buy the book. Perhaps by stating that some will not survive gives the game away too much but at the same time it certainly raises interest.

Today I spent about six hours reading and refining my draft. I believe that I have nearly taken it as far as I can although I still have to strengthen the Te Puke sections. I plan to make a hard copy on Monday or Tuesday so that A and P can read it and make their own assessments. I can also start investigating the Reed and Harper Collins publisher options, even if they are very long shots. My focus should be on self-publishing, probably using Authors on Line in the UK. I will probably go with the more expensive editing/proof reading package because I think that my punctuation is poor and they may also be able to propose some important improvements to the storyline.

Once I have completed my writing input I will have to return to the sad reality that I don't have any obvious source of income. Things look pretty bleak and therefore I must give the book my very best shot. I really don't want to spend the rest of my days in some soul destroying job.

Friday 14th January 2005

And so on the 10th January I was finally satisfied that my book had reached a stage at which I could feel fairly happy for others to read it and make their own assessment, identify any grammatical errors, and generally give me feedback on how they rated the effort.

My brother read it in three days and his overall opinion was that *"he had read worse books."* Now clearly that was not a ringing endorsement by any means but he did say that the storyline moved on very well after the first thirty pages. He identified that I had used the first person and the third person in a confusing and incorrect way. I will have to look into that and get the book professionally edited before publication. Overall I think that my brother is probably too close to me to give the best opinion of the book since he knows that there are certain autobiographical sections in it that would not be fresh to him.

The very strange thing is that in todays New Zealand Herald a front page headline was *"Tramper sacrifices his life for partner."* Now how weird is that? The accident took place on the Cascade Saddle which forms a key location in my book, the Scorpian's Tail Saddle. Perhaps I can use this event to support my case to the publishers about the relevance of the book. At least I can prove that I did not base it morbidly on this tragedy but actually finished the book days before that event.

At present I am sitting on an Inter City bus to Auckland. Martin has asked me to advertise his apartment overlooking the harbour and he wants me to show any prospective buyers around in return for a fee if successful. I am not at all keen on staying in Auckland but perhaps that fact can provide the basis for another short story.

Friday 21st January 2005

I have managed to offload the marketing of Martin's apartment to someone more suitable since they live in Auckland and therefore this will reduce Martin's costs substantially. The backpacker where I stayed in Parnell was very friendly although it was rather lacking in facilities. Whilst I was there I tried to locate an iron but the only one was being used by a Canadian girl who was working there for a few days. She offered to iron my shirt and shorts for me and in return I offered to buy her a beer. In the end I took her out for a pizza but it cost one hundred and sixteen dollars for the two of us! The wine alone cost fifty dollars. At least we had a very enjoyable time and I don't regret the expenditure. However, I think that I will be doing my own ironing in the future!

Over the last two weeks I have failed to keep up with my diary. Perhaps having completed the book on the 10th January the motivation to record progress on that project disappeared. Whatever the reason there are now considerable gaps in my record which are unlikely to be filled. This is a pity since I was doing so well.

The good news is that today I sent off a synopsis and the first two chapters of my book to three New Zealand based publishers, Reed, Harper Collins NZ and Penguin NZ. I am not expecting a positive outcome because it would appear that very few writers are published, particularly first time authors. However, it is worth a try since one never knows. My main thrust will still be on self-publishing and this I can investigate in detail on my return to the UK. I continue to improve the book in minor but nevertheless important ways. I honestly believe that it is a good read and once it is produced in book form with an attractive cover I believe that it will gain additional credibility.

I have no idea what I will do with respect to employment on my return. There is a possibility I could return to my old green keeping job at Slinfold but that would be a backward step since I do not see it as being the future that I am seeking. In any case the green keeping job may not be available if the Head Greenkeeper has moved on. I can work on my website for a week or two to try to generate more income. In some ways I might be better just staying here and going up the East Cape to write or just try to get some work apple picking. But on reflection I should get home to get my book published after which I can reassess the employment situation.

Sunday 30th January 2005

On Friday I received my first rejection from Harper Collins. It was a polite letter and no doubt they have to send out many rejections in the same standard format. I guess I was disappointed but not at all surprised. Tramping is not a subject which is likely to excite too many people even though it only acts as a backdrop to the main story. Although the book has little depth I feel that I should publish it in it's present form. The next stage may be to take the existing book and develop it to the next level where the characters and relationships are more fully explored. Rather like John Fowles later did with his book The Magus, or perhaps Shrek 8!

I bought Witi Ihimaera's 'The Whale Rider' last Thursday and read it within the day. It again demonstrates that to be successful a novel does not have to be long. Overall it was a good read but I don't think that it can be classified as a great book. It was actually reassuring to me since if a film can be made out of that standard of writing then I see no reason why The Track should not be similarly adapted. It was quite surprising how the film changed so many of the events in the book and somewhat difficult to understand why this was really necessary. I still think that the heroine, Kahu, should have saved the whales and the community but should have disappeared over the horizon. I believe that the happy ending seriously weakened the impact of the book.

It is quite surprising that I have now been in Taradale for over three weeks. I believe that the increasing gaps in my diary illustrate that I have now lost much of the purpose of my journey to New Zealand. I think that it is the equivalent of getting into a rut and it is certainly time to move on. The main reason that I haven't left before now was that I played in a golf tournament with my brother A and with his stepson R, just as we have over the past three years. It was a lot of fun and we did as well as we could have hoped, each winning an electric fan as a prize.

The question of, Where to Now, again raises it's head since my future employment situation again looks as doubtful as ever. I guess I just have to get home and apply myself to the task once more. And so folks, The End of a Journey. Well at least for now.

14. Hostage Postcript

<u>Tuesday, February 21, 2006</u>

Hostages released on 23 November 2004 after 27 days in captivity unharmed. The threat from kidnapping to employees of NGOs and foreign companies throughout Afghanistan remains.

15. Mamoe Track: fact or fiction?

Friday, March 31, 2006

One question that has been asked from time to time is *"Do the Ailsa and Mamoe tracks exist?"* The answer is that if you look on a detailed map of South Island you will not find tracks with those names. At least I don't think so. However the Ailsa and Mamoe are based on my own personal experiences of the Dart River/Cascade Saddle, Kepler and Routeburn Tracks. I have walked the Cascade Saddle only once on a glorious summers day after having been turned back a few days before by lightning and floods. The Cascade Saddle can be dangerous and two fatal accidents have occurred in recent times. If you have time to wait for good weather it is a really fantastic experience. The Kepler I have walked twice and the Routeburn four times.

The book opens on the "Ailsa" at the Lake McKenzie hut on the Routeburn and follows Alexander, Kathy and Sonja's path to the Routeburn Falls hut and down to the Glenorchy side exit. The town of Mamoe does not exist. I could have used Te Anau, Wanaka or Queenstown but somehow I wanted to create a fictional town west of Lake Te Anau, possibly on the far side of Lake Manapouri. The "Mamoe" track starts quite close to the Murchison Mountains and the description used is based on the Kepler track. After the the second hut by the swimming hole Alexander and Sonja decide to take the Scorpian's Tail route, which is actually the Cascade Saddle. After reaching the saddle the descriptive passage relates again to the Routeburn between the Lake McKenzie and Routeburn Falls huts. Between these huts Alexander and Sonja's refuge, the rock, actually exists, and it used to be marked as an emergency bivouac. I have climbed down to it and it does indeed have a significant overhang which provides shelter from the elements. If you do climb down be very careful since there is a significant drop hidden by some gorse bushes, where I nearly came unstuck. The emergency shelter where Alexander seeks assistance is located on the Harris Saddle.

It is very difficult to follow the fictional tracks in the correct order since that would mean walking the Routeburn twice. Since the Routeburn is my favourite walk that is not a bad idea but not very practical. I would therefore recommend that you start with the Kepler track, then the Routeburn from the Te Anau side, then the Dart River/Cascade Saddle route. Whilst on the Routeburn pay special attention to the walk between

Lake McKenzie and the Routeburn Falls hut since this is where the book ends at the rock. Happy tramping.

16. Final Track Synopsis:

Tuesday, 29 March 2005

"Every year the major walking tracks of New Zealand act as a magnet to thousands of visitors from all corners of the world. A large proportion of those visitors will be backpackers in their early twenties who are testing their adult wings for the very first time. Others may be older and some may be trying to solve the riddle of their lives. And foremost among the backpackers are those who travel alone. Sometimes their paths interact with each other in unexpected ways and strangers may become friends, lovers and even victims in an environment which can show its many faces within a single day. Set against the backdrop of the majestic Southern Alps "Track" follows the story of three such people and the relic of an earlier era, Te Puke. Te Puke of One Thousand Battles. And the enemy that they all face is the power of nature itself."

The End

About the Author

Trevor Cree was born in Steyning, Sussex, and has lived there most of his life. He studied agricultural engineering at the University of Newcastle upon Tyne and spent his professional career working in over 30 countries worldwide undertaking short-term consultancy assignments for various international entities, including the UN Food and Agriculture Organization (FAO), European Union (EU) and UN High Commissioner for Refugees (UNHCR). Travel to countries such as China, North Korea, Sudan, Yemen, Iraq, Iran, Syria, Moldova, Albania, Liberia and Sierra Leone influenced his views on the importance of democracy and democratic accountability. From 2012 onwards he took an active part in parish council affairs in Steyning in an effort to increase openness and transparency in local government.

'Track', originally published in 2005, was the result of a long-term love affair

with New Zealand and its people.

Books by the same Author

Track (2005)

Random Journeys - New Zealand (2011)

Modbury Tales (2022)

The Writer's Diary (2022)

The Clock Tower Affair (2025)

Printed in Dunstable, United Kingdom